ALL THE EVIL SCATTERS

All the Evil Scatters

— A Novel —

Irene Fantopoulos

IFP

All the Evil Scatters
Copyright © 2022 Irene Fantopoulos
All rights reserved

First Edition

No part of this book may be used or reproduced in any manner, stored in a retrieval system, stored in a database and / or published in any form or by any means, electronic, mechanical, photocopying, recording or otherwise without prior written permission by the author or her agents, except in the case of brief quotations embodied in critical articles and reviews.

This is a work of fiction. Except for references to certain cases involving other serial killers and locations in and around Toronto, the characters, incidents and dialogue are the product of the author's imagination or are used fictitiously. Any resemblance to actual events or persons, living or dead, is entirely coincidental.

IF Productions
33 Delisle Avenue
Toronto, Ontario M4V 3C7

@renafanta

TITLE: All the Evil Scatters / Irene Fantopoulos
NAMES: Fantopoulos, Irene, author

ISBN 978-1-73875-1-9 (softcover) / ISBN: 9798358361966 (softcover)
ISBN 978-1-73875-2-6 (hardcover) /
ISBN 978-1-73875-0-2. (kindle) /

For George and Mary

PART 1

All the Evil Scatters

1

The boy shifted carefully and reached out sideways; he was unable to fully extend his arms, his elbows bending in protest as the tight sleeves of his shirt pinched his skin. He brought his hand to his face and imagined seeing his fingers as he wiggled them. Tiring of that he stumbled to his feet and reached, as he always did, for the handle, hoping the door was unlocked.

A rustle of noise beyond the door made his heart somersault in his chest. He trembled, awaiting whatever fate was beyond the door that day. He heard the Man's footfall and recoiled backward as if the knob were on fire. The Man's feet moved closer to the closet. The boy peeked through the keyhole seeing Him in bits and pieces, parts of a whole, never one full person. His hair was black as tar and hid a long scar from one end of his forehead to the other. The Man's steely eyes shifted from side to side as if he couldn't focus on one thing. Fear rose in the boy and he pushed himself back into the deepest corner of the closet, as far away from Him as possible. The hem of a young child's coat hung in the closet, grazing his face like soft feathers, comforting him, protecting him, the scent familiar. Someone who had once held him close, but he couldn't picture who it was. The image faded as quickly as it had come.

The boy couldn't remember how long he'd been in the closet, most days he was confused and disoriented, his days broken up by the Man's readings and punishments. Sometimes he tried to pull out a memory from another place. A better place. A place without pain or fear.

Light filtered through the keyhole giving him a small, distorted view of the world beyond: pieces of metal, legs from a chair, and a dirty spot on the linoleum. The Man must have turned on the lamp that stood in the middle of the room. He couldn't make out the space beyond the outer edges of the keyhole.

The key turned and clicked three times. The boy held his breath so that the Man wouldn't hear it, fearing His retaliation. The rusty creak of the knob snapped open; the light cascaded into his dark cavern, blinding him momentarily.

All the Evil Scatters

"Come and sit in your usual spot, Gabriel Santis," the Man said. "And remember. No looking. You know what will happen if you do."

Gabriel released his breath and shivered. He rose and edged out into the room beyond the closet, using his arm to cover his eyes, allowing them to adjust because the Man didn't want him to look directly into His eyes. The Man had told Gabriel that his eyes held evil and that if He ever caught him looking, He would gouge out his eyes. Gabriel believed Him and focused on the Man's shoes, which were scuffed and ugly. He imagined the shoes walking on their own, away from His body, floating outwards beyond the paper-covered window.

He was mesmerized by the dust particles dancing inside the beam of mottled light. The space beyond the closet was sparsely furnished with two chairs, a table, and a small television with a humped back. There was also a cot that the Man sometimes slept on and a toilet that He used. Gabriel wished that he would be allowed to pee there.

The Man kicked him in the shin, causing his knees to buckle.

The boy stifled his pained scream.

"Concentrate! How will you ever learn if you space out? You're just like her."

Gabriel wondered who "her" was but instead of asking, he looked down at the floor, his eyes focused on the black "X," his designated spot outside the closet, and scrambled toward it. He looked closely at the frayed edges of the duct tape, where the "X" had been extended over time to account for his growth spurts. But with each addition of tape, the boy was punished as if getting bigger was his fault. Not wanting to anger the Man he tried to make himself as small as possible. He remained on the "X," shifting his body to fit within it and tucked in his knees.

"Here," the Man said handing him a bowl containing a sludge so thick that the spoon stood straight up like an obedient soldier. "Eat this."

The "X" was positioned beside the Man's chair where Gabriel listened to Him read from books ranging from history to science and mathematics, to fables and fairy tales, to stories that took place in faraway lands.

Gabriel didn't know many of the words, and when he once asked a question it angered the Man. "How dare you challenge me!" the Man had said and picked up Gabriel by his collar, shoving him back into the closet and locking the door. He didn't understand why he deserved such punishment but

All the Evil Scatters

had learned to accept it. He stopped asking questions and concentrated on the Man's scratchy voice. He enjoyed the stories about faraway places. And other stories about children being chased by wolves and grandmothers who tried to eat them. He didn't know whether he had a grandmother, but he knew he never wanted to meet one. Although these stories were his favourites, they always came with a warning: *If you don't behave, Gabriel, I'll feed you to the wolves.*

As the Man read, Gabriel ate whatever food He gave him, swallowing without tasting. Eating the food calmed his thoughts. Thoughts of light and music, of people and places and of being happy. But he knew that it was just a dream, distant and out of reach. He tried to recapture those moments but they trickled out of reach like water through his fingertips.

"Today we will vanquish them," the Man said. "Look at them, Gabriel!"

The boy focused on the book with pictures of beasts with clawed fingers and creatures spewing fire.

"This is the real world," the Man said. "We're safe here. You know I have to lock you up to keep you safe, don't you? In there you're safe from the monsters that make up the world outside."

Gabriel's eyes widened in fear, finally understanding why the Man had brought him this particular book. It was like none of the other books He'd read to him. The Man was saving him from the monsters.

When the boy didn't say a word, the Man said, "Show a little gratitude for everything that I'm doing for you."

"Thank you," Gabriel said, and when he felt the Man's piercing eyes on him, he added, "for all that you're doing fo…for me."

The Man furled his lips and began to read. As the Man read to Gabriel about hell and damnation, he wished that he was back in the closet where he could dream about light and music. The day seemed to go on forever as the Man read the book from cover to cover and then started from the beginning again until He slumped over in His chair and fell asleep. Gabriel scurried back into the closet, closed the door behind him, and fell into a disturbed sleep, drifting in and out, waking several times throughout the night. At one point he woke up and felt his clammy clothes against his skin. Gabriel wondered if he had wet himself or worse, knocked over the bucket full of his shit and urine. He avoided inhaling deeply, hoping to block out the

All the Evil Scatters

overwhelming stench, hoping that the man would clean it out soon. Then he remembered his dream filled with monsters chasing him, finding him in the closet. They were monsters with eyes that spewed fire, claws that could cut through you like a knife, and breath that was so hot, Gabriel felt that he was on fire.

2

Gabriel woke to the Man's angry voice and the rotting smell of something burning. Instinctively, Gabriel moved to the back of the closet and covered his nose with the hanging coat. Smoke clawed beneath the door's jamb, reaching for him like talons. He coughed, unable to breathe and as he was about to lose consciousness, the Man swung open the door and yanked him out, pushing him down onto the floor. Gabriel scurried dizzily to the "X", sat on it and watched the flames engulf whatever the Man had been heating on the stove. The Man grabbed a towel and threw it over the fire, patting it down until he'd snuffed it out. Gabriel coughed, choking, his eyes watered from the acrid smoke that had filled the room and cast a haze around them. The Man yelled and cursed as He tore at the paper covering the sealed window. He whacked at the window with a broom handle, shattering the glass and causing the pieces to fly in all directions. Gabriel saw blood trickle down the Man's hand, a piece of glass stuck in it.

The air changed. Gabriel took in the sweet, crisp smell of the world full of monsters, so different from the stale and stinky air to which he was accustomed. His breathing steadied. For the first time, he heard birds chirping. A car backfired in the distance and from somewhere inside the house, a woman screamed.

"Shut up," the Man hollered at the ceiling. And when the woman didn't stop, he repeated, "I said: SHUT. THE. FUCK. UP!" He pounded his fist on the table and when the screaming stopped, He said to Gabriel, "Take a deep breath before the monsters come for you."

The Man pulled out the piece of glass that was sticking out of his finger. Swooning from the fresh air, Gabriel watched the blood drip onto the floor, leaving red dots on the linoleum. The Man rifled through the cupboards, finally locating a needle and thread; with his right hand, he sewed the gash on his left index finger. When the Man finished, He pulled viciously

All the Evil Scatters

on Gabriel's hand causing him to teeter unsteadily as he rose and met the Man's penetrating stare.

"I told you never to look at me! There will be consequences." The Man smacked Gabriel across the face so hard that he went reeling toward the closet, falling with a thud on his buttocks. While still on the floor, he shimmied backward the rest of the way into the closet, focusing anywhere but on the Man. He feared that the man would hurt him bad, gouge out his eyes.

He reached for the boy's legs, pulled him out of the closet, and lifted him by the back of his shirt. He dragged him to the sink, the glass piercing Gabriel's bare feet. He winced in pain but said nothing to avoid provoking the Man. He tried to avoid some of the larger shards and was thankful when the Man said, "Sit down. Don't move! I have to remove them."

The Man picked out the pieces of glass from Gabriel's feet with a pair of tweezers and when he was done, he wiped the blood away with a towel. He looked up at the Man with gratitude, but the Man hadn't seemed to notice.

The Man opened the drawer and pulled out a small flat knife. Before Gabriel realized what was happening, he felt the cold blade of the knife cut into the skin above his eye. The warmth of his pee trickled on the inside of his pants and down his leg. *No. Not my eyes*, Gabriel thought, panic overtaking him.

The Man's hand shook as He tapped the knife on the side of Gabriel's face. Gabriel clutched the side of the chair, closed his eyes and prayed that it would be over quickly.

Gabriel felt the stinging cut as the knife pierced deeper into his brow and travelled toward the temple. *It hurts so bad,* he thought. He wanted to scream at the Man, tell him to stop. Instead, he gritted his teeth and hoped to dull the pain. His flesh was on fire and when he could no longer stand it, he pulled away from the Man. He knew instantly that he'd made a mistake. The blade cut into his forehead. He clenched his fists as the warm blood streamed down his face.

"I told you not to move! Now look at what you've done," the Man said.

As the blood flowed, blinding Gabriel, the Man stopped and said, "I can't do this!" He pushed Gabriel away from him, threw the knife into the sink and left the room.

Gabriel grasped his bleeding head and bit his lip, trying to stop himself from crying out and causing the Man to return and finish what he'd started.

All the Evil Scatters

When he was certain that the Man would not return, Gabriel rose still holding his face where the knife had sliced him. The blood flowed through his trembling fingers and dripped like a leaky faucet onto the floor. He felt dizzy and grasped the countertop to steady himself, taking a few deep breaths to calm his unsteady body. He saw a large spoon on the counter, and when he saw his reflection in it, he gasped at the blood-spewing gash.

Time passed and when his shaking stopped and his breathing steadied, he rummaged for something bigger so that he could have a better look. In the back of one of the junk-filled drawers, he found a small mirror. He propped it against the wall behind the counter and then grabbed a rag, pressing it against his forehead. Gabriel reached for the needle and thread that the Man had previously used on Himself. He sat
nervously in front of the mirror, glancing over his shoulder from time to time. He was afraid the Man would return and make him suffer even more.

He gritted his teeth, and as he'd seen the Man do, pierced the needle through the two pieces of skin above his brow. He stifled a scream as the needle's point went in and out, in and out of his tender flesh. Each time the needle met with his skin, he gritted his teeth, swallowing the pain. When the blood flow stopped and the throbbing in his head subsided, he opened his mouth and screamed silently into the empty room.

Gabriel picked up a shard of glass and returned to the closet.

3

As the weeks and months moved forward, Gabriel accepted the revolving pattern of listening to the Man read to him, scream at him, or punish him for no reason. He ate and then he slept. His thoughts and memories were so scrambled that he didn't know what was real and what was fantasy. Monsters reached for him in his sleep. Trees beckoned to him with their woody limbs. He was in a car. He couldn't breathe. There were voices, but the words were unclear. When he awoke, he realized that he was in the safety of the closet, away from the Man.

From time to time he heard the voice of a woman from the floor above him, but he never knew if her voice was real or imagined. Sometimes he was whipped with a belt, scars forming upon scars and sometimes he returned to the closet with leftover scraps from whatever the Man had cooked. Gabriel

All the Evil Scatters

became accustomed to the smell of his bodily waste; it now seemed like it was a part of him. He was given new clothing as he outgrew the old ones. He could no longer extend his arms and legs along the length of the closet and often curled up in a fetal position as he slept, turning to change positions when the cramping in his back became unbearable.

One night, the Man left the floor lamp on and the closet door unlocked. He waited for the Man to return, and when Gabriel was certain that the Man would not come, he inched his way out of the closet for the first time on his own.

Gabriel walked around the room, stretching his arms and legs. Remnants of the fire were everywhere: black streaks on the walls, broken glass that he avoided stepping on, and the burnt pot on the stove.

Gabriel went into the closet and brought out the bucket filled with waste and, as he had seen the Man do, he flushed it down the toilet. He rinsed out the bucket in the sink and let the water wash away the stench. Water ran through his fingers, the droplets caressing them, taking away the smell that permeated his skin like a second layer of clothing. He closed his eyes and imagined what it would be like to immerse his entire body in the wetness.

The extra space was like a dream from which he never wanted to wake. Occasionally, he heard pacing on the floor above, back and forth from one end of the room to the other.

He heard a thud from above. Afraid that the Man would come and punish him, he darted into the closet, closed the door and waited. His breathing was heavy, his heart throbbed against his chest and sweat dripped down his forehead.

The Man did not come.

This went on for months. The Man didn't come, but signs of Him were always present: food and clean clothes were left behind, and sometimes the gooiest, yummiest chocolate treats he'd ever tasted. Gabriel figured that these items had been left while he'd slept. He tried opening the door that led to somewhere beyond the room and his closet, but it was locked. He soaked his shoulder-length hair with warm water and when he was done, shook his head like a dog.

Then one night, as suddenly as the Man had disappeared, he reappeared. The door clicked open; Gabriel darted into the closet.

All the Evil Scatters

"Where are you going?" the Man said in an almost kind voice. "I have a surprise for you. You like surprises, don't you?" When Gabriel said nothing, he repeated, "Don't you?"

Without looking, Gabriel nodded and said, "Yes."

"Today is a special day," He said. "Do you ever wonder what's above you? Upstairs? Well, today is your lucky day. I'm gonna give you a tour of the rest of the house. I have a special meal planned for us. I think you'll like it — it's pizza."

Pizza. Gabriel savoured the word in his mouth, familiar, but not familiar. *Have I had pizza before?*

Gabriel followed Him up the steps, counting 15 of them before they reached another door. When He opened it, the light's intensity seemed to push Gabriel backward, but the Man grabbed his arm, saving him from taking a tumble down the steep steps.

They walked out into a long hallway, its walls adorned with photos. They stopped before each one and the Man explained that it was Him and a woman called, Eugenia. Gabriel looked inquisitively at her image and wondered if she was the one he'd heard screaming. There were pictures of the Man when He was younger. There were fewer smiles in the photos as the Man aged. There was a picture of the Man and Eugenia, His arm over her shoulders. She looked like she was in pain. Gabriel saw that he was in one of the photos, standing alone, the background a dense forest. And he looked happy. He tried to remember when and where it was taken, but he couldn't.

"Don't you have any questions?" The Man said, but Gabriel said nothing even though he wanted to ask Him: Who is the woman? Where was she? Why was there only one picture of him?

"Do you want to know about your mother?" The Man said, pointing to the woman smiling in one of the pictures.

"Mo…mo…mother? That's my mother?" Gabriel said incredulously. He tried to remember her, but couldn't except for something to do with a car. Had she driven him somewhere?

"Of course, that's your mother and I'm your father. Who did you think we were?"

Gabriel had never thought of the Man as his Father. Or that he had a mother. He only wondered why He kept him locked up in the closet.

"Wh…wh…where is she?" Gabriel asked tentatively.

All the Evil Scatters

"I'll tell you the story when you're ready to hear it. But for now, it's pizza time!" He said and Gabriel followed Him to a room that was painted yellow, the light pouring in through the window, casting a beautiful glow in the room. Everything glistened. It was different from the room downstairs. Gabriel hoped that he'd never have to go back to it ever again.

His Father put down two plates, one in front of each of them. A white box, with the word "Pizza" written on it, lay in the centre of the table.

A small hope stirred in Gabriel. He wondered if his confinement was over.

He looked at his Father who sprinkled something white on the pizza and pushed a plate with a slice of it closer to him, his eyes encouraging him to eat. Gabriel wanted to ask what his Father had put on the pizza but thought better of it. He took a tentative bite.

"Go on. Eat it," his Father said, laughing and chomping hungrily on a cheesy slice with loads of pepperoni.

"You know that I love you and that I want you to be happy."

Love? Happy? Gabriel wondered if he dared believe in those words. Words he knew, but never dared hope for. Both words chimed like a bell from long ago. At that moment, Gabriel knew that he had been loved. That he had been happy. He began to hope, once again.

Gabriel nodded, his fear replaced with warm feelings that he never thought possible.

"Thank you," Gabriel said, and started coughing as the food went down the wrong way.

His Father smiled. "Easy," he said. "You'll choke and then where will we be? Right?"

Again, Gabriel nodded. He devoured the pizza. It was the best meal he'd ever had. He ate slice after slice until he began to feel nauseous. His head felt heavy, but he saw His Father smile at him. An almost kind smile. In that smile, Gabriel could see that things were going to change. *Why am I so sleepy,* he thought?

After they ate, they climbed another set of stairs that led to more rooms. Gabriel took one laboured step after another. Sunlight shone through the open doors and onto the landing lighting it up as if it were on fire. Gabriel had never seen so much light, its brightness keeping him awake. He heard

All the Evil Scatters

someone, a woman's voice coming out of one of the rooms, and wondered if that was his mother. He dared not ask.

They stopped in front of a closed door, Gabriel's legs threatening to collapse under his weight.

"Now this is a special room, a room only for you. You won't need to go back into the closet. This will be yours forever. I will visit you when I can, but first, there's something that we must do to cleanse you of all the evils that live in your body. All right?"

Gabriel nodded, his head heavy but he managed a smile for his Father as if He had transformed into an amazing person. If this was happiness, he never wanted it to stop. Gabriel drew an imaginary line in the sand; on one side was the before and on the other, the after.

The room had a toilet, a sink with a mirror above it, and a bathtub. Beside the tub was a pole with a thick clear plastic bag hanging from it and before Gabriel could ask what it was, his eyes widened as his Father pressed the lever on a needle and squirted liquid into the air a couple of times.

"What's th— ?"

"This will help us get rid of the monsters. Don't worry. It's safe. I'm a paramedic after all. I have years of training."

Gabriel wondered what a paramedic was but he couldn't string the words together to ask.

"Come here," He motioned.

Slowly, Gabriel inched toward him. His Father smiled, but he knew it wasn't a real smile and took a couple of steps back. His Father grabbed his arm, pulled him close, and covered his mouth with his hand.

Everything went dark.

When Gabriel woke, he was lying naked in the bathtub, his right hand tied to his right foot, both pointing toward the ceiling; the other hand had a needle buried in his arm. He winced in pain. Gabriel saw that the plastic bag which had been clear and empty before everything had gone dark, was now full and red with his blood.

Gabriel passed out and when he came to, his Father was replacing the full plastic bag with a clear empty one until it too was filled with his blood. From time to time his Father made him drink orange juice and eat cookies. Gabriel lost all sense of time.

All the Evil Scatters

When he woke up the next time, the plastic bag, needles, and bindings were all gone. He was lying on a bed, his arm was blue and yellow where the needle had been; it was sore to the touch.
"I had to, Gabriel," He said. "I had to get you ready."
His Father walked out of the room and the door clicked shut.
Get ready for what? Gabriel wondered.

4

"Come on. We have lots to do to get ready," His voice wafted through the air, pushing itself into Gabriel's consciousness. "You're recovering now. You lost lots of blood. But there was no other way."
Gabriel glanced at the Man who was his Father and thought, *Why are you doing this to me?*
"I prepared a wonderful meal. Come on, I'll help you out of bed."
Gabriel remembered the pizza and wondered whether his Father would once again drain his blood after he'd eaten. "I'm not hungry."
His father looked at him in disappointment and said, "There's someone I'd like you to meet."
Gabriel's eyes widened in surprise.
"Of course. You've seen her photos. I want you to get reacquainted with your mother. She wants to see you. It's been a long time for her. Don't look so surprised. She loves you as I do."
Gabriel doubted the truth of his Father's words. He hoped that his mother would be different. "Wh...wh...where is she? Why hasn't she been around?" Gabriel said, remembering the screams he'd heard that time during the fire.
"She's always been here, Gabriel. It's, um… The time hasn't been right for the two of you to be together again."
"Why didn't she ever come to see me?"
"I told you about the monsters, didn't I?" And when Gabriel nodded, He continued. "We had to cleanse your blood first so that we could be sure the monsters will no longer detect your scent. You see, I never told you. But the monsters like a certain blood type, and you had it. But not anymore. You're pure now."
"I want to see mother," Gabriel said.

All the Evil Scatters

His Father arched his eyebrows and said, "Yes. But first I have to tell you how special your mother is so that you will understand the way she is. Long ago, when she was a young girl, maybe about 10 or 11, just like you are now, her head hurt so much that her vision blurred, she was throwing up and couldn't keep food inside of her. The doctors couldn't find anything wrong with her. Her headaches continued until her *yiayia,* her grandmother, surmised that the only explanation was that someone had cast the evil eye on her. Someone who envied her beauty and indeed, your mother was a beautiful young woman. *Yiayia* told her that for the evil eye to be potent and inflict harm on someone it would have to be someone with blue eyes, just like your mother's. Your mother believed that someone had wished harm on her. Your mother knew right away who it was."

"Who was it?" Gabriel said, his eyes widening in anticipation.

"It was Christina, one of her classmates. And you know how she knew it was her?"

"How, Father?"

"Christina's eyes were so blue that your mother didn't doubt that she had cast evil on her, making her sick."

"What happened to Christina?"

"Christina? Ah, yes. Christina moved out of the neighbourhood shortly after that and as far as I know, your mother never saw her again."

"What happened next?"

"*Yiayia* filled a small bowl with holy water that had been blessed by the priest. *Yiayia* was a religious woman. She went to church every Sunday and on significant days of worship to honour the many saints like John, Christos, Maria, and Eleni. Your mother was skeptical because she'd been raised in an agnostic household.

"*Yiayia* drizzled some oil into the holy water and added frank and myrrh, swirling it around before lighting it. Your mother watched the flames consume the oil. The mixture emitted a sweet aroma, like the flowers that bloomed in her mother's garden. *Yiayia* said, *ready* and grabbed a bunch of rosemary, held together by a string, and dunked it in the liquid. She sprinkled it in front of your mother's face several times. As the droplets dripped down your mother's face, *yiayia* chanted, *Jesus Christ is victorious, and all the evil scatters by Him* three times, representing the Holy Trinity."

"What does it mean?" Gabriel dared to ask.

All the Evil Scatters

"It means that there is one God who forever exists in three persons: the Father, the Son and the Holy Spirit."

Gabriel nodded but wanted to understand more about this God and his three persons.

"When she finished chanting," his Father continued, *"yiayia* crossed herself and then your mother, three times, ending with and mock-spit, *ftou, ftou, ftou*. Your mother was surprised to see tears flowing down *yiayia's* cheeks and, just like that," His Father snapped his fingers, "her headache disappeared."

"Forever?"

"Yes. As *yiayia* wiped away her tears, she said, I *have taken the evil onto me. You are free.*"

"Wow," Gabriel said.

"You believe this, don't you? Because you have to believe it so that you are protected from the evil eye."

Gabriel nodded, fear replacing interest.

"And you know why you must believe this?"

"Why, Father?"

"Because I also suffered from headaches for a long time. Your mother cured me of them. Since she performed that ritual on me, the pain and the headaches disappeared. Now she uses her special skill to rid us of the evil and monsters, like Christina, who want to harm us." His Father gave him a rare smile and said, "Let's go!"

Gabriel rose to his feet, the sheet falling away exposing his nakedness. Feeling vulnerable, he stooped to pick it up and wrapped it around him, its warmth immediately calming him.

"Don't be shy," his Father said and gently tapped him on his arm. "Put this on. We don't want you naked in front of mother, now do we?"

Gabriel took the robe, put it on, and tied the belt around his waist. He took a few tentative steps toward the door, wondering if this was all part of his Father's punishment. He walked unsteadily as he followed Him out of the room and down the long hallway.

They stopped in front of another door that was different from the others. This one was painted white, but all over its surface were images of eyes: some were small, others large; all of them were the same colours of

All the Evil Scatters

white and blue with a big large black orb in their centres; some had tears of blue, others red.

He fixed his eyes on them, dread washing over his body.

He was startled to hear whispering from behind the door. The more he concentrated the more the whispers turned to chanting or singing, repeating the same words, words he couldn't make out.

"Gabriel," his Father murmured, "I want you to be very quiet. When your mother goes into one of her trances, she doesn't see anything or anyone else."

"What's a trance?" Gabriel dared to ask.

"A place, like another world that she enters."

Gabriel wondered if she too escaped into a world similar to the one that he had created. Was her other world full of light and music and happy people? Was it a place where she was happy like he was?

"Don't look at her. Remember what happened to you the last time you looked at me? I'd say you got off easy."

Gabriel touched the scar below his brow. It was a constant reminder of the knife cutting into his flesh.

His Father reached above the door's frame and grabbed a key. Gabriel anticipated hearing a click, but there was no sound at all. It was a different lock from the one on his closet door; no light could get in or out. Gabriel watched his Father's hand turn the knob; he anticipated the appearance of his mother. *Had Father given her the same punishment as He had with me?* Gabriel wondered. *Was He keeping her safe from the monsters?*

The door creaked open, like the one to Gabriel's room. The overwhelming and familiar stench floated toward him, a fetid combination of shit and urine. Mixed in with that was another odour, a sickly sweet one that wafted out of the myriad of large, small, and in-between vessels in the room: some of them were colourful like the rainbows he'd read about; some were made of glass; some looked like soup bowls.

She jerked up from the floor when they entered.

Gabriel recognized her from the photos; she looked different, not as pretty. Her long, wiry hair fell like a rope down her back; her clothes were dirty. Her eyes were unable to focus on anything in the room, darting from Gabriel to his Father, to a glass charm of an eye made of blue, white, and black which she held in her hand. She scurried to the other side of the cot and

All the Evil Scatters

clasped her hands atop it. She chanted repeatedly — the chant that Gabriel had heard from the other side of the door — *Jesus Christ is victorious, and all the evil scatters by Him*. Only now the words were clear to him. They were the same as the words her *yiayia* had used to rid her of her headaches.

"When she finished she crossed herself three times, ending with a mock-spit: *ftou, ftou, ftou."*

His Father pushed him into the room, the surprise of it causing Gabriel to stumble toward his mother and land in the spot in which she'd been sitting when they'd entered the room. He noticed that the same images of the eye that adorned the exterior of the door were everywhere: on the walls; on the window; and, one had been painted by a hurried hand at the foot of the bed where he now crouched.

"Come," she said, crossed her fingers against her chest three times, and reached her hand out to him.

He pulled back apprehensively.

"Just for a few minutes, Eugenia," his Father said, eyes riveted on Gabriel. "Say hello to your mother."

"H...h...hello," Gabriel said.

His mother's eyes focused on him now. They didn't dart back and forth. "Stand up son," she said. "Let me look at you. I've missed you so much." She then glanced at Aidan and said, "Please let him stay."

"We did well Eugenia, don't you think?"

"Oh yes, Aidan. But we must rid him of evil," she said.

"Work quickly," his Father said. "Look what I have for you Eugenia," He said and showed her one of those pieces of cake that he frequently gave to Gabriel.

Eugenia leaped toward Him, grabbed the cake and stowed it under the bed.

"Yes, Aidan," she said and chanted, *Jesus Christ is victorious, and all the evil scatters by Him* several times before crossing herself and mock-spitting, *ftou ftou ftou.*

"You've seen enough for now. Let's go, Gabriel. We've lots to do before bedtime."

As the door closed behind Gabriel, he heard, "Bring him back to me, Aidan."

After his Father locked the door, they returned to Gabriel's room.

All the Evil Scatters

"Take off your robe and let me look at you," his Father said.
Gabriel slowly removed the tie that bound his robe and let it drop to the floor. His father's stare never left his body as he said, "Your body is transforming, here, here, and here is where you'll see the most changes," he said.
Gabriel shivered as he looked at the tufts of hair growing under his arms and around his groin. He pulled away, sensing that the Man was going to hurt him again.
Thwack.
His face burned as his Father's piercing slap landed hard across it, causing him to reel backwards. "I'll have none of that. Do you understand me? Try to control yourself." Gabriel had no idea what his Father was talking about but shuddered as his Father's eyes roved over his body.
Gabriel closed his eyes.

5

The next day his Father took him to see his mother again.
"He has the evil in him, Eugenia. We must hurry to rid him of it."
Eugenia stared up at his Father, reverting to her chanting without taking her eyes off Him.
"Stop looking at me. You know what will happen if you don't." He said and rubbed his belt. She flinched and then beckoned for Gabriel to come to her.
Gabriel heard the door click shut. Eugenia lolled her head back and forth and began praying, repeatedly crossing herself and chanting, *Jesus Christ is victorious, and all the evil scatters by Him*. Gabriel lost count of the number of times she did that until the room fell silent once again. When she finished chanting, she mock-spat, "*Ftou, ftou, ftou,*" at Gabriel
He flinched.
"Don't be afraid of him, Gabriel. He's not a bad man. He wasn't always like this. He used to bring me flowers, so romantic, we took long road trips, until, until... " Her voice trailed off; she looked away.
"Until?" Gabriel said.

All the Evil Scatters

His mother prayed under her breath, "Jesus Christ is victorious, and all the evil scatters by Him, Jesus Christ is victorious, and all the evil scatters by Him, Jesus Christ is victorious, and all the evil scatters by Him."

"Tell me what happened, um, mother."

"One day he came home and he had a headache. He was in so much pain. I prayed for him as I pray for you. I took on his pain. My tears filled with his pain as they trickled down my face. That was when everything changed. You were a little boy. Now I have to rid you of the same evil. He wants you pure."

"What will you do?" Gabriel said.

"I'm going to do a special incantation to rid you of any evil that has entered your body. Come sit while I prepare the holy water."

He watched her pour some water and something else into one of the vessels and light it up with one of the many candles. He remembered his Father's story and imagined that this was how her *yiayia* had made her feel better. Gabriel wondered if she knew about his headaches. How sleepy he felt all the time and how sometimes his head hurt so much that he thought it would fall off his neck. "Yes. I want you to rid me of all evil."

She nodded and went over to him. She dunked her fingers into the liquid and flicked the water across his face. Startled, his head flinched backwards, the coolness of the water catching him off guard. She chanted repeatedly, "Jesus Christ is victorious, and all the evil scatters by Him." This was followed by crossing her fingers, first against his chest and then, against hers. He saw the tears stream down her face and reached out with a trembling hand to touch them, but before he could, she mock-spat and called out, "He's ready, Aidan." She grabbed the chocolate cake that his Father had left for her. Soon, her shoulders slumped as if she were going to sleep; the room filled with silence and the smoke from the vessels billowed upward.

His Father appeared, assessed Gabriel from head to toe, glanced at his mother, and said, "He is free of all evil. I am pleased, Eugenia," He said, took Gabriel's hand, and led him back down the hall.

They stopped in front of another door and opened it.

Gabriel gasped, admiring the magnificence of the room. Shelves adorned all four walls; they were all filled with hundreds of books, newspapers, and magazines.

All the Evil Scatters

"I want you to learn about everything," His Father said. "I'd send you to school, but there are monsters out there that are ready to take you."

School, Gabriel thought. He had a vague recollection of three kids, walking and playing with him. He couldn't see their faces; their names were at the tip of his tongue. Before he could figure out who they were his Father continued.

"You're curious about school aren't you? You remember the story about Christina? There are many Christinas out there. Evil. Monsters. I had to take you out of school to keep you safe. This is why I read to you. Why you must read. Never stop reading. You need to learn so that one day you will fight the monsters that I fight every day."

The library became his favourite room where he read as much as he could. Gabriel had vague memories of many kids like him, sitting at a small desk; someone, a teacher he believed, was talking at the front of a room. He wondered if it was real or if he'd dreamt it. In the books he read monsters weren't gobbling up people; there were only books with beautiful lands and great blue skies. Only the fairy tales had monsters. He often wondered about his mother and how he might be able to find a way to get her out of that room. Maybe when his Father leaves for work, he could let her out, even for a bit. But there was no predictability to his Father's schedule. He was gone at all hours of the day and night. "I have a very important job," He said proudly to Gabriel. "I take care of the sick and the wounded."

Gabriel sat at a makeshift desk made of particle board which looked as if it had been constructed in a hurry; his Father sat at another desk, a beautifully crafted piece of furniture that Gabriel imagined was made by someone who had cared about putting pieces of wood together. Gabriel saw a similar one, in the style of French provincial, in one of the design books, *Furniture through the Ages.* Some books were piled high around them; there was no room for them on the shelves.

Gabriel read everything that he could.

*

One day as they were reading in the library, his Father began to speak, his tone wistful and almost kind, startling Gabriel.

"When I met your mother. I didn't know what to do. Your mother was so beautiful. I was with a couple of my buddies. We went to Greek dances every Saturday night. I'd never seen her before. She was not like any of the

All the Evil Scatters

other young women her age. She was 18; I was 28. She was there with her parents. I remember her beautiful blue eyes. Eyes that pierced through me, seeing into my soul. I wanted to meet her and never let her go. I fell in love with her the moment I saw her."

"What happened next?" Gabriel said his voice filled with interest.

"We started dating. But it wasn't like normal dating because we had to meet secretly — her parents wanted her to marry someone different from me. Someone smarter, like a doctor or a lawyer. Someone who made good money. At that time I wasn't working. But I decided to go to school to become a paramedic. Two years later, I started working with EMS. I went to her father and asked for her hand in marriage. He despised me even more and forbade me to see his daughter. "You will never have my blessing. Leave Eugenia alone!" He told me, fist raised in the air as if he was going to take a swing at me. I told him that I was a paramedic and that I made good money and that it was the closest I could get to being a doctor. Maybe I should have become a doctor. Her father never wavered from his position till the day he died."

"How did he die, Father?"

"You're interrupting! Do you want to hear this or not?" His Father said eyeing the belt that hung loosely against the wall on the hook.

"I'm sorry. I'll be quiet," Gabriel said not wanting to be punished for asking too many questions. He pushed himself back into his chair trying to make himself invisible because he wanted his Father to continue with his story. He wanted to find out more about the woman, his mother, Eugenia who was locked up in that room and wondered if his Father would tell him.

His Father continued. "It was really hard for us to be together alone. Her parents had a tight leash on her, shall I say. We continued to date, but her father found out about it and made sure that her older brother kept an eye on her. I schemed to get her alone and finally decided that if she would have me, we'd elope. One of her girlfriends, Sylvie, gave her my note, telling her that I'd made arrangements for us to marry at City Hall in a few days. I didn't know if she would obey her father or come to me and be my wife. The rest, as they say, is history."

His Father rose and went over to the bookshelf and pulled out a book. He opened it, revealing photos of Him and his mother. But before Gabriel could have a good look, he snapped the book shut and returned it to the shelf before sitting down to continue reading.

All the Evil Scatters

Gabriel wanted to know more. But he could tell that he would get no more information that day. He would be patient.

6

A few weeks later when his Father had left for work, he opened the door with its many watchful eyes that led to his mother's room. He wanted to know what happened to her. Why was she locked up? His Father didn't finish his story. As much as he wanted to know more, fear kept him from asking any questions.

He reached for the key that his Father kept on the doorframe. When he opened the door, she scurried to the corner, the same one she'd gone to the first time he'd seen her. He walked slowly toward her and opened his palm, revealing a small piece of cake like his Father had done. She looked at him suspiciously, grabbed it and she had done with his Father, she stowed it under the bed.

He kneeled before her and said, "What did he do to you?"

She crossed her chest and chanted. Then she patted the floor beside her; Gabriel sat down. The two of them surveyed each other, she with her glassy look, he with inquisitive eyes. He saw the faintest movement in her eyes, and then she reached for him, her fingers travelling gently along the scar on his brow. She stopped where it stopped and began to cry.

"You took him away from me," she said.

"Who?"

She rocked herself back and forth and chanted. She crossed her chest and then crossed her fingers in front of Gabriel as if she were praying for him.

"Him. You! Monsters," she said, pointing her bony finger. "Bad. Aidan is a good man. It's your fault I'm here. He replaced me with you." She crossed herself and mock-spat, "*Ftou, ftou, ftou.*"

Gabriel tamped his hands over his ears, shutting out her words, and said, "I'm not a monster!" *Why is she saying these horrible things to me? Is she right? Am I really a monster?*

"You are!" Her accusatory words spilled from her lips, "Go Monster!" She screamed and her finger pointed to the door. "Go."

All the Evil Scatters

He stumbled out of the room and as he did, he swept his hand across one of the tables that contained the vessels billowing with incense; they crashed onto the floor, fracturing into many pieces. He stared at the broken pieces, turned to look at her before locking the door.

Gabriel went to the welcoming darkness of his closet. He pulled out the hidden shard of glass and cut into his flesh, making a thin line along the soft skin of his elbow. He couldn't see his work, but the action calmed him. The warm blood trickled down his sleeve. Gabriel closed his eyes, breathed deeply, held his breath and then exhaled. The word, *Monster,* floated out of him with each exhalation.

He muttered, "Jesus Christ is victorious, and all evil scatters by Him. Jesus Christ is victorious, and all evil scatters by Him. Jesus Christ is victorious, and all evil scatters by Him." He crossed himself three times and fell asleep.

7

One day his Father said, "Let's go out for a stroll. I want you to see the changing leaves."

"What about the monsters?"

"They're gone. Washed away through the cleansing of your blood and your mother's prayers," his Father said and opened the door.

Gabriel reeled backwards as the brightness of the outdoors pierced his eyes like a knife. He squinted, feeling the tears trickle down his cheeks. He closed his eyes and wiped away the wetness.

"Here," Aidan said, handing him a pair of sunglasses.

Gabriel put them on, his eyes quickly adjusting to the light. He took a deep breath and inhaled the air, faintly tinted with the decay of fallen leaves that blanketed the ground.

"Watch your step," Aidan said holding Gabriel's arm at the elbow, easing him down.

The world beyond the house was beautiful. Gabriel heard the whispering leaves as they succumbed to the fall air, twirling their final dance before landing on the ground. Cars swooshed in the distance. He welcomed the wind on his face, breathing in so deeply it made him swoon.

All the Evil Scatters

"Now we can't be out for too long. Small doses for you until you get used to the fresh country air. But you've earned it. You've been good. How old are you now? Thirteen?"

Gabriel shook his head, wondering how old he was and whether it mattered. Time seemed unimportant when your days were the same. But being outside had changed everything. He should care about how old he was. Maybe his Father would tell him more about the bits and pieces of memories that wove in and out of his dreams. He knew now was not the time.

"Father," he said. "This is wonderful. Let's stay out here a bit longer. Please?"

"We'll stay as long as I think it's necessary! Do you understand?" He said, grabbed Gabriel by the elbow, and pushed him back into the house. This time Gabriel's step did not falter; he maintained his balance as he entered.

"Now, go take a shower. You stink."

"Ye…ye…yes, Father."

"And when you're done come to my bedroom. I want to teach you a few things."

*

Gabriel scrubbed away any possible smells that could upset his Father. He dressed and made his way to His bedroom.

His Father lay naked on the bed, smiling and patting the spot beside Him, "Come to me."

Gabriel froze; the hairs on his skin tingled as if a cold wind had injected itself into the space between him and His father.

"I said, come here!" He patted the space again.

Gabriel didn't move. His Father reached underneath the pillow and pulled out his belt. He shuddered, slowly made his way to the bed and stood before Him, his eyes never leaving the floor. He lowered his body and sat beside his Father; he felt every muscle in him tense, his fists formed into balls.

*

"Remember when I told you that I had something special planned for you today?" His Father said and pulled out some clothing from the closet. "These will look better on you. Matches your eyes and you'll be able to show off your long hair."

Gabriel stared at his Father.

All the Evil Scatters

"Put them on," He said holding the clothes in front of Gabriel.

Gabriel slowly put on the clothes terrified by this new torture of His, but he felt His eyes drill through him. He looked everywhere, but at his Father's face.

"Now come back here and lie down," His Father said.

Gabriel froze in place.

"You know what I can do to you," his Father warned.

He moved forward, his gait stilted and edged his way onto the bed, lay on his back, and closed his eyes. His Father turned him over on his stomach and straddled him, his fingers working their way over his body. Gabriel tried to pull away, but his Father tightened his grip, punching him hard enough on his lower back, causing him to gasp for air.

*

His Father was shaking him, "Get up!"

Gabriel woke, the memory of the nightmare still with him. For a moment, he was uncertain of where he was, but as his eyes adjusted he remembered the pain that he'd endured. His heart raced. He blamed himself for being weak and incapable of defending himself. He pursed his lips, balled his fists, and closed his eyes. He saw his clothing lying on the floor beside his bed and noted the blood on them; he was certain that it belonged to him. He swung his legs over the bed, not daring to look at his Father who was shuffling around the room.

"There it is!" His Father said as he rolled a metal stand with a pole across the floor as if they were walking together. Gabriel's eyes widened in horror. It was the same stand with the clear plastic bag like the one his Father had used to cleanse his blood.

Am I full of evil again? Gabriel wondered. Then he heard the chanting. It was near him, filling the air with prayer, "Jesus Christ is victorious, and all the evil scatters by Him."

Gabriel scanned the room to see from where her voice was coming and felt a jab in his arm. The last thing he saw was his mother cowering in the corner, feverishly crossing herself, repeating her familiar chant.

All the Evil Scatters

8

"Now, don't you feel better?" His Father said when he saw that Gabriel was awake. "The final monster is gone."
    Gabriel could barely move from the pain. He saw blood on the bedsheets; beside him was a silver tray with medical instruments and a threaded needle, similar to the one he'd used to sew up the gash above his eye. The pain in his groin was excruciating. He closed his eyes. When the pain subsided slightly, he lifted his head and saw dried blood between his legs. His trembling hand reached down and gently touched the area; he felt a line of sutures and a cavern where his testicles should have been. *The pain. Oh, the pain. What has He done to me?* He pulled his hand away as if it were ablaze. As realization sank in, he hung his head over the side of the bed and vomited.

*

    Gabriel came in and out of consciousness for the next several days, his entire body sore. He stifled his screams that, if released would only bring more pain upon him. In his delirium, he remembered his mother wiping his forehead and cleaning his groin. She made him drink water as she chanted and crossed herself. Gabriel tried to speak to her, but she always shushed him and crossed her fingers against his lips. Through his grogginess, he saw her pin one of the charms that looked like an eye on his t-shirt.
    "I'm not a monster," Gabriel said.
    "I know. Sshh," his mother said, "you have to be quiet. Don't upset him."
    "He. He did this to me. Why?"
    "He is sick. I hope this time it works."
    "This time?"
    "Do as he says. We must both do as he says."
    For the first time, Gabriel sensed that his mother was not as lost as he'd thought she was.
    As if reading his mind, she said, "I have to save myself. He is in control. This will be our secret. Now sleep."
    "I will save you, mother," he said to her and thought, *I will kill the Man who is my Father. My Father is the Monster.*

All the Evil Scatters

He howled like a wounded animal, his convulsing body intensifying the pain. He stopped when he realized that the noise would alert his Father. He waited for the door to open, but his Father never came. He closed his eyes and cried until the pain subsided and thoughts of how he would kill his Father replaced the throbbing in his groin.

9

Gabriel woke to voices coming from outside of the house. He didn't know how much time had passed since his castration, but he felt it was many, many days. The pain had subsided and he was getting used to the numbness that occupied his now mutilated groin. The first few days were out of this world painful, a burning, cutting pain.

Beside his bed were two items: a piece of paper with information on how to properly clean the area to minimize infection; and, a container of antibiotics with a scraggly note: *Take 2 daily*.

He remembered the voices he'd heard moments earlier and lifted his legs over the bed, the pain punching his body as if something was being forced through him from the bottom up. He slumped over like an old man, moving step-by-step toward the window.

The voices from outside continued, but became more distant, the closer he got to the window. When he reached the window, the voices had stopped and there was no one there. He wondered if he'd imagined them.

*

For the second time in one day, Gabriel woke to noises. At first, he thought it was his mother's chanting and strained his ears to listen. But unlike earlier that day there were no voices, only the repeated pattern of *che, che, che, psshh, psshh, psshh* coming from somewhere on the property. He hobbled over to the window. The night had taken over the day and beyond the trees, he saw a figure. When the figure stood up, holding a spade in his hand, Gabriel recognized his Father. *What are you up to Father?* Gabriel thought and hoped that the digging had nothing to do with him. He shivered.

He dreamt that his Father had buried him alive; he woke up shaking at the thought of the cold earth covering his body, choking him.

All the Evil Scatters

10

Gabriel and his Father sat at opposite ends of a small table, reading from their respective books. Gabriel tried to concentrate on his book, entitled *Psychology for Today,* but the burning question about his mother's whereabouts had taken root and he needed to know where she was. He cleared his throat and said, "Is mo...mo... mother sick?"

"Why do you ask?" His Father said without looking up from His book, *Culture and History Throughout Time.*

"I haven't heard her praying. And I, um, wondered if she was okay?"

"She left us. She left you!" He said. "She left because she couldn't handle it. She doesn't love us anymore."

Did she leave? Gabriel wondered.

"She pried open her door and escaped," his Father explained. "By the time I realized what she had done, she was long gone. I looked for her, but I knew I was too late. Now you know why I had to lock her up. We were happy in the beginning. Then she became pregnant with you."

As his Father spoke he noted a scowl on his face when he looked at Gabriel. He cringed, fearing that his Father was about to punish him. He didn't move a muscle, waiting for whatever fate would befall him.

Gabriel was surprised when his Father went on, "She gave birth to you and that was when everything changed. I started to get these excruciating headaches. I couldn't sleep. I couldn't eat. Work was becoming a burden. Then your mother told me the story about her *yiayia,* remember?" His Father paused and Gabriel nodded. "She told me that she had learned the incantation that would help to rid me of the pain in my head. The pain eased with aspirin, but it didn't completely go away. Things went back to normal for a few years.

"You were about seven years old, in Grade three when things worsened. Whenever you came home from school, the headaches intensified. I started putting things together. My headaches started when YOU were born. You didn't have blue eyes, but I wondered if the eye colour mattered. I also wondered if you were bringing evil upon us. So I locked you up in the closet." His Father stopped and looked as if he was far away, remembering. "Your mother said that I was crazy, locking you up like that. I hit her so hard that she reeled backwards before falling to the floor. I locked her up in the

All the Evil Scatters

room from which she escaped. My headaches stopped. I knew that I was right."

Gabriel was silent, horror creeping into his body. All the things he had endured were because his Father believed that he was evil. *Am I?*

"Now do you see why I had to lock her up? If I hadn't, she would have run away long ago. Leaving us both. Leaving us before we could rid you of your evil."

Gabriel didn't see. *Why didn't you take me with you, Mother? Is it because I'm hideous to look at now that He took that away from me? I would have saved You!* Gabriel clenched his fists at his side, feeling a dull ache in his groin. "Jesus Christ is victorious, and all evil scatters by Him. Jesus Christ is victorious, and all evil scatters by Him. Jesus Christ is victorious, and all evil scatters by Him," he whispered under his breath.

His Father looked up and smiled. "At least she taught you that."

11

As time passed, Gabriel stopped believing that his Mother would return. He hated Her for abandoning him, almost as much as he hated his Father. He swore that one day he would find Her. Gabriel knew that his Mother was as guilty of what had happened to him as his Father.

"You'll never leave me like she did, right?" His Father said.

He didn't look up as he said, "No, Father."

Gabriel vowed to escape as his Mother had. He would find Her.

*

His Father started more consistent working hours, mostly in the afternoon and into the late evening, leaving Gabriel to freely roam the house. Gabriel was the happiest when his Father left him all alone. He cherished his freedom. Since the operation, his Father's beatings had stopped. Over the coming months, the changes in his body were subtle: the little hair he had in his pubic area and tufts of hair growing on his chest and chin became more sparse after the operation. Even his voice had taken on a high-pitched tone, often catching in his throat when he tried to speak, making him sound almost like Her.

All the Evil Scatters

During his Father's absence, he roamed the house looking for things to help him escape. He tried all the doors and windows; they were bolted shut, the windows protected by bars. There was no way out.

Gabriel approached one of three doors that his Father had forbidden him to enter. His need to know what was behind those doors intensified.

One day when he was certain that his Father would not be back for several hours and that he'd completed all of his chores, he stopped in front of the door that was between his and his Mother's room. He looked over his shoulder, a reflex, ensuring that he was still alone. He twisted the knob; it was locked. He reached atop the door frame. He'd seen his Father place his Mother's key above the door, on the frame, and wondered if he'd done the same for all of the doors. His fingers travelled along the wood frame, feeling the layers of dust and when he felt a small piece of metal, he knew he'd found what he was looking for.

He grabbed the key, unlocked the door, and entered. The room wasn't like any of the other rooms he'd seen. This one was painted a light blue; the shelves along one wall were filled with books, toy trucks, airplanes, and baseballs. A poster of a football player was taped to one of the walls. He closed his eyes and reached for a memory of having played with these toys. *Why did You keep me from this room and lock me in the closet?* He hit the sides of his legs with his fists and pursed his lips.

The bed was covered with a checkered black and blue blanket; He lay atop it and inhaled the dank and mouldy air. The blanket's rough fibres scratched his skin. The ceiling was painted black, coming alive with eyes of many different sizes drawn upon it. *Don't judge me,* he said and stared defiantly at the sky of eyes above him before rising from the bed. He looked around the room, saw a small box sitting on top of the desk, and went over to it; like the room itself, it was oddly familiar. He sensed that this box had been very important to him, but he didn't know how or why. He tried to recall the last time he'd seen it, but couldn't, almost as if a curtain was separating him from his memories. He was about to lift the lid, but before he could look inside, he heard a door opening downstairs. *Father's home.*

Gabriel scurried back to his room and waited for his Father to open the door, His after-work ritual.

His Father peered in and said, "Is dinner ready Gabriel?"

"I'll set the table."

All the Evil Scatters

Gabriel went downstairs while his father changed out of his uniform. He nervously set the table, glancing up from time to time, making sure that his Father didn't arrive before everything was ready. He folded the napkins in a triangle as his Father had instructed. The flatware was placed in its appropriate place on either side of the plate.

He thought about the room and the box he'd found. *I must get back in there,* he thought.

12

Following his Mother's abandonment, His Father rarely punished him. But when He did, He'd hang the belt on the back of the door and lock him in the closet. Gabriel saw it as his reprieve. Once a place of darkness it was now his haven. He pulled out his shard of glass, finding an uncut patch of skin among the rivers of cuts on his upper arms and muttered his Mother's words, "Jesus Christ is victorious, and all the evil scatters by Him." Gabriel mock-spat, *ftou, ftou, ftou,* three times as she'd done. Each time he said those phrases, he placed his thumb over the index and middle fingers and crossed himself, feeling one step closer to ridding himself of all evil.

There were also rewards, like reading and walking through the brush and trees on the property. They stopped at a mound of dirt and his Father told him to pray. "Jesus Christ is victorious, and all the evil scatters by Him. Jesus Christ is victorious, and all the evil scatters by Him. Jesus Christ is victorious, and all the evil scatters by Him." When his Father was satisfied, they moved on. As time passed the mound was swallowed up by weeds, but he still prayed.

During these outings, Gabriel looked around him, familiarizing himself with the property: the distance from the house to the road, where the animal traps that his Father had set up were located; and the gully between the road and the edge of the property. There were no other homes visible. As he scoured his surroundings, he mapped out how he would escape when he got the chance.

His Father bent down to examine one of the traps where a small gopher lay dead under the toothlike vice. Gabriel moved away slowly, never taking his eyes off Him, and edged backwards onto the gravel path. The sound of shifting pebbles crunching under his feet alerted his Father.

He looked up from what He was doing and leaped to His feet, grabbed Gabriel by the arm and yelled, "Where do you think you're going?"

"N...n...nowhere," Gabriel stammered.

"Doesn't look like nowhere to me," He said and punched Gabriel in the face, knocking him backwards onto the gravel. Gabriel winced from the pain as he landed hard on his buttocks.

"You're exactly like her! Always wanting to leave. But you're not going anywhere. Come with me!" He picked Gabriel up and pushed him toward a clearing. A rope with a noose hung from a tree. Gabriel tried to shake himself free from his Father's grasp, but He was bigger and stronger; the more Gabriel pulled, the angrier his Father got.

"Now I'm going to show you what it will feel like to die, to slowly take your last breath."

Beads of perspiration dotted Gabriel's forehead, and he recalled his dream of being buried alive. His head swirled like a maelstrom.

*

Gabriel woke in his bed. He couldn't remember how he'd gotten there. He swallowed, but it pained him. He felt his throat and moved his fingers along the rough skin which had not been there before. He bolted out of bed, took two steps to the mirror, and saw the fiery red track marks around his neck. He balled his fist and punched the mirror shattering it, oblivious to the shards of glass that pierced his skin, the blood dripping onto the dresser like an out-of-control tap. Gabriel picked at the skin on his neck with a piece of glass until dots of blood fell onto the dresser.

13

Many months passed and the routine of being trapped in the house with his Father continued. Reading, walking the grounds with his Father and being punished for misbehaving were part of his routine. Gabriel cooked and cleaned, leaving no speck of dust lest he garner his Father's wrath. With Mother gone, the house was mostly silent, particularly when his Father was working. He loved the solitude, the silence. But the spectre of his Father persisted.

All the Evil Scatters

One Sunday afternoon, the hair on Gabriel's neck tingled. He knew his Father was in the room before he saw Him. He tensed and waited for punishment.

"I have a surprise for you!" His Father entered the library with a box in his hand and put it in front of Gabriel. It was the same box he'd seen in one of the forbidden rooms. Gabriel was curious to see what was inside but feared that somehow his Father knew that he had been in that room and that it contained some new punishment.

"Go on. Open it! It's your birthday today."

"Birthday?" Gabriel had a vague recollection of birthday celebrations from long ago and reached for a memory that was no longer there.

"I know we don't normally celebrate, but today is special — you're sixteen. Too bad your mother isn't here to see all of your accomplishments. She deserted us too soon. No matter. We'll celebrate them together."

What accomplishments? Does reading books, preparing meals, and being obedient count? What's Father talking about? Gabriel was afraid to ask.

"Open it!" Aidan said, the excitement on his face urging Gabriel.

Gabriel lifted the lid apprehensively, wondering if it was a trick. He opened the lid fully, half expecting something to leap out and pull him into the box. He knew that his thought was absurd but he peered hesitantly inside the box: it was an eviscerated rat. Gabriel cringed.

"Well? Isn't it great?"

Gabriel wondered why his Father was doing this and fixed his eyes on the eviscerated rat remains, taking in the disgusting odour of rotting meat, sour and musty at the same time. The bile rose into his mouth, but he held it back. He was sickened by the appearance of the rat and wondered what horrible things his Father may have done to it. He wondered how long the rat had been in the box. "Thank you, Father," he stammered.

Gabriel watched his Father reach under the rat, removing a smaller box. His Father opened it and took out a long needle and what looked like thread and began sewing the rat's skin back together, hiding its entrails with every stitch.

"This is how you suture," his Father said. "One day it might come in handy for you. Show me what you got." His Father sliced through the stitches he'd made and waited for Gabriel to take the needle from Him.

All the Evil Scatters

The bile rose once again, but wanting to avoid his Father's wrath, he took the needle; his hand trembled as he pinched it between his thumb and two fingers. Slowly, he sewed the skin back together again hoping to avoid any further indignity that his Father might inflict on the poor creature.

"Not bad," his Father said when he was done. "You'll improve."

"May I take these Father?" Gabriel said, looking at the boxes.

"It's your party."

Gabriel gathered the boxes and took them to the basement. There was a hole in the far corner of the room that had been filled with pebbles. When he had removed enough stones to make a hole big enough to bury the rat, he took it out of its box and placed it in gently in the hole. He covered the rat with the pebbles, tamped them down with his hand and whispered, "Jesus Christ is victorious, and all the evil scatters by Him. You are safe now."

He placed the boxes in the back of his closet and before returning to his Father, he said, "One day, I will become a better paramedic than you." He hurried back upstairs, hoping that his Father was still in a good enough mood not to notice that Gabriel had been gone longer than was necessary.

He had nothing to worry about. His Father had fallen asleep, but when he heard Gabriel he opened his eyes and said, "Too much excitement for one day. I'm going to bed."

His Father dropped his house keys into a bowl and staggered up the stairs. Gabriel knew that his Father kept them in the bedroom. *Why the change?* He thought. *Another test?*

"I'll make your bed, Father," Gabriel said.

Up in the bedroom, Gabriel saw his Father's keys in their usual place on the nightstand. *Two sets of keys!* He thought. *This might be my chance.*

*

Later that night, when he was certain that his Father was asleep, he dashed into the kitchen and grabbed the keys. He fumbled, trying to figure out which one belonged to the front door. He was about to turn one of the keys when he heard:

"Where the fuck do you think you're going?"

Gabriel froze in place. "I, um. I wanted to see the full moon. Would you like to see it with me?" Gabriel smiled.

"There's no fuckin' full moon. You're running away! I knew I couldn't trust you. You are as predictable as she was!" His Father grabbed Gabriel,

All the Evil Scatters

punching him until he fell to the ground, hitting his head hard on the floor. He winced from the pain; his vision blurred. His Father pulled him up, grabbed him by the hair, dragged him toward the basement, and pushed him down the stairs. Gabriel's arms flailed wildly as his attempts to stop his descent failed. He landed on his back, feeling a sudden piercing pain in his ankle.

"Stay there until you repent for your sins!" The light behind His Father obscured him, but Gabriel sensed His seething anger.

Then all the light disappeared with the closing of the door; Gabriel was left in the dark at the bottom of the stairs. "Jesus Christ is victorious, and all the evil scatters by Him," he whispered.

*

His eyes became accustomed to the darkness; he made out where the chairs were and attempted to lift himself off the floor, but he felt as if a giant version of the truck he'd seen in the forbidden room had plowed over his entire body. His head ached and when he touched his body, it felt tender to his touch.

He rolled over onto his knees, steadying his body, and waited for the dizziness to ease before rising. "Owww," he howled, the pain in his ankle causing him to drop back down to the floor. *I will not fail next time, Father,* Gabriel thought as he hobbled over to where he knew the lamp was, fumbled for the switch, and turned it on.

He assessed the weird angle of his ankle and wondered if it was broken. He half-crawled, half-walked over to a chair, and plunked himself on it, taking a few moments to catch his breath. On his good foot, he hobbled around the room, looking for something with which to support his ankle. He found two pieces of wood and wrapped a towel around them, tightening it enough to support his weight. He smiled at the brace he'd created, proud of his ingenuity, and knew that soon he would put an end to his Father's torment.

I will stop You!

All the Evil Scatters

14

Several days passed. Every day was the same: the house upstairs was silent with no sounds of footfalls: no clanking around in the kitchen. The pain and swelling in his ankle receded but Gabriel had no food.

Hunger gnawed at this stomach. His Father hadn't left him any food. He drank water to curb his appetite and wondered how long his Father intended to keep him locked up with no food. Panic overcame him as he wondered how he would get out of there if his Father never came. No one would know that he was alone, imprisoned without hope of escape. He looked for something strong with which to pry the bars on the window, but he found nothing useful.

On the fifth day, he heard voices coming from above — three distinct male voices. Gabriel recognized his Father's, but he'd never before heard the voices of the other two men.

Gabriel clasped the handrail for support, hobbled up the stairs, and edged himself toward the door, placing his ear against it.

"Aidan," Gabriel heard. "Is there someone who can help you get around? Bring you food?"

"Thanks, Hisham. I'll call my son. He lives with his mother," Aidan said, laughing nervously. "We split a few years ago. He's a good son. I'm sure he'll come and help out his old dad."

Gabriel pictured his Father fake-smiling to convince, whoever Hisham was, that all was well in the Santis's residence. He wanted to scream: *I'm down here!* But instinctively he knew that he wouldn't win against his Father. Not yet. He would wait for the perfect opportunity, remembering his two failed attempts to escape that had landed him back in the basement because he'd been impatient and hadn't planned enough. *I will not make another mistake.*

"You'll need to rest. Make a concerted effort to walk each day. Want me to sign your cast?" The man named, Hisham, said.

"Nah. I like it clean."

"All right then. You've got everything that you need?"

"Got my cane," He said. "And my pills!"

"Don't overdo it. Oxycodone is addictive," the voice of the other man said.

All the Evil Scatters

Gabriel felt the throbbing pain in his groin and balled his hands. He made his way back down the stairs and retreated into the closet, wondering about his Father's injury. He heard footsteps move toward the front door and then its unmistakable opening and closing. A single set of footsteps and the *clop-clop* of what Gabriel assumed was his Father's cane retreated toward the kitchen.

Gabriel heard the creak of the basement door open. His Father's figure stood at the threshold and said, "Come up. I hope you've learned your lesson. I'll give you one more chance to prove to me why I shouldn't let you rot down there."

Gabriel made his way slowly up the stairs, the pain in his ankle was almost gone, and followed his hobbling Father into the kitchen. Gabriel suppressed a smile at the irony of both of them being incapacitated by leg injuries.

"Make us something to eat. I've missed your cooking. Why are you hobbling?" He said as Gabriel made his way to the refrigerator. "What did you do to yourself?"

"I, um, tripped and fell," Gabriel said and thought: *Seems like you've forgotten the push you gave me.*

"We're a pair, aren't we?" His Father said and snickered.

Gabriel prepared sandwiches for the two of them and set two plates, one in front of his Father and one in front of him. Even though Gabriel was hungry, he waited for his Father to eat first. When his Father finished eating, Gabriel wolfed down his food, barely taking a breath between biting and swallowing. In one gulp, he downed his juice. Gabriel still felt hungry but couldn't risk a second helping.

"I can't believe that this happened to me," Gabriel's Father said and tapped the cane against His cast several times.

"If that stretcher hadn't collapsed on my leg, shattering my tibia, I wouldn't have to be here all day with you. The recovery is three to six months."

Gabriel was heartened that His recovery would be long, a slow smile formed on his lips, but he stopped himself, lest his Father saw him and relegated him back down to the basement. *This will give me lots of time to plan my escape.*

"Help me upstairs," his Father said.

All the Evil Scatters

The weight of his Father crunched down on Gabriel's ankle. He worked through the pain by shifting his Father's weight onto his good leg. They stopped in front of his Father's bedroom, Gabriel hesitated before helping his Father into the bed.

His Father took out a couple of pills and swallowed them without any water. He placed the bottle of pills on his nightstand. Gabriel waited until His Father's snores rumbled through the house. Gabriel sighed with relief, hobbling toward the basement and slowly making his way down. He went to the closet and took out his shard of glass, picking at the scabs on his neck until the blood flowed.

*

Gabriel woke the next day with an idea. After bringing his Father breakfast, he gave him two pills. His Father fell asleep quickly. He memorized the name of the drug and when he was certain that his Father was asleep, he went into the library and pulled a book on pharmacology and looked up Oxycodone: highly addictive, and in large enough doses, it could incapacitate; too much and it could be lethal.

15

At the beginning of His convalescence, his Father went into town every couple of weeks, for groceries and to renew His prescription. He'd hobble down the stairs, aided by Gabriel, open then lock the door from the outside. Gabriel heard the engine spring to life and then the unmistakable sounds of pebbles hitting the side of the car as He drove away from the house. When He returned, He had more pills, promptly putting the bottle on display on his nightstand. Soon, the frequency of His outings increased, sometimes to twice a week, bringing home more pills than food. The pills were no longer in a bottle but in a small plastic bag.

During his father's absence, Gabriel scoured the house looking for things that he might use to escape. He found tools that would come in handy and hoarded food which he stowed at the back of his closet, ready for that moment when he would put his Father and this place out of his life forever.

Gabriel monitored his Father's sleep pattern. When he was certain that his Father was asleep, His snoring signalling that He was, Gabriel took one pill at a time, being careful not to take more in case his Father noticed the

All the Evil Scatters

missing pills and became suspicious, foiling his plan. Gabriel learned that the best time to take a pill was when his Father returned with a fresh batch. He wasn't quite sure how he would use the oxycodone but knew that it was his best option.

He put the pills in the pocket of his baggy pants and took them to the kitchen. He crushed the pills into a fine powder and stored it in a jar that read *sugar*. He placed it in the back of one of the cupboards. *The kitchen is your domain, Gabriel,* his Father had said. His father barely entered the kitchen these days, preferring sleep and popping pills to eating.

Gabriel cut himself more these days as the gravity of what he was planning to do became more real. More real as the amount of finely crushed pills filled the *sugar* jar. When he ran out of space on his arms and neck, he cut into his upper thighs, invisible, hidden from Him. And as the blood flowed it cleansed him of evil, like the time his Father had drained him of his evil blood. With every cut, he thought of ways to kill his father after he'd fed him enough oxycodone to render him helpless. *Strangulation. Quiet but not sufficiently painful to make Him suffer. An oxycodone overdose would be too quick a death and He wouldn't suffer or be aware of His horrible crimes, going into a comfortable sleep and then, death. Perhaps a slow painful death by cutting Him into pieces, starting with His eyes, then working my way down and cutting off His balls.*

*

One day, as Gabriel watched the news, he jolted with interest when the chyron: *Arsonist at large; Another barn in the area torched,* flashed along the bottom of the screen. The news anchor went on to say that they had no suspects and that the residents were taking measures to protect their properties in the small hamlet in northern Ontario.

I will burn You alive, he thought.

*

Gabriel planned his escape. He circled the date on the calendar and gathered newspapers, lighters, and other flammable material. An old lamp with enough kerosene would help start the fire. He'd pocketed coins and bills that he found lying around the house. He'd taken some of his Father's oxycodone. An old duffel bag, which he stored in the closet, contained a change of clothes, cans of food, a science book and the box with the needle and thread.

All the Evil Scatters

The night that he would execute his plan arrived bringing with it a clear sky; stars that looked like thousands of shimmering eyes danced around the moon, watching him, guiding him toward freedom. He didn't know where he would end up, but he didn't care, as long as it was far away from Him.

He inserted the key, its bow the shape of an evil eye, and licked his lips in anticipation. The bit clicked, unlocking the door. Gabriel paused and glanced behind him, expecting his Father's sudden appearance. When he felt it was safe to do so, he placed the duffel bag on the porch where he'd grab it on his way out.

As was customary, Gabriel made dinner for his Father. He poured beer into a glass and watched it fizzle and foam. When the head disappeared, he stirred in enough of the powdered oxycodone to render Him helpless, but still aware of what was going on. He put everything on a tray, grabbed the kerosene lamp, and made his way up the stairs to his Father's room.

He placed the lamp by the side of the door jamb and entered.

"Hello, um, Father," Gabriel said, knowing that soon he would be saying goodbye.

"I feel so much better tonight, Gabriel. I think I'll come downstairs for dinner."

"I've brought it here for you. With some beer," Gabriel smiled encouragingly.

"I'm bored of lying in bed. Help me downstairs."

Gabriel was dismayed; his careful planning was now uncertain. He had to think fast to persuade his Father to stay in bed. "I, um. I was thinking we might celebrate your recovery and fix you a proper meal tomorrow night. Make it special."

His Father looked at him, considering what Gabriel was saying. "You're a good son. All right. Tomorrow it is," He said and winked. "Come over here. I've missed you."

Gabriel stopped in mid-stride; the hairs on his nape tingled as if an evil breeze had entered the room.

"Come," he said.

Gabriel balked at the thought of having to endure any of that again.

He placed the tray on the night table and slowly approached His bed. He needed to make sure that his Father didn't suspect anything. "How about a sip of beer, Father? It always makes you happy."

All the Evil Scatters

"You know me so well," He laughed that evil laugh of his. "Give it here."

Gabriel watched Him gulp down the beer. Then he burped. "They say that beer is like a meal. I feel full already."

Gabriel smiled, patiently waiting for the effects of the beer and oxycodone to usher his father into his last slumber. As His father ate through his dinner, quickly at first but then, as time passed, his movements slowed, the food dribbling down his chin. He imagined the drug flowing through His father's blood like a river, the specks of the drug embedding themselves like grains of sand. His Father's focus waned, His gaze was distant and sleepy.

Gabriel's thoughts drifted. What would it be like out there? In the world where his Father had said monsters lived. But he knew now that the only monster was his Father.

Gabriel watched his Father's feeble attempts to rise from the bed, but the effects of the drug had slackened his body. He blubbered something that Gabriel couldn't understand, letting him know that it was finally time to put the rest of his plan into action.

He left the room and returned with the kerosene lamp.

"You...you...!" His Father gasped, and with a tremendous amount of effort lifted an accusatory finger at Gabriel before it plopped back down beside him.

His Father closed His eyes.

"Open your eyes, Father! You're not getting off that easy. Tell me why you hurt me all these years. What did I do to you?"

"I...I...I saaaaved you," his Father's slurred speech made Gabriel wonder if he'd given him too much of the drug before he could execute his plan. "From...from...monsters."

"That's a lie and you know it, Father!"

"No. No," his Father gasped as he tried to rise from the bed. "Monster. Evil. You."

"Why did you do this to me?" Gabriel said, pointing his finger at his crotch and then at his brow. "And this?"

"Rid you of evil. Monsters won't...won't get you."

"That's not true."

"What...what... did you put... in beer? Why?"

All the Evil Scatters

"Because tonight you are going to pay for everything that you and Mother did to me. And when I'm done here, I will find Her and do the same."

Gabriel pulled a knife out of the back pocket of his pants and moved over to his Father. He pulled his Father's pants down and made an incision. His Father screamed and squirmed to get out of bed as he realized what Gabriel was going to do to him. "No. No. No."

"You never gave me a choice? Why should I give you one?"

"I saaaaaved you,"

"You destroyed me. You're the Monster," Gabriel said and leaned in with the knife.

*

When his Father regained a semi-state of consciousness and Gabriel was certain that his Father would be aware of his next move, he removed the lamp's glass funnel and drizzled the oil onto the foot of the bed and whispered, "Goodbye, Father."

His Father's eyes tried to take in what was happening to him. A faint glimmer of fear passed across his face and then his eyes widened despite the drugs and the cuts that Gabriel had made to his groin area. Gabriel wanted his Father's horror to be a thousand times worse than what he'd endured.

He flicked on the lighter. Threw it at the oil and listened to the hissing and snapping of the flames gnawing hungrily at the bedsheets, like hundreds of mouths multiplying, as they travelled upwards and sideways. His Father's attempts to get out of bed failed. The flames bit into His legs, quickly devouring the skin as the blood dried on impact with the fire. His Father howled. Soon, the smell of burning flesh consumed the bedroom like the time he burnt a steak and the fat sizzled and sent smoke into the air.

His Father's lips moved, His words inaudible over the crackling flames. He screamed again.

At the foot of the bed lay his Father's belt. Gabriel reached into the growing flames and grabbed the belt, burning the hairs on his arm in the process. *It will be a reminder of what he did to me.* As he ran from the fire, he tripped on the carpet's edge, hitting his head against the banister.

Everything went dark.

*

Smoke tickled Gabriel's nose. He coughed. His confusion was replaced with a sense of urgency. The flames had engulfed his Father's room, gaining

All the Evil Scatters

momentum as they edged close to him, reaching out like burning hands from hell. "Jesus Christ is victorious, and all evil scatters by Him. Jesus Christ is victorious, and all evil scatters by Him. Jesus Christ is victorious, and all evil scatters by Him," he said and rose to his feet. Still woozy from the fall that had knocked him out briefly, he grasped the railing and moved slowly down the stairs ever-aware of the fire's long fingers were reaching for him. He made it down the stairs, but stopped to grab the frame that held his photo, put it under his arm, left the house and picked up the duffel bag that waited for him on the porch.

He heard the hissing snap of wood and turned around for one more look. He watched as the staircase collapsed into itself, the fire eating its way through the wood like a giant termite. Windows from above him shattered, hitting his head with scraps of glass and wood. He ran. He ran from the flames. He ran away from the stinging smell that filled the fresh summer night. He ran from the horrors that he had endured.

As he ran, Gabriel thought he heard his Father screaming his name, but he knew that by now He was long dead.

He ran out onto the road and came to a screeching halt when a small van swerved to avoid him, missing him by inches. The van's driver corrected it straight back onto the road and continued on his way.

A while later, Gabriel heard a fire truck barreling down the country road, heading in the direction from where he'd come. He dropped himself into a drainage ditch and waited for it to pass. When the fire truck disappeared over the hill its siren faded into the distance, he rose, wiped at his clothes, and clambered back onto the road.

Gabriel walked and ran, forever it seemed until the ache in his legs overcame his need to continue. He was far enough away now to rest; he found a place in the woods and decided to sleep there for the night, his only companion, the moon and its many shiny eyes, watching over him, like they always did.

I'm finally free. He closed his eyes and slept.

All the Evil Scatters

16

Over the next few days, Gabriel continued walking and running until the soles of his feet burned. His head throbbed and his body felt like something with enormous force had hit him. But he was free at last — nothing could overshadow his freedom.

He came upon a gully in the woods and dropped his bag, deciding that it would be his bed for the night. He inspected the blisters that had formed on his feet. *Tomorrow I will double up on socks.*

He looked at his scant supply of food: one jar of fruit and a can of tuna remained. On the fourth day since his escape, he came upon a sign that read, *Welcome to Erin,* and saw the beginnings of a town, houses rising in the distance like beacons of hope. He sat on a boulder by the side of the road and cried. He wiped away his tears with his sleeve and looked with hope at the road which turned into a tree-lined street where majestic houses stood guard. He edged into the town, and as he rounded the bend in the road, he saw Him.

No. No. You can't be here. His Father loomed ahead of him. *Alive. How can it be? I killed you. I heard you scream.*

Gabriel turned back the way he'd come, but his Father was right there, only a few feet away, His charred skin crumbling away from His body, falling slowly, as if in slow motion, onto the ground.

Gabriel closed his eyes and whispered his words of safety, "Jesus Christ is victorious, and all the evil scatters by Him, Jesus Christ is victorious, and all the evil scatters by Him, Jesus Christ is victorious, and all the evil scatters by Him." He crossed himself three times and mock-spat, *ftou, ftou, ftou.* His Father disappeared.

Retail shops, eateries, and businesses lined the street. He found himself among a crowd of people who had stopped to admire one of the buildings. A woman with the bluest of eyes Gabriel had ever seen, was telling the group about the architecture of the red brick building with white columns on either side of its entrance.

Gabriel backed away, never taking his eyes off the woman with eyes just like his Mother's. He shuddered, fists clenched at his side.

Beep. Beep. Beep.

The sound broke his gaze; he narrowly missed the oncoming car and darted to the side of the road. Gabriel's hands went up apologetically.

The man behind the wheel waved his hand, indicating that it was all right.

He kept walking until he saw a diner, stopped in front of it and opened the door.

A server named Daisy showed him the way to a booth where there was a discarded newspaper. She picked it up to clear the table.

"Do you mind leaving the paper for me if it doesn't belong to anyone? I haven't read the news in days," Gabriel said and flashed a smile and, as he reached for the paper, Daisy's eyes landed on the scars on his arms. He quickly pulled his sleeves over them. Daisy left the menu and the paper on the table.

He ignored the menu and flipped through the newspaper, scanning it for news of his Father's death, finally seeing an article at the bottom of page four. *Not even worth being on the front page,* Gabriel thought as he read:

Orangeville. The remains of the victim found in the old Orchard House were identified as those of Aidan Santis, a paramedic who had been injured on the job four months previously. Significant amounts of oxycodone were found in his bloodstream suggesting that he'd taken too much of the highly addictive opioid which rendered him incapable of escaping the flames that eventually consumed him. The cause of the fire is believed to have been started with kerosine fluid leading authorities to suspect that the Orangeville arsonist, who has plagued the area for over a year, may also be responsible for this fire.

Police are looking for Mr. Santis's wife, Eugenia, and son, Gabriel, who according to friends, was separated from Aidan Santis. Mr. Santis lived alone. To date, authorities have been unable to locate Mr. Santis's next of kin.

Advocates and experts for the regulation of prescribing highly addictive opioids for pain management took to the media urging lawmakers to restrict their use.

The investigation continues.

That's good. They think I am with Mother, Gabriel thought and tore out the article. He put it in his bag. *One day, I will find You and ask why You abandoned me.*

All the Evil Scatters

Using some of his meagre funds, Gabriel bought a bus ticket to Toronto. He'd read about the big city in one of his Father's books. A huge place filled with millions of people.

17

For the next several months, Gabriel roamed the streets, taking shelter on top of the warm sidewalk grates when he could find one that was unoccupied. Other times he folded pieces of cardboard over himself, protecting his body from the rain that pelleted him or the snow that whipped across his body.

Gabriel shuddered, the January air nipping at his face and fingers. *I need to find better shelter*, he thought. He'd saved some money, but one night while he was sleeping he'd been robbed. He now knew exactly where to keep the money. He created a makeshift sack from a discarded piece of cloth, tying it with a strand of yarn, that he'd pulled from a wool top, and hung it on the inside of his pants. The coins jingled whenever he moved, comforting him in the knowledge that as long as he could hear it, it was safe.

*

He jerked his head up and peered out from his cardboard shelter and saw a scrawny, mangy cat with a missing eye; his motley-coloured, long-haired coat reminded him of a checkerboard. The cat poked its nose under the cardboard, finding a nook at the back of Gabriel's bent knees and purred. Comforted, Gabriel cleaned around the cat's eye with some of the alcohol that someone had left for him. He hadn't drunk any of it, saving it in case he needed it for bartering. He shared his meagre food with it, and slowly the cat put on weight and didn't look as malnourished.

"I will call you, Cat," he said, as the cat meowed and sidled up to him, rubbing his head against his leg.

One day, Cat was gone. He called out to it as the snow fell around him, but Cat never returned.

*

One surprisingly warm day in February, two men approached him and without warning kicked him a couple of times.

"Wh…why'd you do that?" Gabriel said, wincing from the pain, remembering the assaults inflicted by his Father.

All the Evil Scatters

"This is our turf, man! Get the hell outta here or next time we won't be so gentle," said the man with the long grey beard and fingers thick as sausages.

"I didn't know. Sorry," Gabriel said grabbing his duffel bag and the few dollars he'd earned. He turned to leave.

The bearded man grabbed Gabriel by the scruff of his neck, slightly lifting him off the ground. "And where do you think you're going?"

"Leaving your turf."

"Wise guy, huh?"

The two men laughed and the bearded man, without warning punched Gabriel in the face. He raised his hands to protect his face from further assault and, in so doing watched as the bills he was clutching fell to the ground.

"Now that wasn't so hard was it?" The bearded man said and scooped up the money. "Now get the hell outta here!"

Gabriel scurried away, smarting from the pain in his jaw and side.

He roamed the streets, looking for another neighbourhood; he found an area where the smell of food tickled his nose. A sign on one of the windows said, *Welcome to the Danforth.* He saw the same phrase repeated in several places.

He walked up and down the avenue, scouring the area to make sure he wasn't on anyone's *turf*. He looked through the windows — people were eating, smiling and chatting.

On one of the windows, he saw a sign: *Dishwasher wanted.*

He entered the restaurant. Four booths with well-worn upholstery were toward the back of the restaurant, near the kitchen from what he could tell. Another four tables were set up toward the front. Five swivel stools were lined up like soldiers along the long bar. Gabriel inhaled the pungent aroma of cooked food. His mouth watered, realizing that he couldn't quite remember when he'd had a proper meal. He took another deep breath, filling his chest with the greasy air that consumed the diner. The unmistakable smell of meat cooking tickled his nose; he closed his eyes, feeling faint from hunger. When he reopened his eyes he was startled to see an elderly man in front of him, waving a menu in his hand.

"Allo. Eat alone?"

"I, um, no. I came for the job."

All the Evil Scatters

"Oh," the man said, disappointment in his voice as he put the menu down on the table and wiped his hands on his food-stained apron.

"I, um, could have something to eat," Gabriel said, searching his pocket for money and felt a few quarters, hardly enough for a meal.

As if sensing Gabriel's hesitancy the old man extended his hand and said, "I'm Stavros Patris. My restaurant. You want job?"

"Yes," Gabriel nodded, his eyes focusing on his shoes.

"Good. But first, you eat," Stavros said. "Dimitri, give friend daily special. On house. He gonna work here."

A tall, thin young man, probably in his 20s, appeared from the back of the diner and said, "Yes, *baba*."

"How old?" Stavros said.

Gabriel took a moment to think and said, "Seventeen."

"Hmm," Stavros said, his eyebrows arching as if debating the authenticity of Gabriel's age.

"I'm 17," Gabriel said, this time with authority.

"You have papers?" Stavros said.

"Papers?" Gabriel repeated.

"Yes. Social insurance number, something with name." Stavros said.

Gabriel shook his head, perplexed that he would need to show who he was.

"No matter to me," Stavros said and winked. "I still hire you. Will be secret."

Gabriel wondered how he would get the things that Stavros talked about. Gabriel hadn't thought to look for any before he set fire to his Father.

Stavros motioned to a table near the front of the restaurant.

Gabriel sat, happy that he would soon make some money and that his new boss was going to feed him. And then he saw it, his Mother's talisman, the evil eye, painted above the doorframe. *This place will protect me,* Gabriel thought and under his breath said, "Jesus Christ is victorious, and all the evil scatters by Him, Jesus Christ is victorious, and all the evil scatters by Him, Jesus Christ is victorious, and all the evil scatters by Him."

*

Gabriel was thankful that Stavros would pay him cash. No one asked Gabriel any questions about where he was from or what his story was.

All the Evil Scatters

Gabriel put the past out of his mind. Stavros paid him seventy-five dollars for eight hours of work.

Stavros' wife, Xanthi, took orders at the front of the restaurant; his son, Dimitri was always cleaning the floors and tables.

During the day, Gabriel slept on the street, ensuring he wasn't on anyone's *turf*; he worked at night until he'd made enough money to rent a room in a house that he shared with two other men. By then the days were getting longer, the wind was warmer; the city came alive with budding trees and tulips peeking up through the skim waking from their slumber. The cramped quarters didn't matter to him. It was like a luxury resort compared to the confinement in that large house. He was free to come and go as he pleased. Gabriel shared a bathroom, a Coleman stove, and a bar fridge, but he didn't need the latter as he had plenty to eat at the restaurant: food orders that went wrong; too much pre-cooked food; expiry dates.

*

"Looks like you knows way around kitchen," Stavros said a few months later as he watched Gabriel flip his omelette in the pan, fold it with his spatula, and slide it onto his plate.

"Years of practice," Gabriel smiled for the first time in a long time.

"You cook for me? Yes?"

"You want me to cook?"

"Yes. You everything Dimitri not."

*

"You never learn. What they teach you in school?" Stavros yelled at Dimitri, spittle spraying from his mouth as he spoke. Dimitri scampered away and cleaned the tables, taking care not to miss any crumbs.

On several occasions, Gabriel witnessed Stavros slapping his son on the head for no apparent reason.

Gabriel learned to chiffonade herbs, coddle an egg, and finely slice through meat.

"One day, you own place like this, yes? My son. He stupid," Stavros said. "You don't need education to own a restaurant. You smart."

Gabriel nodded, but he knew that the only thing he wanted to do was to become a paramedic. But he would be better and smarter than Him. There was one problem that Gabriel had. He had no school diploma, he had no identification. He had nothing to show who he was. *I will ask Dimitri. He will know how to help me.*

*

"Petros, my cousin will help you with what you need," Dimitri said.
"Really?"
"Yes. ID. Stuff. Papers," Dimitri said.
"Social insurance number? Driver's licence?"
Dimitri nodded and said, "It's none of my business, but were you in jail? You running from something?"
Before his escape, Gabriel felt that he was in jail. He shook his head and said. "I lost my ID in a fire." It was partially true. Gabriel had never thought to look for any papers that confirmed his identity. Any papers that were in the house had been destroyed by the fire. But it was all right, he would recreate everything based on information that he already had. He thought of changing his name, but it. Gabriel Santis would be a reminder of who he had been and who he would become.
"We all have story, yes? Petros take care you," Dimitri said and jotted down an address.

18

Petros wanted three thousand dollars to get Gabriel what he needed. Gabriel balked at the amount. He would need to work another six months to amass that kind of money, but he pulled out a few hundred dollars and said, "I'll give you some more at the end of the month and the rest by August."
"That's four months from now," Petros said, counting the months on his fingers. "You pay. You get," Petros said. He was older, in his early thirties and was already balding, a few hairs remained atop his head.
"I promise I'll have it. Dimitri can vouch for me."
"My cousin's a good boy. He needs to get away from the restaurant. You should too. Make something of yourself. Okay. I'll do this for you. When I have half the money, I'll give you what you need. You can pay me the rest in instalments. I'll charge you low interest. Fifteen percent," Dimitri said, scratching the top of his head.
Gabriel nodded. He had no other choice.

All the Evil Scatters

The following month, Gabriel returned and gave Petros some more money. In exchange, he received three plastic cards: social insurance, a birth certificate and a driver's licence. He also gave him an envelope from which he withdrew a high school graduation diploma. *My graduation diploma.*

"Thank you. I will give you the balance with interest in four months."

"Yes," Petros said dismissively.

When Gabriel received his next pay, he opened up a bank account, using his identification and deposited his earnings.

*

Gabriel exited the kitchen and caught the tail end of what appeared to be an argument between Stavros and Dimitri.

"... you no good for nothing, lazy, *sommamabitch*. Work and we talk," Stavros said.

Gabriel was surprised to hear his boss accusing his son of not working. He pushed the tip of the knife that he was holding against his thigh, feeling it pierce his pants and find skin. *How could Stavros say those things? Dimitri worked all the time, non-stop, doing everything his father told him.* He felt the throbbing in his groin and tightened his grip on the knife cutting his skin, oblivious to the small bloodstain on his pants.

"You think you too good for this? Go! Come back when ready to start from bottom!" Stavros said and spat on the linoleum floor.

Gabriel clenched the knife and wondered if Stavros had ever inflicted on Dimitri the kind of pain that his Father had on him.

19

By his eighteenth birthday, Gabriel had saved enough money to pay off Petros. He spent days on end at the library, where it was a welcome escape from the August humidity. There he researched science and medical journals. He studied anatomy and physiology; learned about the layers of the skin and the musculoskeletal composition of the human body. He reviewed pharmacology books and looked for information on drug interactions and their effects on the brain. Drugs for pain relief. Drugs for sleep. Drugs for incapacitation.

The animosity between Stavros and Dimitri intensified over the coming months. The verbal and physical abuse continued. Gabriel found himself

All the Evil Scatters

thinking of ways to deal with Stavros: set the place on fire with him in it; stab him; poison him. He didn't act on any of his thoughts, choosing instead to cut himself with a small hunting knife he'd bought at a thrift store. He cut into the epidermis on his arm, above the elbow. He didn't want his scars to be visible and made sure that he wore long sleeves. When the blood flowed, he felt a release.

*

After he'd paid off Petros, he applied to paramedic school and was excited to get the confirmation letter for his acceptance a few weeks later. He would start the first semester in January, and by the time he was 21, he would be a college graduate. Gabriel hurried to the restaurant. He wasn't on shift that day, but he wanted to share the good news with someone. Dimitri, the ever-obedient son, was there clearing tables.

"Hey. What are you doing here? It's your day off. Wish I had a day off."

"I've been accepted to paramedic school and I wanted to share it with someone," Gabriel said.

"I wish I could do something like that. But dad has enslaved me to this crappy restaurant life."

Dimitri reached under the counter, grabbed a couple of shot glasses and a small bottle containing a clear liquid and propped them on the counter. Gabriel read the word *ouzo* on the label. He poured some of the liquid into their glasses and said, "To you, Gabriel. I wish you much success."

20

Gabriel was fascinated by suturing methods: folding the skin and sewing it together; watching the skin tighten over the wound, the blood protected from seeping out.

Gabriel researched the material used for suturing wounds. Catgut, although no longer widely used for stitching up people, piqued his interest because he was certain that he could make it himself. It reminded him of the suturing material he'd used long ago to seal the gash on his brow, and then to resew the eviscerated rat he had gotten for his birthday. Gabriel began making catgut from the leftover lamb or goat intestines that the restaurant discarded and brought them back to his room.

All the Evil Scatters

To prepare the catgut, Gabriel cleaned the intestines by meticulously cutting out the fat and scraping off the external membrane with a blunt knife. A small bucket, filled with epoxide, alcohol, and boiled water, served as a vessel for soaking the slippery fibres.

His roommates didn't seem to mind it when he draped the prepared strands on a makeshift rack, drying them as one might if they were making pasta.

"Whatcha got going on there?" Said Ivan, his short, scrawny roommate with the pimply face.

"It's part of my paramedic training. I need to know how to make this and be able to use it on the job if I need to," Gabriel lied.

"Cool. There's nothing like that in my accounting classes," Ivan said. He laughed and went to the refrigerator, pulled out a drumstick, and chomped on it as if he hadn't eaten in days.

When the strands had dried and were clean and malleable, he twisted them together to make a long piece of string. "This will be fine," Gabriel said out loud as he wrapped the finished strands onto a spool as if it were thread and put it in his duffel bag. The entire process took Gabriel less than a week to make enough catgut to begin his practice.

*

While his roommates slept, he left the apartment and prowled the streets for injured animals upon which to practice his suturing technique. He started with squirrels and cats, being especially excited when he came upon an injured dog. He took the whimpering animals to the ravine near his rooming house, where he tried to sew them up, to save them. Gabriel liked the bigger animals as they gave him a larger surface with which to work.

Gabriel was pleased every time he was able to save an animal. Every once in a while, the animal died because and infection would set in. Even though he disinfected the wound the animal's injuries had progressed such that he couldn't save it. Gabriel remembered Cat and wondered if she'd died alone and injured on the streets. When he lost one of the animals, he carved a notch on his skin as a reminder of his failure to save it. He took great care to sew their eyes shut so that they would be protected from any evil.

With time he mastered his stitching technique, but soon realized that he wanted to work on larger specimens; dogs and small animals were no longer enough. But something intense, something insistent began to grow inside of him. It was like a hunger that he couldn't satiate it. In those moments, his mind was a blur, but he saw Them very clearly: his Father and his Mother. The pain of what they had done to him, returned. And each time it did his fury grew as did his ability to control his urges. *I will stop You or Anyone who harms me. No one will ever hurt me again!*

21

"Gabriel!" Stavros called from the front of the restaurant.

Gabriel pushed open the door from the kitchen and went to him. He saw a young boy who'd sliced his finger with one of the steak knives. Blood was everywhere.

"Get some towels," Gabriel said.

"We've already called 9-1-1," the boy's frantic mother said.

"I can fix this. Stop the bleeding," Gabriel said.

"You do that?" Stavros said.

"I'm in paramedic school," he said. "I can take care of it. I've done it many times." When the mother hesitated, her eyes shifting from one person to another and then to her son, Gabriel continued, "Your son needs attention right away."

The mother nodded her consent.

"You're such a good young man," Stavros said. "Where's that *sommamabitch* son of mine?" He looked around and spotted Dimitri clearing the tables toward the back of the restaurant and motioned for him to come.

"I'll be right back," Gabriel said, went into the kitchen, and returned holding his medical kit.

"Now this will hurt a bit, but it will be over quickly," Gabriel said as he threaded the needle, poured alcohol on it, and cleaned the boy's wound. "Two stitches oughta do it."

The boy nodded, tears trickling down his cheeks. He winced as Gabriel threaded the needle in and out two times, cinching it at the end and cutting off the excess. "That will hold."

"That's some fine work, dude," Dimitri said.

"You could learn a few things from him," Stavros said.

That night, Gabriel returned to his apartment and was elated at what he was able to do. *Much better working on humans than on animals,* he thought,

All the Evil Scatters

grabbing his pocket knife and cutting himself a couple of times on his lower abdomen. He inhaled deeply and slowly released his breath. With each breath he remembered the belt whipping against his young flesh, the blade of the knife slicing his brow, and the ultimate humiliation, his castration. Gabriel vowed that he could always be in control and never be taken advantage of again.

He cut into his skin and turned off the light.

That night his dreams were like a film montage: a car racing into the forest; a boy, him, going down the steps of a big building; three kids his age picking up a broken chair from the side of the road; Father driving to a hospital; Mother holding him tight; Someone was hurt; a car door slamming shut; darkness.

*

The next morning, Gabriel walked into the restaurant and heard Stavros berating Dimitri once again, but stopped when he saw Gabriel and said, "Hello my boy."

I am not your boy, Gabriel thought and knew what he had to do. It was clear in his mind. This man was like his Father. This man had to die, just like Him.

22

"I have the perfect drug for you," said Norman, the drug-peddling pimp Gabriel met on the streets when he first came to Toronto.

"I want something swift and not immediately detectable. Something that will kill," Gabriel said as he glanced around Norman's garage which looked more like a storage facility than a place to park your car.

"Okay. Okay. 'Nuff details," Norman said and opened a neatly organized drawer filled with row-upon-row of pills of different shapes and colours; some vials contained powder, others liquid.

He opened another drawer and pulled out a plastic vial with something that looked like water. "Give him or her, this," Norman said and handed Gabriel a thimble-sized container with a colourless liquid.

"What is it?"

"Good, old-fashioned cyanide. It's fast-acting and can kill within minutes or a few hours."

All the Evil Scatters

"How do I use it?"

"Put all of it in their food or drink. Ipso facto they're dead."

"Sounds good," Gabriel said and handed Norman some money.

*

As Stavros ate the breakfast that Gabriel had prepared for him, Gabriel prepared the grill and turned on the ovens in preparation for the morning rush.

From time to time, he glanced over at Stavros who sat in the corner booth at the back of the restaurant. Gabriel heard a thud from the corner booth and went to have a look. Stavros sat lifeless, his eyes staring up at the ceiling. He checked for a pulse. Nothing. His chest didn't rise and fall and when he put his hand near Stavros's mouth, there was no breath.

Gabriel removed the dirty dishes, flushed the leftovers down the toilet, and washed the dishes. He wiped the bowl clean and dialled 9-1-1.

He crossed himself and said, "Jesus Christ is victorious, and all the evil scatters by Him. Jesus Christ is victorious, and all the evil scatters by Him. Jesus Christ is victorious, and all the evil scatters by Him. *ftou, ftou, ftou*"

23

Later that night, Gabriel read an article in the Toronto Star with interest:

Toronto. Stavros Patris, the owner of the popular eatery in the heart of Greek town, has died of a heart attack. Mr. Patris was known to have suffered from heart disease. Many patrons have laid flowers and other tokens in front of the restaurant. Many remember him as a generous and kind man.

He is survived by his wife, Xanthi and son, Dimitri. It is unclear whether they will keep the restaurant open.

Gabriel cut out the article and placed it in the box and put it on the shelf with the news articles about his Father's death. Beside the box was a row of videotapes of the animals he'd operated on. Another small box, the one from his birthday that used to contain a needle and suturing material now contained many charms of the evil eye.

All the Evil Scatters

24

Gabriel pulled out of the ambulance station, turned on the siren, and eased the emergency vehicle onto the road. That day, like most other days for the past few years when Gabriel was on shift, he was paired with Duke, an emergency medical technician.

He glanced at his colleague and said, "Ready?"

"Yes, sir," Duke said inflecting the "i" as if it were an "a", making the word seem much longer than its three letters. Duke was a recent transplant to Toronto from Birmingham, Alabama. His laid-back attitude, aloof manner and eagerness to please suited Gabriel. They were about the same age, in their mid-20s. That's where the similarities ended. Duke was almost half a foot taller than Gabriel. Where Gabriel was quiet and spoke only when necessary, Duke filled every gap of silence with entertaining stories about his life in the South, often equating Canadian polite society to southern hospitality. Gabriel didn't agree with Duke's point of comparison but didn't see the need to debate a subject in which he had no interest.

Gabriel turned on the siren and alternated the car's flashing lights, switching adeptly back and forth, depending on the traffic congestion. He gunned the accelerator and sped off down the street.

"Get out of the way, dude," Duke said, waving both hands at the driver in front of them.

Gabriel saw the driver's head bopping up and down to the tune of some unknown song. The driver was oblivious to the ambulance charging behind him, trying to get through the busy street. When the driver finally realized that the ambulance was almost on top of him, he stopped directly in front of it. Gabriel swerved around the car, narrowly missing it and continued to their destination.

"Toronto drivers," Duke said. "Not so polite." He laughed with the mirth of a child.

Gabriel shrugged his shoulders and said, "No matter. One day they will understand."

"Raaaaght."

Gabriel parked the ambulance in front of a duplex on a quiet street in Cabbagetown. They carried the stretcher up the stairs, acknowledging the two police officers who were already at the scene. A remorseful, seemingly

All the Evil Scatters

distraught husband sat handcuffed and blubbering like a baby at the top of the stairs, repeatedly saying, "Didn't mean it. She wasn't listening. I grabbed the knife. Now she's bleeding."

Her wounds aren't deep, but she'll have scars, Gabriel thought. *I know I'm not supposed to do this, but I need to do it. I can do this.* Gabriel looked into the woman's soulful brown eyes. A memory of a dog, a black lab with similar eyes, crept into his consciousness. He tried to remember more, but before he could, the woman's nails jabbed his arm and the memory evaporated.

He finished cleaning her wounds, looked around the room, and knew from Duke's animated gestures that he was telling one of his stories; the two cops tried to hold back their laughter, but Duke's engaging manner had them in stitches in no time.

"Duke? A hand please," Gabriel said.

Duke was at Gabriel's side in an instant.

As a precautionary measure, they were going to take the woman to the hospital for observation. They put her on the stretcher, strapped her in, and carried her down the stairs and out onto the street where neighbours had gathered to gawk at their fallen neighbours. *I wonder which one of them called it in?* Gabriel thought.

The police had already brought down the handcuffed husband who was securely seated and belted in the back of the cruiser. His door was open and Gabriel heard his blubbery litany: "Sorry, honey. Sorry, honey. Sorry, honey."

When they had secured the woman inside the ambulance, Gabriel said, "I'll stay here with her. You take us into Emerg."

Duke nodded, sat behind the wheel of the ambulance, adjusted the seat, and turned on the radio.

Gabriel cleaned the woman's wound; from his pocket, he pulled out the already prepared needle and began to suture it.

All the Evil Scatters

25

Gabriel drove out of the city later that evening, the darkness giving him both silence and anonymity. Last year, he had opted for a rental in the country, a place much cheaper than his bachelor apartment in the city. It was far from prying eyes, enabling him to practice and prepare.

Once inside, he emptied his pocket, filled with three half-used vials of medication that he'd collected during his shift. He opened his refrigerator and placed them on the top shelf among dozens of similar vials. A carton of eggs, milk, and an orange were the only other items in the fridge.

He carefully withdrew a couple of unused syringes, from his other pocket and put them in the plastic Sharps container. There was another Sharps container filled with broken and used needles.

He made his way to the basement where a whimpering dog lay on the floor, barely able to open its eyes when it heard Gabriel approach. His moaning increased; his tail wagged slightly as if he were trying to tell Gabriel how happy he was to see him.

"It will be over soon, dog," he said, grabbing one of the needles with the ketamine. This dog was beyond saving, his injuries too severe. Gabriel was mad at himself for not being able to properly stitch up the dog. He patted the dog's head gently before piercing him with the needle. He held the dog as it whimpered, its pain slowly subsiding until it sputtered its last breath.

"Sorry, Dog. You know I wanted to save you." Gabriel's tears fell on the animal's fur.

He grabbed the dog and took it out to the yard.

26

"I'm sorry Gabriel, but you know the rules. Unless you have the proper designation, you are not allowed to stitch up people," his boss, John Hanani said.

"But she was bleeding," Gabriel stood up, anger sparking in his eyes.

"That's not your job. You don't yet have the credentials; there are medical professionals equipped to do that."

"I wanted the blood to stop," Gabriel said.

All the Evil Scatters

"Her wounds were superficial. The doctor or nurse at the hospital would have taken care of that. You had no right."

I have more experience than you know, Gabriel thought; instead, he said, "I'm sorry. It won't happen again."

"Make sure it doesn't. If it does, you'll be suspended without pay," John said.

*

Gabriel seethed from the encounter with his boss. He had saved that woman. *No. This won't work. I need my autonomy. I'm not going to wait for my "designation". I'll pick and choose who I save. I don't want to listen to people who feel they have the right to tell me what to do. I listened to Him all those years. Now, I will do it my way.*

He exited the station, immediately finding himself caught up in a swarm of people, buzzing around leaving or going to work. A woman bumped into him; she glared at him, her lips curled in disgust, blue eyes penetrating right through him causing him to stop in his tracks. She didn't stop, but Gabriel heard her whisper, *Monster.* As she wove in and out of the crowd. Gabriel said, "It's been a long time, Mother. I'm glad I finally found you."

He followed the woman down the street and around the corner.

*

Gabriel and Duke zipped up two dead adolescents into black body bags; a young male and female who had made a pact to die together.

"I dunno if I'll eeeever get used ta carting dead bodies," Duke said.

The sombreness of death had no impact on Gabriel who zipped the vinyl bag without lament or comment.

*

He looked about his workshop. On the wall hung a grey plywood board with many holes in which he'd hung medical instruments, such as scalpels, scissors and tweezers of all shapes and sizes. Empty IV bags and spools of suturing thread hung from nails that he'd affixed to the board. On each corner of the board, he had painted eyes from which red tears flowed. "See Mother? You've taught me a few things too. Eyes are evil."

He clenched his fists at his side and felt the dull, familiar ache. The only way to curb the feeling was when he practiced his craft. *I need something bigger. Something better to perfect my skill,* he thought.

All the Evil Scatters

"Did you ever imagine my success, Father?" He said "That I would even follow in Your footsteps? And You, Mother. Where did You go? I've scoured the Internet for signs of Your whereabouts, but You vanished like a ghost. Why didn't you stay and protect me? You were a coward, just like Father said. You will pay for Your role in all of this! I thought I found you the other day, but I was wrong. That was not You."

He crossed himself three times and said: "Jesus Christ is victorious, and all evil scatters by Him. Jesus Christ is victorious, and all evil scatters by Him. Jesus Christ is victorious, and all evil scatters by Him."

"I am ready."

PART 2

All the Evil Scatters

27

It's a busy Saturday afternoon in the downtown core of the city. People milling about — shopping, eating and walking, and talking into their phones. The past two days had alternated between heavy rains and sunshine, not unusual for April. Climate change, I suppose.

No one notices me. Ahh. The beauty of living in Toronto. I'm anonymous in my jeans, sneakers, sunglasses, Toronto Blue Jays sweatshirt and baseball cap. A black t-shirt and hoodie complete my outfit. I look like one of the thousands of white suburban dudes roaming the streets before the baseball game. I reach for a memory of someone, me, playing baseball. People who I don't know cheer me on, but then it vanishes as these unbidden snippets often do. They seem real, but were they? I've tried to understand it, but nothing.

I fasten my duffel bag over my shoulder and weave my way through the crowds. The bag contains a hand-drawn image of the evil eye which I'd picked up at a flea market a few weeks ago. I saw it as a good omen — the evil eye used to be Mother's talisman to ward off evil — my protection. I'm not yet sure how I'll use it, but I'll know when the time is right. Syringes filled with ketamine, my sedative of choice, are in my bag's flap, ready to be used. I've researched ketamine's effects until I was certain that I could precisely dose my victims. They are colour-coded according to their strength. Green for mild; orange for moderate and red for an intense out-of-body experience. The drug works as a general anaesthetic, reducing bodily sensations, giving the recipient a floating feeling and rendering them immobile but still able to experience the events that would unfold.

I stole discarded vials of medication from the hospitals where we'd drop off patients. There was always residual medication left in the vials and I've collected enough of what I need to begin my practice. No one ever suspected anything. A bunch of black cable ties, used for binding, are held together by an elastic band and a wrinkled change of clothes. The photo frame of a younger me, the only photo of myself that I'd snatched from the fire, is wrapped with a towel, completing the contents of my duffel bag.

I wait and watch. I am prepared today to move with my plan, to rid the world of evil. I spot a male and a female probably in their early 20s getting

All the Evil Scatters

off the GO train at Union Station. Her graceful gait tells me she's had many years of ballet practice. A blond pixie cut frames her strawberry-shaped face. Her tight, purple t-shirt and white jeans fit her body like a glove. He's more goth and wears a black t-shirt and jeans; his shoulders are hunched, probably from being one of the tallest kids in his class. They are the right age, aloof and self-absorbed, chatting and laughing without regard for anything around them. Their hands, intertwined like tree roots, made me wonder if Mother and Father were happy like these two when they first met. What might it have been like for me if I hadn't been at my Parents' mercy? Had They too been full of hope, or were They always horrible human beings? Her blue eyes are what draw me in as they glance in my direction, somewhere to my left. I have made my decision. These two will never have the opportunity to destroy someone else's life; the world will be safe.

A lanky dude with frameless glasses and hair doused with gel that created stiff spikes, joins them. He's not much taller than I am. He leaned in to hug each one, in turn, taking a bit longer to release his grasp from the girl. I see the way he looks at her — a love triangle. Amusing. I briefly consider doing all three of them, but that's not my plan. Only Mother and Father must pay. "Consider yourself lucky, buddy,*"* I whisper.

The female crooks her arm between the two males. They lead me to a seedy part of Toronto filled with the homeless, the drug addicts, and the yuppies who want to capitalize on the area's gentrification efforts. There are cheap places to stay, like the *Inn on Jarvis*, where they enter. I walk in after them, so close I can smell her intoxicating aroma, a mix of strawberry and vanilla. I sit in the lobby within earshot; they check into room 619.

I take the stairs two at a time to the sixth floor and wait in the hallway. When I hear the *ping* of the elevator, I fidget with one of the doors pretending I'm going into my room and watch the three of them enter their room.

They don't notice me. I wait.

*

After about an hour, I hear the click of their door opening. I pull the hoodie over my head and pretend that I'm leaving my room. They pay no attention to me, once again engrossed in themselves. I run back down the stairs and spot them as they are about to exit the hotel.

All the Evil Scatters

    I follow them to a street filled with Victorian brownstones — a mix of frat houses, residences, and businesses. One of those brownstones is the *Helion Pub*. They enter.
    I am close behind.
    I sit on a stool at the bar and position myself to better see them from the mirror behind the assortment of liquor bottles. I sip my cola; they eat and drink and, just when I think they've had enough food, the female orders more chicken wings. At this point, I consider giving up on my plans, but I persevere. I've been waiting for this moment for a while now, so I must be patient.
    The friend from the station says something to the young woman, she laughs unabashedly, eyes so blue, they hypnotize me. I shake my head, feeling a headache coming on. She is willing her evil on me. I know what I need to do. He isn't her only admirer; a man, twice her age, sends her a cocktail. She bats her lashes coyly at him and I am more convinced than ever that for her, *time's winged chariot [is] hurrying near.* As I finish my third cola, I know exactly how I will use the hand-drawn image of the evil eye.
    When they rise from their table, I follow them to a brownstone house that's not far from the *Helion Pub*.
    "This is a nice area, Donald," the female says to the friend who met them at the station.
    "I need to grab some weed," Donald says. "The party's at number 53 Bernie, just around the corner. I'll meet you there; Kayla's down with that."
    The couple disappears down the street.
    The shrubs shield me as I wait for Donald to come back out.
    I don't have to wait long. He whistles as he traipses down the stairs, but he spots me and says, "You all right, man?"
    "Looking for my phone," I say, "Ahh there it is." I reach as far into the bushes as I can, making sure he doesn't get a good look at me. A thorn jabs me, tearing the skin on my finger. I suck on it, applying pressure to stop the bleeding.
    "That's dope, bruh. Later," Donald says walking away from me and disappearing around the same corner as the couple had done earlier.
    I climb the steps and look for his apartment: *Donald Spielman* is scrawled beside unit #2. The door leading to the foyer is unlocked, his apartment was down the hall. Everything is falling into place: it's meant to

All the Evil Scatters

be. My eyes take in the most disorganized room that I have ever seen: books piled high like Doric columns; food containers strewn all over the place as if I'm in a landfill; half-full garbage bags are everywhere. And that smell. Reminds me of all those years I'd spent in that closet — a Petrie dish of disgust. I gag but manage to control myself.

I look around for somewhere to place the image of the evil eye, somewhere conspicuous, but not too conspicuous. I pull it out of my bag and lay it on a pile of books beside the sofa where someone with a keen eye for detail would spot it if they were looking for it in this dump.

I exit as quietly as I enter.

28

I wait on the steps of one of the brownstones close to where the party is being held. I'm not sure how much time has passed. And then, angry voices coming from up the street, startle me, breaking the quiet of the evening. It's them.

"Donald did that?" The young man says.

I wonder what he did?

"He's supposed to be our friend. How could he hit on me?" I hear the angry voice of the young woman as they walk toward me. I pull the hoodie over my head and pretend to scroll through my cell phone.

"Let's go to *Victor's*. The place that they were talking about at the party," the boyfriend says.

I type *Victor's* into my phone's GPS. It's a bar on Bloor Street — I will see them there.

*

I arrive at *Victor's*, a bar with a grunge band playing songs by Nirvana. It's half-full which helps my anonymity. I spot a camera in the corner of the bar and hide my face. An empty booth situated in the camera's blind spot is perfect for me.

When the couple arrives they take two stools at the bar. They dance. When she tires she returns to her seat; he continues dancing.

Their friend Donald enters the bar. He looks around, spots her, and takes a seat on the stool beside her. His back is toward me. I can't hear what they're saying, but I can see from the tensing of her body that she's not happy

All the Evil Scatters

with whatever it is. He's wearing a hoodie. We could be twins. I chuckle and sip my cola.

Donald rises after a few minutes, shoulders sagging in defeat, and heads for the door. The boyfriend spots Donald and moves toward him. They exchange words before Donald walks out the door. The young woman watches the altercation, shakes her head and covers her face with her hands.

The couple leaves five minutes later.

I am close behind.

The man has his arms around the woman. She's sobbing. I take that as my cue and say, "You okay?"

The man turns around and looks at me, ready to attack, fists balled. "Hey. I thought you were someone else. S'up?"

The woman wipes her eyes and looks at me, hesitant at first and then with trembling lips, cracks a smile.

"I have a bag of bones. My girlfriend missed her flight into Toronto and I have no one to smoke them with. Interested?"

They look at me and the boyfriend says, "We're on our way home. Later dude."

"I don't wanna toke alone," I say focusing my eyes on her evil blue ones.

She smiles and turns to her boyfriend and says, "Why not Bo?"

"It could be laced with anything. We don't know this guy, Pen," Boris says.

"He looks fine to me."

I smile and say, "No worries. Getting stoned on my own seems to be the story of my life lately." I turn to leave and head in the opposite direction from which we'd come.

"Hey wait," Pen says. "I guess one joint won't hurt. Right, Bo?"

I stop in my tracks and wait for them to come to me.

"All right. Why not, dude? Light it up," Boris says.

We pass the joint among us, take a couple of short inhales and exhale slowly, savouring the skunky smoke. We walk along Bloor toward Bay Street. Few cars are on the road and even fewer people. During the day, these streets are filled with cars; people bustling along, shopping or going to work, or seeing the sites. I inhale the stale air and look about me, the darkness comforts me.

All the Evil Scatters

"What's your name?" She says.

"Gabe."

"Nice," she says.

"How long have you two been together?" I say, feigning interest.

She laughs and says, "All our life, Gabe." Noting my surprise, she crooks her arm in mine. "He's my brother."

Inwardly, I'm disappointed because I thought that they are a couple. But that's all right. I'll adjust my plan. I'll have to pay more attention next time. "That changes things," I say and squeeze her arm. She glances up at me and pushes her body closer to mine. I try not to pull away.

"Are you from Toronto?" Pen says.

"No. I'm from Bowmanville. I came down to spend some time with my girlfriend who lives in Vancouver. But you know. She didn't make it," I say. "Are you from here?"

"We're from Waterloo."

"What are you doing in Toronto?"

"Went to a friend's birthday," she says.

"Some friend Donald is, was," Boris pipes in.

I guess Donald is the birthday boy. I wonder if he'll appreciate the gift I left for him. "What happened?"

"Don't worry about him," Pen says, her blue eyes, evil and determined to cast harm on me as Mother had. I now know that Mother's blue eyes were not used for good, but for bad.

We walk and I steer them toward where I've parked my car. I stop and say. "You guys have been great. Thanks for the company. Good—"

"Wait. Is this your ride?" She says.

"Wanna check it out?" I say focusing all my attention on her.

"Yes," she says and climbs into the passenger side. "Come on Bo! Get in."

He hesitates, but I pull out another joint which is laced with ketamine and offer it to him. He takes it, opens the door, and climbs into the back seat.

"Put your seatbelts on," I say.

They pass the joint back and forth between them and when it's my turn, I shake my head and say, "I'm driving."

"You're all right, dude," Boris says and takes a long drag.

I don't have to wait long for them to pass out.

All the Evil Scatters

The ride home is quiet and calming.

29

Pen wakes first. She notices she's naked, looks around, spots me, and screams — the gag stifles it. The terror in her eyes tells me everything I need to know. I am pleased. "You will not harm me, Mother. I will take care of Your eyes."

Her body writhes on the floor, but her feet are bound and her arms are tethered behind her.

I see the pleading in her eyes and say, "Don't worry. It will be over soon. I promise. You won't be able to harm anyone ever again."

I leave her for a moment and walk over to the tripod where I've mounted my video camera. I like old technology; cell phone videos don't appeal to me. Tapes are more concrete. I can touch them, rearrange them on the shelf, view them whenever I want. They allow me to relive these moments at a later time — a memorable token of my work!

With the needle threaded, I lean into her. Her horror intensifies as she realizes that my face will be the last thing she sees. She screams her silent scream, moving her head from side to side in defiance.

"If you don't stop moving, I may make a mistake and pierce your eyeball."

Her eyes expand in horror; she stops moving.

I work the needle through the muscle of the upper lid, piercing it together with the cartilage of the lower lid, and stitch them together. It feels like gristle as she pushes her eyelids open. I give her another shot of ketamine. She passes out. I continue suturing, taking my time to perfect each stitch. Red tears of blood stream down her cheeks.

Boris stirs and wakens. A perplexed, dopey look clouds his eyes. He spots his sister's naked and inert body lying beside him, blood streaming down her face. He shakes his naked body, trying to free himself, but soon realizes it's futile. He spots me. Fear and understanding fill his eyes.

I stand above her with the hangman's noose in my hand, I swing it back and forth over her face like a pendulum, "*...the agony of my soul found vent in one loud, long and final scream of despair*", I say quoting from one of my favourite writers, Edgar Allan Poe. Boris shakes his head. Trying to tell me to

All the Evil Scatters

stop, I assume. Is he in for a surprise. I lean in and slip the noose over her head. She stirs but doesn't wake. "It's alright," I whisper in her ear, and then to him, I say, "Your time will come."

He shakes his body in a feeble attempt to loosen the black cable ties. I have to admit that he's a fighter. But he will soon realize that he's not going anywhere. Not now. Not ever. Just like Father as he took his last smoke-filled breath.

I explore her face, blood tears continue; a rivulet of my sweat drips and mingles with her blood. We are one.

I straddle her torso to minimize her movements, fasten the rope around her neck and slowly tighten the hangman's noose. Her body flails as I pull on the knot, tightening, feeling her resistance. Her breath shallows as I squeeze tighter; the more I tighten the shallower it gets. Shallow. Shallow. Shallow. *Snap*. Her windpipe cracks and she exhales one last, gurgled breath. The room is quiet. Boris has stopped moving, eyes riveted on his sister, tears trickling down his face. Lamenting her death, I suppose. My body shudders as waves of triumph wash over me like a turbulent sea.

Once my breathing returns to its regular rhythm, I remove the noose from her neck, rise and move over to where he lies. He starts moving again as he realizes that there is no escape. His eyes plead with me to let him go. It's all there on his face: horror; anger; sadness; and, defeat.

I grab my knife and move toward him.

*

I gather their clothing, which I've piled neatly. Their documents lay on top. I go to the backyard and stare at the crackling flames that light up the night, intensifying as I toss in their belongings. The flames eat their way through everything, swallowing hungrily, consuming everything that I feed it. The crackle and pop of the flames satisfy me; soon there will be nothing left. The flames are mesmerizing as Father's screams reach out to me from the past.

I return inside and marvel for a few minutes at their two inert bodies and whisper, "Jesus Christ is victorious, and all the evil scatters by Him. Jesus Christ is victorious, and all the evil scatters by Him. Jesus Christ is victorious, and all the evil scatters by Him. *ftou, ftou, ftou*."

With the scalpel in hand, I make an incision to the man's groin area.

All the Evil Scatters

When my work is complete. I stop the video recorder, take out the tape and write *Mother and Father #1* and return it to the shelf with the other videotapes, depicting my successful suturing of the animals I'd saved over the years.

*

I wipe them both clean, taking care that there is no caked blood around the sutures. I like clean wounds. I rinse any excess spatter from the floor, watching as the blood swirls, round and round, finally disappearing down the drain. I wrap their bodies, first one and then the other, in a plastic tarp and haul them into the car's trunk. It took me longer than I thought it would.

I open the driver's door, sit back and take a few gulps of air before starting the engine.

I obey the rules of the road and end up in the alley close to *Victor's*, but not too close. I want them found — everyone will know that I exist to save them from the monsters and evil of the world.

30

The weather had turned quickly. Yesterday had been sweltering; people were wearing shorts. Today they're back to heavy coats. Staff Sergeant Melissa Hargrove and her partner, Staff Sergeant, RJ (Ryan John) Otombo got out of the cruiser and felt the chill cut through their bodies like a knife.

"Well, there goes a nice morning with the family," RJ said.

"I haven't seen Ari and my nephews for weeks," Melissa said.

"Know what you mean. I was looking forward to some time with Carla," RJ said.

They approached sergeants, Paul O'Brien and Greg Monaghan; they were talking to a man holding onto his dog's leash.

"This is Mr. Hamilton and his dog, Zane. They found the bodies," Greg said.

"Thank you for staying at the scene, Mr. Hamilton," Melissa said.

"Let's secure the perimeter before the media hounds and other gawkers smell blood and ruin valuable evidence," RJ said and turned to Paul who had already grabbed the yellow crime tape. There was no knowing at the initial

All the Evil Scatters

stages of an investigation which piece of evidence, even the smallest, could be the key to unlocking the mystery behind the crime.

"Hey Monaghan," Paul called out to Greg. "Give me a hand will ya?"

RJ pulled out a cigarette, lit it, and took a long drag. He watched as Greg and Paul, with rolls of yellow police tape in hand, work their way from one end of the laneway to the other, wrapping it around one pole, then another and around the last pole. They made sure to protect everything within the crime scene, including the dumpsters, the concrete slabs discarded by some construction crew and the back entrance to *Nona's Variety*.

Melissa bent down and removed the rest of the debris found around the bodies, bagging everything that looked relevant, careful not to overlook anything. She looked at the backside of the body and that's when she saw the eyes on the body underneath. Eyes which, although they were sewn shut, seemed to stare at her.

She shuddered as she touched the male's bare back; the coldness of death coursed through her fingers. "Please help me turn over the body," she said and grabbed her camera, viewing the victims from the lens, a welcome layer of distance, as RJ and Greg turned over the body.

Melissa inhaled, counted to ten, then exhaled, her breath forming a misty cloud in the frosty air. She wanted to run but stilled herself by taking several deep breaths.

"Jesus, fucking Christ. What kind of a sadistic son of a bitch would do this sorta shit?" RJ spat out the words and placed his hand on her shoulder.

She looked up at him, visibly shaken, and then shifted her focus on Paul and Greg who had returned to the task of taping off the scene.

After the shock of seeing the disfigured corpses dissipated, she snapped photos from all angles as if she were shooting a couple of models in a studio set. There were two bodies side-by-side, the female's eyes had been sewn shut and the male had been castrated. They were young, in their early twenties, maybe in their teens. She homed in on the mutilated areas, continuously clicking her camera.

Melissa and RJ were an odd team in some ways, but they worked well together. She was tall and slender; the first signs of grey were evident in her auburn hair that she kept in a ponytail. Almond-shaped green eyes, that rarely exhibited any emotion on the job were her trademark in the Force. The crimes she dealt with had no room for subjectivity. She had hardened herself to the

All the Evil Scatters

vile human acts that she had seen over the last twelve years with the Toronto City Police Force since graduating with a Master's degree in forensic psychology. Becoming a police officer seemed like a natural transition

RJ was her foil in his outlook and approach. He was a striking man with olive-toned skin; his rigid jaw gave his face a stern look that almost bordered on anger. Where many of his friends were losing their hair, he shaved his daily, leaving no strand on his scalp. He tended toward the emotional. His outbursts around the department were commonplace. He didn't care who was around. When he had something to say, he said it. Life was too short to play the game of political correctness. He'd been a cop for 25 years and planned to retire soon.

Melissa recalled his recent outburst in front of the Chief, Tara Stanton, about one of the newly elected city councillors. "He's an asshole," RJ said pounding his fist on Tara's desk. "He doesn't give a shit about the community, only about making his rich friends richer."

"I'm not going to warn you again, RJ," Tara said. "No dissing the politicians. You hear me?"

RJ had seemingly acquiesced, but Melissa could tell from the glimmer in his eyes that when the opportunity arose, he would not hesitate to repeat his comments.

Melissa, although younger than RJ, was one of the few people that could temper his emotions, making sure that he didn't get relegated to desk duty, working on some obscure policy. He was too valuable on the ground. She needed him.

*

Melissa and RJ looked on as the coroner, Frank Williams and his staff hoisted the bodies onto a gurney and then onto the ambulance. But before they could zip up the body bags Melissa said, "Wait a sec, Frank." She walked over to the female's body and saw something white sticking out from her hair. Melissa pulled out a pair of tweezers, carefully prying the piece of paper which looked like a rolled-up cigarette. *How could I have missed it,* she thought?

RJ looked over Melissa's shoulders as she unfurled the paper. They read:

Welcome to my beginning.

"Holy shit," RJ said.

All the Evil Scatters

"It's a warning. He's going to strike again!" Melissa said.

31

Back at the station, Melissa and RJ filled out forms for toxicology, serology, DNA and fingerprinting, and a slew of other tests. They reviewed Frank's initial conclusions on pathology: the female victim's eyes had been sewn shut while still alive. They were then strangled and the man's testicles removed posthumously; they'd been dead for about seven hours given the state of rigour mortis. They'd been killed elsewhere — no blood spatter was found anywhere near the crime scene.

RJ and Melissa's cell phones beeped simultaneously with a text message from Tara.

"I guess she wants a debrief," RJ said as he and Melissa exited the elevator, walked the few steps to Tara's office, and stopped in front of her door. RJ rapped on it to indicate their presence.

"Come in," Tara said, motioning for them to enter. "I can see from your faces that the news is grim. Tell me what we have."

It was customary for Tara to take a personal interest in some of the more high-profile and heinous crimes. She was likely already getting pressure from the politicians. Tara was a 'hands-on' leader and often wanted to be informed every step of the way in such cases. She didn't believe in hierarchical management. To her, everyone was equal which commanded her the utmost respect from her team, unlike her predecessor. Her officers had the facts and she wanted to hear from them directly.

They entered her stylish office, furnished with a mahogany desk and matching credenza, circa the 1950s. Always an environmentalist, Tara had retrieved the furniture from surplus assets — a place where unwanted furniture went to die unless someone found a use for them.

"What do you have for me?"

"Here's what we know so far, Tara," Melissa began. "The two victims are a male and a female in their early 20s. Caucasian. We were unable to identify them at the scene. We're running tests — blood, DNA, toxicology and we're running their prints through our system. They had no ID or any personal effects on them."

"What else do we know?" Tara said.

All the Evil Scatters

"We found the male on top of the female with his face down. Her eyes were sewn shut. Gruesome. When we turned the body over the male had been, um, castrated," Melissa said.

"He worked them pretty good. The removal of the testicles was postmortem, given the lack of blood surrounding the man's wounds," RJ said. "The SOB stitched her eyes shut with what the coroner thinks is catgut while she was still alive."

"Frank's running tests to confirm that the stitching material is catgut," Melissa said.

"Hasn't catgut been replaced with synthetics?" Tara said.

"Which makes this a unique signature of our perp or perps," Melissa said.

"Perps? Do you think there's more than one?"

"Possible," RJ said.

"And why is that a possibility?" Tara said.

"Because there are two bodies. And because the bodies were moved from the primary crime scene. Doesn't seem feasible that one person could do this alone unless he is a big man with extraordinary strength," RJ said.

"There have been cases where murderers have acted alone, wiping out entire families. Right?" Tara said.

"Correct," Melissa said.

"Anything else?" Tara said.

"We are fairly certain that the deaths occurred sometime between midnight and 2 a.m.," Melissa said. "We have only one witness — the person who found the bodies — Marty Hamilton."

"Could he have done this?"

"No," RJ said. "He was a poor schmuck walking his dog. His daily routine. We confirmed with area store owners who reported routinely seeing him with his dog. His being there was nothing unusual."

"He was fairly shaken up, but we'll interview him more extensively later. For the most part, he hadn't seen or heard anything," Melissa said.

"Except he said that he had the eerie feeling that he was being watched. But when he turned to look there was no one. Of course, this is a normal reaction for someone who'd made a horrific discovery."

All the Evil Scatters

"So, for now, we're thinking it was probably nothing, but sometimes you never know. We've all seen criminals return to the scene to relive their crime," Melissa said.

"Check the CCTVs," Tara said.

"We're on it," RJ said.

"Do you think it's random or did the victims know their killer," Tara said.

"Too early to say. We also think he may strike again. We found this at the scene," Melissa said and handed Tara an image of the note they found embedded in the female's hair.

Tara glanced at it, reading the perpetrator's scrawl and said, "Do you have any theories about why this particular method of killing? Seems ritualistic."

"We're working on some assumptions about the underlying psychological trauma, but can't say much at this time other than that in such crimes, the perp always identifies with the victims who are somehow symbolically associated with a significant and traumatic event or events in his or her life."

When they finished updating Tara, the three of them sat quietly, each contemplating aspects of the case: the limited information; the bizarre mutilation of the victims; their age; and, what the public and politicians would need to be told.

"Everyone will be watching us," Tara said.

RJ and Melissa looked at each other and nodded, both understanding that they would be on the proverbial "hot seat" until they solved the case.

"What are your next steps?" Tara said.

"We're going door-to-door to make inquiries," Melissa said. "Someone might have seen or heard something. Maybe someone knows the victims?"

"I want the two of you to keep me in the loop," Tara said. "I don't care which one of you does it. Just do it. I want to hear from you first thing in the morning and before you leave for the night. I want to know everything. Leave little in writing and, no email until we know more. I can't stress enough that we must work quickly to find this killer. I've allocated the necessary resources to help with the investigation."

Melissa and RJ headed back to the briefing room. Heather Catsell, a rookie officer, had laid out photos of the evidence on the whiteboard. The timeline below the images gave them approximate time of death and when the bodies had been discovered. Everything before and in between was blank.

"Well, the easy part's over," RJ said.

Melissa sighed, her emotions a mixture of apprehension, revulsion, and a hint of exhilaration at delving further into the case so that she could give closure to the families, if there was ever such a thing. "There's no time to waste. I need the lab techs to analyze the samples and conduct toxicology, entomology, and hematology tests. Frank started the autopsy. That may tell us where the victims were before they were killed and any distinguishing marks we may have missed."

Melissa looked over the ominous note and hoped that they weren't dealing with a serial killer.

32

❝ I am triumphant! Do you see that, Father?" I laugh as the video of Bo and Pen's deaths plays in the background.

I read the article about them with interest.

Toronto. Police have uncovered the unidentified bodies of two caucasian victims: a young male and a young female. A man walking his dog discovered their naked bodies in a laneway as if in a lover's embrace. The bodies had been mutilated, but police aren't disclosing further details.

There is no apparent motive at this time as police try to piece together what happened to these two young adults.

Anyone with information is requested to contact the police.

I cut out the article and place it with the rest of my collection.

All the Evil Scatters

33

Later that day Marty Hamilton found himself in the police station waiting to recount his horrific discovery while his recollections were still fresh. As if he would ever forget. He knew that it was routine. He'd seen many episodes of *Cardinal, Law and Order* and the like.

Marty sat in what he suspected was a typical interview room. *It doesn't look anything like the ones on television,* he thought — this wasn't a dingy, boxy room with a metal table in the centre, the witness on one side of it, the cop on the other. There was no fluorescent light dangling from the ceiling as if it was holding on for dear life. This one had a window looking out onto College Street; there were four cops in the room, not two. He'd met them all at the crime scene.

RJ positioned the cell phone on a tripod, pointing it at their witness.

"Mr. Hamilton, can we get you something to drink?" Melissa said.

Marty shook his head, thinking that the faster they got his statement, the faster he'd be able to take Zane out for his evening walk before they both settled in for the night. How could he have ever imagined that he and Zane would be cast in this real-life crime drama?

"Ready Mr. Hamilton?" Melissa said and when he nodded, Paul clicked on the cell phone's camera.

MELISSA: 4:57 p.m. Interview with Marty Hamilton, In attendance are Staff Sergeant Otombo, Sergeants Monaghan and O'Brien, and myself. Mr. Hamilton. Thank you for coming in this afternoon. Take a moment and get settled. I want you to relax and try to remember everything that you can about your discovery this morning.
MARTY: I'll do my best.
MELISSA: That's all we ask. Now can you please tell us how it was that you found the bodies, beginning from when you left your home this morning?

All the Evil Scatters

MARTY: We, Zane and I, took our usual path up through the side streets, through the university, up Bloor and then to the area with those Victorian brownstones.
MELISSA: Please tell us where you live.
MARTY: I live in a rental near the University of Toronto Campus. Been there for years. Rent controlled.
MELISSA: Can you tell us what time you found the bodies?
MARTY: It was, let me see, probably around 7 a.m.
MELISSA: How do you know it was that time?
MARTY: Well, I, um, usually take Zane out around six for his walk. We'd been walking for a while, by the time we came upon... um, you know, the bodies. You see, I grew up there and the old hood gives me a sense of belonging. I like looking at the old houses, the bustle of activity as people wake, get their kids ready for school, and rush out their doors. I'm sorry, I'm rambling.
MELISSA: No problem. Tell us how you came upon the bodies.
MARTY: It wasn't my discovery. It was Zane's.
RJ: Tell us about that.
MARTY: Zane started whimpering, sniffing, and scratching at something under some cardboard boxes that were sopping wet. He's always sniffing out something or other. Usually, he gets bored and moves away, but he wouldn't let it alone.
RJ: Then what happened?
MARTY: I gave in and got down on one knee and began peeling back the layers of cardboard. They were heavier than I'd anticipated. You know, on account of Toronto being deluged with torrential rains. I remember hearing that Union Station had become a pond; the Bayview extension had been closed due to

All the Evil Scatters

pooling of water at its south end, and — I'm rambling again, aren't I?
MELISSA: Please take a deep breath and continue, Mr. Hamilton.
MARTY: I wanted him to stop making those sounds so I picked up the pace. And then...
MELISSA: Take your time.
MARTY: At first I thought they were two nude mannequins, facing each other. I edged closer for a better look. Zane was spinning around frantically and finally settled beside me. The dolls had an odd hue. A bit too blue for a mannequin. I remember thinking that perhaps technology had advanced such that they now make mannequins more life-like. There wasn't anything fake about them.
RJ: What happened next?
MARTY: I touched them. They were so cold.
MELISSA: How did you feel at that moment?
MARTY: At first I was surprised, then shocked, and then horrified. I saw one body peeking at me from beneath the other one. Not exactly peeking because the eyes were sewn shut. Horrifying. Still, I felt they were staring right at me. Poor kids. Who would do such a thing? I think I'll take that water now.
MELISSA: Are you able to continue, Mr. Hamilton?
MARTY: Yes. I tried to make sense of what I was seeing. Gruesome. I'd never seen anything like it. My stomach somersaulted, the bile rising. I puked up my breakfast of bagel and cream cheese.

All the Evil Scatters

MELISSA: It must have been horrible for you, Mr. Hamilton. No one should ever have to bear witness to such events. Are you able to continue?
MARTY: Are you sure you want to hear this?
RJ: We're conducting an investigation. Of course we do.
MARTY: I spat, trying to clear the aftertaste of vomit. I turned to look back at the bodies and wondered how the poor souls had ended up there. And that's when I felt it.
RJ: Felt what?
MARTY: Goosebumps on my arms and down my spine. I looked around, half expecting to see someone behind me.
RJ: You think someone was watching you?
MARTY: There was no one.
RJ: What did you do next?
MARTY: What I wanted to do was run, put distance between me and the atrocity. Instead, I put back the cardboard over the bodies. No one else should have to see what I'd seen.
RJ: What happened next?
MARTY: I walked a few meters from the bodies and tried to compose myself. When I felt that my nerves and my stomach had calmed down, I called 9-1-1.
RJ: About how long after you discovered the bodies did you call for help?
MARTY: Five minutes. Tops.
MELISSA: What did you say to the dispatcher?
MARTY: I told her that I found two bodies and she asked for my location. I told her and waited for the police as she instructed. She said that you, the police, would have questions for me. But I

wanted nothing more than to be as far away as possible. I wanted to take shelter in my apartment, wash the stink of death from my body and Listerine away the taste of vomit.

MELISSA: I understand, Mr. Hamilton. Is there anything else that you recall?

MARTY: No.

MELISSA: Thank you for your time. If you remember anything else, please contact us. Sergeant O'Brien will give you a direct line for you to call. If we have any further questions as the investigation continues, we'll be in touch.

MARTY: I hope you catch whoever did this.

RJ: We will.

RJ clicked off the camera and nodded at Melissa. They watched Greg and Paul escort Marty Hamilton out of the room.

34

A few hours later, Melissa's phone went off. She answered, "Staff Sergeant Hargrove."

"Hello, officer. Ma'am."

She recognized the voice on the other end, "Mr. Hamilton? Did you remember something else?"

RJ arched his eyebrows in interest.

"No. And I know this is going to sound disgusting, but Zane pooped something out a few minutes ago. I thought it might be related to the case."

"I'm going to put you on speaker. Staff Sergeant Otombo is with me," she motioned to RJ.

"Mr. Hamilton," RJ said.

"Please tell us what you found and why you think it's relevant to the case," Melissa said.

"It's probably nothing, but I found a trinket in Zane's stools," Marty said.

All the Evil Scatters

Melissa and RJ looked at each other, eagerly anticipating what their witness had found.

"What kind of trinket?"

"It's a circle with a dot in the centre of it — looks like an eye. It's blue on the outside and the centre dot is black. I thought…I thought maybe it belonged to one of them."

"Can you send us a picture and then we'll send someone to pick it up?"

Ping. The photo arrived in her mailbox. *Did it belong to one of the victims? Probably had nothing to do with the case,* Melissa thought.

"Thank you, Mr. Hamilton," she said and ended the call.

"Do you think it's relevant?" RJ said.

"Hard to say. For now, we'll file it as evidence."

"I'll see if Greg can pick it up — maybe there are some latent prints on it."

"We need to identify our victims as quickly as possible so that we can notify their next of kin."

*

There was a knock on Melissa's door. Greg and Paul entered.

Greg waived a piece of paper and said, "We've compared the DNA of the two victims — they're related. There are sufficient markers in their DNA to suggest that they are siblings."

Melissa downloaded the photos from the crime scene and zeroed in on the victims' faces. "I see a slight resemblance."

RJ walked over to the desk, looked at the photos, and said, "The bone structure is similar, as is the cleft chins, the angle of their cheekbones. Even the bump on their noses is virtually identical. Why didn't we see this before?"

"We see it now," Melissa said.

She continued examining the photos as if by concentrating hard enough their questions would be answered. But all she saw was death.

"I'll crop the photos, add some colour, and then we can take them to the local restaurants, bars, and residences in the area," Greg said. "Someone might recognize them."

"Can you photoshop the eye area? Get rid of the stitch work?" RJ said.

"Sure can. I'll fade out the sutures," Greg said. "No one needs to see her eyes sewn shut."

All the Evil Scatters

35

My hand trembles as I turn the key, slowly open the door, poke my head through it and look around to make sure no one's there. I guess it's from years of being cautious around Him. Even though I know he can no longer hurt me, I still feel Him around me. I half expect to see Him waiting for me, lurking beyond the door, waiting for His supper, and holding His belt to let me know who's in charge.

This room is bigger than the one from back then. I've blocked out the light with thick curtains; no one can see in or out.

I flip the light switch to "on", giving everything around me an eerie glow. The room is plain and simple, almost a replica of that room of long ago.

I laugh out loud; the sound of my voice gives me comfort in the night's silence.

The room has the most basic of furnishings: the Formica kitchen table and three wooden chairs that don't match surround the table, some people might say the chairs are antiques. A bed and a night table with a metal lamp on top of it. Against one of the walls, beneath the below-grade window, is a sink and a toilet. I've recreated the room from back then. No details were spared. Because of how awful it was I'd never forgotten even the tiniest detail. I am saddened, but only briefly that He wasn't around to see that I have succeeded where He had failed.

The room wouldn't be complete without a closet. I go in, close the door and cut myself. It no longer matters where. I've run out of skin surface now, but I cut over the old wounds, creating scabs, one upon the other, like rough patches of asphalt. I feel the safest in the dark. Sometimes I cringe at the imagined footfall coming toward me; relief soon envelopes me because He will never hurt me again like that. Still, the scabs remain.

If I leave the shades open, the gravel path leading to the concession road beyond seems to float into nothingness. The nearest neighbours are probably a kilometre away on either side of my property. This place serves me well, giving me respite from my work as a paramedic.

I walk over to the table and plunk my bag on it; inside is everything I need: His belt, my work clothes and syringes with ketamine all at the ready

All the Evil Scatters

for my next pair of victims. With the death of the siblings, I know now more than ever that this is my true calling. All those years have led me to this.

I grab a paring knife from the drawer and grab His belt. I take off my soiled clothes and put on clean ones. I cinch the baggy pants at the waist with His belt — the only thing I kept from Him. The only thing left to remind me of those years, long ago when I didn't know any better. My faded blood has seeped through the leather, leaving its indelible mark. I shudder as the memory of my kill washes over me. I'm finally able to show Him that He no longer rules over me. Last night's events, from start to finish, were truly exhilarating, cleansing and purifying. The true meaning of my life is clear now that I saved myself and the world from the siblings' evil.

I pull out one of the chairs from under the table and silently contemplate my next move. The deaths of the siblings had gone better than I had ever anticipated. Bo and Pen, as they'd called each other, had been like putty to be moulded and shaped. Sometimes the young are so foolish, so gullible, just as I had once been. But I took my time with them, perfecting my craft from the moment I met them to the moment when their lives ended.

The video helps me relive my work, learn from it and savour every moment, every breath, every whimper and every look of hope for freedom. Oh, how delicious it was watching their lives fade before me, first the female and then the male. He had to see Her go first. She had left Him. That was only right. The last thing that they each saw was my ultimate control. They were helpless, too doped up to struggle, but her eyes, those evil eyes didn't waver until they forced me to shut them forever. As my work unfolds before me like a movie, I quiver with delight. A quiver that soon becomes a throbbing, pounding, unrelenting urge. An urge that needs to be satiated — it comes overwhelmingly and excitedly to the surface once again. I surrender myself to it.

I glance at the closet, its door wide open, inviting.

All the Evil Scatters

36

"How's it going, Mel?" RJ said as he approached her desk.

"Give me a few minutes and we can head out."

"I'll meet you downstairs in fifteen. I need a smoke." RJ had been trying to quit for years. Sometimes he'd stopped for a few months at a time, sometimes days, but always returning to what his wife, Carla, called *his crutch*.

He took a long drag, feeling his chest expand as he exhaled thick smoke into the damp air. He sneezed a few times and thought, *Damn allergies!* He recalled how Carla pleaded with him to quit, almost since the day they'd started dating. But eventually, she realized how hopeless her requests were and stopped. He had once gotten so angry at her, that he chain-smoked for an hour until he thought he was going to cough out a lung. RJ rarely took the advice of others, often rebelling, doing the opposite, first as a youngster, then as a teenager, and then into adulthood. He started smoking when he was 16, sneaking a cigarette from his father and smoking it behind his high school, by the ravine, where all the cool kids hung out. Since then he'd been fighting the battle of, on-again, off-again smoking. But what he craved at that moment was the warmth of a neat shot of Scotch.

Over the years, and especially the last few, he'd felt Carla withdrawing, not only her affection but also the amount of time she spent with him, choosing instead to meet up with her girlfriends, going for walks alone, weekends away without him. Deep down he knew that he had failed her in so many ways. But the biggest failure was not bringing their son, Ryan, home alive. And so he kept his son's memory at the forefront, repeatedly reviewing the case files over the years, grasping on to any idea or any clue that might lead him to find his son's body. A large wall in their basement had been devoted to evidence about Ryan: timelines, photos of scraps of evidence, photos of his bloodied clothing, his shoes, scuffed and dirty like he'd been traipsing through a muddy field. This case would be different. The perpetrator would not escape justice this time.

RJ took a long drag from his cigarette, calming his frayed nerves whenever he thought of that time. That time when everything he had done to find his son, had failed. To this day, RJ never stopped trying to find out what had happened to Ryan. If he did figure it out, maybe she would forgive him.

All the Evil Scatters

RJ puffed on his cigarette and recalled his frenzied search for his missing son, the nights of anguish as he and Carla waited for a call that would tell them that their eight-year-old son was alive and well. But that call never came. For several weeks, the police conducted searches all over the city — in the Toronto ravines, the Humber River to the West, and the Don River to the East until the officers were redeployed to other cases. Ryan's case went cold. That was 18 years ago.

RJ and Carla had posted flyers all over the city and in the Greater Toronto Area. The two of them had gone on television, pleading for Ryan's safe return. They spoke to many people who thought they had seen him, but all of them were dead ends.

Months passed; the trees had shed their green hues for more vibrant reds, golds and shades in-between. The posters that RJ and Carla had put on the hydro poles around the city had fallen off or had been replaced by more current advertisements: someone offering guitar lessons someone seeking a lost puppy, or someone having a yard sale. RJ couldn't remember when the calls stopped, but they did. Everything went cold, including his and Carla's relationship.

Many months later as they accepted that Ryan would never come home to them, they held a memorial service for him at the Catholic Church. A large framed photo of Ryan was propped on an easel, standing vigil over an empty coffin; his smiling image looked straight at him. It was a smile that broke RJ's heart. He watched Carla staring into the distance, her gaze fixed upon the stained glass windows of the old church. Family, friends, and members of the police force filled the pews, many others stood in the back, the heat was unbearable as the ceremony continued. No one gave a eulogy. No one sang hymns. Only the lyrical voice of the priest filled the room.

As the pallbearers loaded the empty coffin, into the hearse, curious onlookers lined the sidewalks, hoping to catch a glimpse of the grieving cop and his wife.

"If a cop can't save his son, what hope do any of us have?" A woman, standing by the side of the road said. RJ shot her a silencing look. *That's right, RJ. You couldn't save your son,* he thought.

That night, for the first time in months, RJ and Carla made hungry, insatiable love, reaching for each other in the dark, replacing their sorrow with the blending of their bodies. But when their heartbeats shallowed and their breathing reached its equilibrium, they felt empty, sad and lost in a world that had taken their son away from them.

Months after Ryan's memorial, RJ reached over to the night table and flipped open his ringing cell phone — it was Tara Stanton, who had been appointed as the Chief of Police for the City of Toronto.

"Chief. Do you need me to come in?"

"Yes. But not for work," Tara said.

"What is it?" RJ said, dread creeping into his voice.

"There's something you need to see."

"What?"

"I don't want to get into it over the phone."

He leaned over and kissed Carla's bare shoulder. She didn't move.

"I love you," he mouthed. On a sticky note he jotted a few words and put it on his pillow.

As he drove to the station, he wondered what it was all about. A new case? Information on an active case?

RJ drove to the station and parked in the underground lot. He went up the flight of stairs leading to the back entrance. He greeted fellow officers as he made his way to Tara's office.

"Tara. What's this all about?"

"Sit down, RJ."

"Uh oh. Did I offend someone? Did they file a harassment grievance against me?" RJ said.

"No. I'll get right to it. We have new information about your son?"

"Wh....What? Did you find him after all these years? Is he alri —?"

"Stop! We didn't find him. Let me tell you what we found," Tara said as she reached into her desk drawer and pulled out a clear plastic bag.

RJ saw what looked like a child's t-shirt, sopped in blood like a bad tie-dye job. "What is this?" RJ said, grabbed the bag, stared at the contents, and looked at her, his eyes questioning what he was looking at. "Where did you get this? Ryan was wearing this the night he disappeared."

Tara nodded. "I'll tell you everything we know."

"I'm listening."

"A man and a woman were out walking in the Bluffer's Park area when they came upon a large pool of blood, this t-shirt was immersed in it. Frank conducted a DNA test; he confirmed that it's, um, your son, Ryan's. The

All the Evil Scatters

blood was fresh, leading Williams to conclude that if Ryan had been alive, he no longer was. Exsanguination. Severe blood loss. No one could sustain such blood loss and live."

"Where's my son? I want to see his body."

"There was no body. We searched the entire area but came up with nothing. Our dogs didn't pick up anything. We've fanned out our search. We'll keep looking. We won't stop until we recover his body."

"Why after all this time? Why did he kill him now and not then? What was he doin—? Oh my God…"

"I'm so sorry, RJ," Tara said.

RJ's shoulders heaved up and down; he clasped his head in his hands. He looked up and said, "How will I tell Carla? It will be as if our son died a second time. Only now we'll never have the hope that he will one day appear at our front door and tell us that he's all right."

RJ brought Carla photos of Ryan's clothing instead of having her come to the station. He didn't want her to be subjected to the other officers' judging her, judging him.

RJ remembered Carla's gut-wrenching sobs, "Noooooo! Noooooo! Noooooo! You promised me you'd find him. You lied to me and now he's dead," she'd said, scrunched up the photo and pounded her fists against his chest. He let her hit him — he felt numb from the guilt of not having kept his promise to find their son. He had no tears to shed, few words of comfort. He wrapped his arms around her.

RJ never stopped searching for the person or persons responsible for killing his son and, when he had time, looked for clues under the Don Valley viaduct where Ryan's bloodied clothing had been found. He never told Carla what he was doing, hoping to one day recover his body and have a proper burial for him. These actions kept the memory of Ryan alive as did the wall of evidence that lined his basement wall. The only thing that had kept him sane all these years was the belief that he, in a small way could chip away at the injustices and—

"Hey! Ready to go?" Melissa's voice wove into his thoughts. She put a hand on his shoulder, noting the distant look in his eyes — a look filled with pain, anger and guilt that she'd seen many times before. She sighed, understanding that like the death of her parents, RJ may never get closure.

All the Evil Scatters

"Sure," RJ said, sneezed a couple of times, a nervous reaction, and stubbed out the cigarette on the wall and put the butt in the makeshift ashtray. "We'll start our search at one end and work our way to the other."

They got into the car and Melissa said, "I'll review the reports while you drive."

37

Melissa and RJ went door-to-door, walked up and down the streets surrounding the crime scene, looked behind bushes and inside garbage bins. They asked residents and retailers the same questions which always yielded the same answers — no one had seen or recognized either of the two victims.

Melissa and RJ ended up on Bloor Street at a watering hole, simply named, *Victor's,* and pulled open the door. They approached the bar, showed their badges and asked the bartender to see the manager. Moments later, a woman wearing a white shirt and black, bell-bottomed pants emerged from the back.

"Hi," she said. "I'm Jan. How can I help you?"

"We're here about the two homicides that occurred not too far from here last night," Melissa said.

Jan silently nodded in respectful understanding.

"We're wondering if you might be able to assist us in our investigation?"

"Sure," offered Jan, "but I'm not sure how I can help."

"We'd like to show you photos of the victims," Melissa said, pulled out the doctored images of the siblings and held them out to Jan. "Perhaps you, or your staff who were working the other night, saw them? Perhaps they're regulars?"

Jan looked at the photos of the male and female headshots taken from above the clavicle. The shoulders were bare. She gasped and held her hand to her mouth.

"Do you recognize them?" Melissa said.

"Yes," Jan said, her voice barely a whisper. "They've, um, been here. But they, um, look different in the pictures," she shuddered as if the cold grip

All the Evil Scatters

of death had clawed its way out of the photos and wrapped itself around her body.

"What can you tell us about them?" Melissa said.

"I'd never seen them before the other night."

"They're not regulars?" RJ said.

Jan shook her head.

"Did they have drinks?" Melissa said.

"Yes."

"Did you notice anything odd about their behaviour?" RJ said.

"Uhm, yeah. Not odd really. The young dude was hitting on every female as if he'd never seen a woman before."

"What about the woman?"

"She started chatting up some guy."

"Oh?" RJ straightened his body as if suddenly waking up from a deep slumber and said, "Go on."

"I'd never seen him before either. We rarely get strangers in here. This bar is frequented by regulars. Some clock in after work; others come in later when things at home get rough or they want to escape into a bottle of booze. There was a grunge band playing that night, so we had more people than usual. Some I didn't recognize."

"What did he look like?" RJ said.

"It was hard to tell. He wore a hoodie. Couldn't see much of him."

"Do you have any video footage from that camera?" RJ said pointing toward the far corner of the ceiling.

She shook her head. "Nah. It's just for show. Boss says cameras, working or not, are a deterrent either way. No one would try anything if they thought they were being watched. Works like a charm. We've never had any trouble."

Melissa and RJ glanced at each other, disappointed.

RJ leaned in and said, "How tall was he? Was he fat? Skinny? White? Black? Brown? Was there anything about his demeanour?"

"Oh, he was small. Thin. About 5'8" or so. But I can't be sure about the height. He was sitting down."

RJ and Melissa looked at each other. Could this be their man? If he were, he'd have to have superhuman strength to overtake both victims. But they'd both seen it before: criminals have a way of overpowering people in non-physical ways, through their charisma, feigning weakness, or enticing them with a cute dog.

"Did they all leave together?"

"I didn't see any of them leave. I was busy dealing with an irate customer. When I was done, the three of them had cleared out. You can ask my server, Stone, who was working that night. Maybe he saw something?"

"Great. Is he here?"

"Stone should be here shortly."

As if on cue, the door swung open and a man in his early 20s with tattoos on his neck and wrist sauntered over to Jan and kissed her on the cheek.

"Hi Stone. These are police officers. They have a few questions for you."

Stone shifted in place and looked nervously around him before producing a sheepish grin. RJ knew the look. He'd seen it many times. Yeah. Stone was guilty of something, probably peddling drugs, skimming from the tips, or hiding the fact that he was gay.

"Look we're not here to bust you for anything if that's what you're worried about," RJ reassured him.

"Have you seen these two before?" Melissa said and showed him the photos.

"Well, they didn't look like that. Are they dead?" He chuckled as if death were a commonplace event in his life. He stopped when he saw RJ's look.

"Sorry man. They're dead, aren't they?"

"What can you tell us about them?" Melissa said.

Stone confirmed Jan's story.

"Did they leave together with the person the woman was talking to?"

"Nope."

"Do you mean *nope* you can't tell us or *nope,* they didn't leave together?" RJ raised his voice, pissed off at the nonchalant demeanour of this millennial.

"The person she was chatting with left before these two."

"How long before?" RJ said.

"Not sure. I was busy. Maybe midnight," Stone said.

All the Evil Scatters

"Thank you for your time, Stone," Melissa said and pulled out a couple of business cards, handing one to each of them. "Call us if something else comes to mind."

RJ and Melissa exited the bar.

"That was something. At least we know they were here, but then where did they go? And who was the guy that the woman was talking to?" Melissa said.

"Could be a person of interest at a minimum," RJ said.

"Let's have Greg and Paul sweep the place for prints," Melissa said.

"There will be hundreds."

"We'll see if there are any hits for any of them in the automated fingerprint identification system database."

*

Toronto. Police are seeking the public's help to identify two young victims, in their early 20s, who were last seen at Victor's, a bar in the city's downtown. Police are releasing little information about how the victims were killed, but sources say that their bodies had been mutilated. A motive for the crime is not yet known. There are no suspects at this time.

Anyone with information is asked to contact the police. The investigation continues.

"I have lots of information," I say out loud and cut out the article for my collection. I put it on the shelf beside the videotape.

38

RJ and Carla stood in their kitchen, tears streaming down their cheeks. "We have to try, Carla. All we've been through," RJ said taking a swig from his glass. He felt the Scotch warming him, numbing him from the pain of what his wife was saying.

"That's just it," Carla said wiping her eyes. "Ryan is dead. You have to accept that."

"I will never stop looking for his body," RJ said, staring at his wife, not believing that she wanted to end their marriage. "Don't do this."

All the Evil Scatters

"Yes. Ryan shouldn't have died. But you can't go on searching for new clues or evidence twenty-four-seven. You need to stop. For your own sake."

"I will. I promise."

Carla shook her head, "No you won't. You've said this before and yet, the wall in the basement is still there, taunting you, pushing you to keep looking. To look for clues that aren't there. You go there every night."

RJ looked at her in surprise.

"Yes. I know you slink out of bed every night. One of those nights, I came down to the basement. You were staring at the wall as if it was going to come alive with the answers you seek. Don't you see? He's gone. I'm his mother. I carried him for nine months, but I have let him go, keeping only the good things about him and the wonderful boy that he was. Dwelling on the past has stagnated our future," Carla ran her fingers through her hair, moved toward the dishwasher and began emptying it. "I can't do this anymore."

"Come on, sweetie," RJ said, his tone pleading. "We can do this; we've been doing it for years."

"I can't do *it* any longer. Whatever *it* is."

"I know we're not the same people we were back then," RJ said. "We're not perfect. I still love you. Don't you love me?"

"I'll always love you RJ, but I don't know who you are anymore. Who we are together."

RJ took his glass and leaned into the counter, looking at her, looking for clues that might help him understand why she wanted to end their marriage. He sighed and said. "Of course, the trauma of losing Ryan will never leave us. He's such a big part of us."

"He *was* a big part of us. He's gone. Gone, forever! Let it go."

"Okay. I'll tear down the wall in the basement. I'll bury everything to do with Ryan." Even as he said it, RJ knew that he would never take down the information on the wall. It gave him strength to continue his quest. To hope. He would never give up.

"When our boy died, he left a black hole in my heart. Staying together won't bring him back. We no longer work together. Please let me go. Let me start a new life."

"But we are stronger together, Carla."

"I can't do this. I can't lie in bed with you and pretend that we're husband and wife. I can't bear the thought of you slinking away every night

All the Evil Scatters

in the hope to find answers. We're like friends sharing a house but nothing else. The rest of the time you're at work, on a case, or on the heels of a new case, the next best thing."

"You know why I work so hard."

"Yeah. To put the criminals away. To make our streets safer. But every day children go missing. Children are killed. And every day a criminal goes free. And every day I'm with you I am reminded that you will never move on from the loss of Ryan. That wall keeps Ryan alive in your mind. I get it, but it's not healthy. That wall separates us. It's been so many years. Ryan is gone forever."

"I would have given my own life in exchange for Ryan's," RJ said.

"You don't get it," Carla said.

"No. You don't get it! I will never stop trying to find our son's remains. They have to be out there somewhere," RJ said, grabbed the bottle of Scotch and made his way to the stairs leading to the basement.

*

RJ examined the evidence board on the wall that he had started and kept adding to over the years. It depicted painstaking work and a never-ending display of his journey to find his son's remains. Everything was there, within reach: strings attached to push pins connected points of interest; Ryan's last known whereabouts were circled in red; the last photos RJ had of his son before he disappeared; and, the final place where his bloodied clothing had been found. He'd even used face-aging software of what Ryan might look like today if he had lived. By looking at that photo, RJ felt that his son had never disappeared, choosing instead to imagine that Ryan was away at University, studying, too busy to call home. *Irrational,* he thought. *But what part of life is rational, if you thought about it?* There were timelines and photographs. He'd shaded the areas that he'd already searched. Every weekend or on his day off from work, he looked for Ryan's remains, hoping that his search would end and he'd find his son's remains and give him a proper burial. But every time he returned, he was back to where he'd started, blotting out yet another area of Toronto's vast ravine system.

He recalled Carla saying on more than one occasion, "RJ. You have to stop. I love our son too. But he's gone." He'd ignored her pleas, determined to keep searching. "I will not stop searching, Carla. Maybe you've forgotten, but I haven't," he'd said. Anger and hurt were evident in her eyes, but she shook her head and left the basement. He sneezed twice and stared at the wall as if by looking at it all the answers would be revealed.

For almost eighteen years, RJ's obsession with finding his son's remains obscured everything else. His son's death had consumed him. He wanted to find the perpetrator who had taken and then killed their son. He had articles and photos of missing children who had also mysteriously disappeared and never resurfaced just like Ryan. He looked for similar patterns or characteristics of the victims and wondered if it could be the same abductor.

RJ glanced at the other side of the room. On that wall there were details of their current case; evidence and photos were tacked on it. The image of the hooded person was in the centre, with all the clues fanning out from it like a spider's web. A drawing of the evil eye, that he had drawn, was at the top of the wall staring back at him.

"Who are you?" RJ said staring at their hooded suspect. He turned back to Ryan's wall and said, "Where are you, son?"

He drank from his bottle of Scotch and then lit a cigarette. He inhaled deeply, the smoke filling his lungs, calming him like an old friend might. RJ wiped the tears from his eyes and took another swig of Scotch. He stared at a missing poster of Ryan — his son's eyes, filled with promise and innocence, stared back at him.

39

I put on a pair of dark glasses, yank the hoodie over my head and pull out my collapsible white cane. The street is deserted, the evening eerily silent as if everyone has taken to their homes to hide from an unseen threat. I tap the cane haphazardly on the sidewalk and walk into the path of an elderly couple, their arms locked together, symbiotic, their heads angled toward each other, almost touching, intimate.

"I'm so sorry," I say. "Are you okay?" I ask them with as much concern as I could muster. "I'm still trying to get used to this cane."

I can see her blue eyes as she says, "We're fine. Happy to help if you're lost." The woman looks at me in that puzzled way people have when their gut is telling them that something is wrong but they dismiss it as nonsense. Her

All the Evil Scatters

blue eyes stare at me, all-knowing, all evil. I am convinced that I'd made the right choice. I will rid the world of these evil eyes.

"No need to apologize," the man says. "Can we help you cross the street?"

I hesitate as if I'm embarrassed to bother them with this debilitating affliction. "I'm fine. Thank you for the offer. I've got to get to my friend who's waiting for me around the corner. He's parked on James and Balmour. Have a good evening." I set out in the opposite direction from where I'd told them.

"You're, um, heading in the wrong direction," the man says. "Why don't we go with you to your friend's car? We're headed in that direction anyway."

"I don't want to bother you. I'll turn around and go the other way," I say sheepishly. "It shouldn't be too hard to figure it out." I chuckle nervously and turn around, dropping my cane in the process. I bend down and fan out my hands, tapping my way on the concrete sidewalk, searching for it. "Where are you?" I say.

The man picks up the cane, cups my elbow, and puts it in my hand. "It's all right. We're all going the same way. We'd be happy to walk with you."

"If you're sure you don't mind."

The woman smiles, her eyes piercing right through me, and locks her arm in mine; our closeness reminds me of how she and the man had been walking, arm-in-arm, minutes earlier. If they only knew that it would be their last embrace. With the other hand, I use my cane to demonstrate to them that I am trying hard to find my way despite my disability. We walk together, the man inching ahead of us as if he couldn't wait to get on with his evening plans, whatever they had been before my appearance.

When we arrive at the intersection of James and Balmour, the man asks, "Which one is your car?"

"It's a blue Oldsmobile."

"Ah, there it is. I don't see your friend, though," the woman says, her breath hot and buttery on my cheek.

"He's probably gone to stretch his legs. Would you mind walking me over there?"

"Of course," the man says, extending his hand to me.

All the Evil Scatters

I ignore it, not wanting to give myself away.

The woman relinquishes me over to the man, takes my hand and puts it in his.

"Honey, why don't you wait here? I'll take our friend to the car. Won't be a minute," he says and crooks his arm with mine.

How delightful. I wasn't sure how I would separate them, but sometimes fate has a way of intervening and giving you exactly what you need at that moment.

"Thank you," I say to the woman. "Sorry to have bothered you."

"Happy to help," the man says.

When we arrive at the car, the man doesn't see the syringe that I'd taken out of my pocket. I quickly glance around me, making sure that there was no one around. I wasn't worried about the woman who shivered in the dampness of the evening, looking about her as if she were expecting someone with nefarious intentions to appear. Little did she know that I'm the one that she should worry about. She clutched her scarf tight around her neck, shielding herself from the Arctic wind that had ceremoniously picked up in intensity. As the man opens the door for me, I jab him in his pectoral area; he clutches his chest and looks up at me, surprised.

I smile.

Terror flashes in his eyes and then the shadow of understanding comes across his face. His grip on the door handle slackens. He collapses to the ground.

I note the scorpion tattoo on the upper part of his neck, below the ear.

"Oh my God! Ma'am!" I call out to her.

At the sound of my voice, she releases her grip on her scarf; her hand falls to her side. In what seems like an instant, she hurries across the street. When she reaches us, she kneels beside her husband and says, "Sweetie? What's wrong?"

His eyes open wide; he moves his lips in a feeble attempt to warn her. But I know that my helpful assistant, ketamine, is the one in charge.

"Let's get him up," I say.

"I know you're scared, Wallace, but we'll get you help." She says matter-of-factly, "I think he's having a heart attack. Did you take your pills today, Wallace?"

All the Evil Scatters

Even better than I had hoped. The man has a heart condition! "Are you sure? Maybe he slipped. There's lots of black ice."
"He's stopped moving." She sprang into action, searching her purse for something. "Where is it? I need to call 9-1-1."
"I have a better idea," I say gently touching her shoulder. "We can take him to the hospital ourselves. If we wait for the ambulance, we might, um, you know, be too late."
"You're right. I'll drive us there."
I liked her strong will and immediate appropriation of the situation. We're similar, she and I. It will be sad to see her take her last breath.
I act quickly. I don't want to attract attention. "Why don't we put your husband in the back seat?"
"Thank you. Thank you so much. You're very kind." She wraps her arms around me. I want to pull away, but her warm embrace comforts me. I inhale her earthy scent and question my decision. My reluctance is overcome by the taste of another successful kill. And so, I argue back and forth with myself. On the one hand, I hadn't planned tonight's kill. Perhaps I should move on? If I let them go, they're witnesses. He'll remember what I did. They'll go to the police. I can't have that. In the end, I pull away from her and say, "Let's get him inside the car."
We hoist him into the back seat, and not without a great deal of effort from both of us. Wallace, as she called him, could stand to lose a few. No wonder he has heart problems.
I give her the keys. She settles into the driver's seat and starts the engine. I make my way slowly, but not too slowly, over to the passenger side and get in.
She pays no attention to me; her attention is focused on the back seat where her husband's inert body lays.
She clasps on her seatbelt.
I lean into her as she's about to shift gears; her pupils dilate with horror when she sees the needle in my hand. I cover her mouth before she can scream. She attempts to extricate herself from her seatbelt, but the needle descends and pierces her chest. I depress the flange and imagine the liquid coursing through her bloodstream, slowly in the first few seconds, but quickly taking over her consciousness with relentless fury. She slumps back into the seat.

All the Evil Scatters

I get out of the car, release her seatbelt, and pull her into the passenger seat. When she's completely situated, I strap on the seatbelt; her head lolls about.

I make my way to the driver's side and as I open the door, I hear someone coughing behind me. I stiffen. Surely whoever it was hadn't been there a moment ago? *Shit! Shit! Shit!* I had made sure that no one was around. Where had he come from? Had he seen anything?

I turn around, look up and see a male in his early 50s, smiling at me. "Would you like some help?" He says.

I second-guess myself. This is a mistake. I should have planned better. I was ill-prepared to go through with tonight's kill. But her eyes, Mother's eyes, compel me to act. I assess the man's weight and size and ponder the idea of taking him with me. But he doesn't fit into my plan. I need to convince him that all is well.

"All good. Thanks." I say. "Mom's tired and dad, well, he's tied one on as usual." I chuckle and wait for him to leave.

"Are you sure you're all right?" He says and glances toward the back seat.

Nosy people! I consider my options: abandon my plan and take him with me; or convince him that all is good. My glasses obscure my eyes from him, the hoodie hides most of my face except for my cheeks and jaw.

"Always happens after dinner. Too many carbs and merlot," I say and chuckle again. "Thanks so much for offering to help."

The stranger appraises the situation, looking first to the woman and then at the man

I reach inside my pocket feeling for that extra syringe with ketamine.

He yawns, takes a final look, and says, "All right then. If you're sure you're fine."

I pulled my hand out of my pocket and say, "Happens all the time."

"Later," he says.

I watch him walk down the street and disappear around the corner and wonder, how many Good Samaritans can there be in one night?

All the Evil Scatters

40

Melissa walked into her Tip Top Tailor loft. It was as if she'd stepped back in time to the 1920s, to the time of art deco. Her apartment was an eclectic mix of mid-century modern furnishings. Prints depicting the original Toronto Star Building on King Street and images of other historical buildings adorned the walls.

There was no clutter here. Soaring ceilings provided enough light to showcase every object that she had hand-picked at auctions and antique shops over the years. From her designer mother, she'd learned about form and function, texture, light, and colour. Melissa had once considered following in her mother's footsteps. In the end, she chose a career in catching criminals — a career as vastly different from design as the proverbial apples and oranges.

She was fortunate to get her condo — a sacrifice sale by the owners who'd both recently lost their jobs. Her agent had claimed it was a great deal, and it was. Melissa had fallen in love with the bones of the old building and its architectural lines. She'd put in an offer; in a matter of hours, the condo was hers. "Mom, you would have been so proud of this place. I miss you so much," she said out loud and then, "if you continue to talk to yourself, Mel, one might think you're losing it." *I should get a dog*, she thought, but immediately dismissed it knowing that the commitment a dog needed was not something she had to give. She sighed, the recent murders weighing her down. She rubbed her neck, hoping for relief. "No wonder I'm talking to myself," she said and laughed. She was wide awake, wired from their gruesome discovery. The events of the past week, the evidence, the castration of the male, a form of emasculation, the stitched eyes, and the lack of clues had her head spinning, rendering her unable to stop the repetitious review of every piece of evidence and every inch of the crime scene in her mind. She'd inherited her father's razor-sharp ability to compartmentalize the facts of any situation, making connections and finding the root of the problem. She kicked off her shoes, shed her work clothes and headed into the kitchen. She pulled out a bottle of Cab Sauv from the wine rack, poured herself a glass and drank from it, immediately feeling its warm liquid coursing down her throat, taking the edge off. She sat on the sofa with its colourful textile of geometric shapes.

She wondered about the identity of the young couple who, according to blood tests, showed that they were likely siblings. How did they come to their

All the Evil Scatters

fate? Who was the unidentified person who had been talking to the female? Was he their killer? What motivated the killer? Why these types of mutilations? Where had they been killed? Did the killer or killers have medical training given the precision of the cuts and sutures?

She grabbed her wine-filled glass, walked toward the bathroom, and placed it on the edge of the Jacuzzi tub. She turned on the faucet until the water temperature felt comfortable to her touch; she added Epsom salts and a capful of French lavender bath foam. Lavender had been her mother's favourite scent. Melissa recalled summer vacations in the south of France, with her brother Ari and her parents. Fields of purple shrubs grew in abundance, infusing the air around them with their sweet aroma as her dad drove through the winding, sometimes precipitous, narrow Provençal roads. She recalled stopping at the Abbaye Notre Dame de Senaque to stock up on soap and honey made by the monks who lived there. Oh, how she missed those summer jaunts to Europe. "How could I have known we'd have so little time left?" And then his face, Nicolas's face, came unbidden, reminding her of that fateful day 10 years ago.

She gulped the rest of the wine and poured herself another before easing her body into the tub. The water washed away her tension and the muscles in her neck and shoulders relaxed. Her eyelids drooped.

She shook herself awake, got out, gently tamped her towel along her skin, went into the bedroom, and buried herself under the duvet. She let her thoughts wander.

Melissa met Nicolas during her second year of her Master's program at the University of Toronto. They were both studying forensics: he anthropology; she psychology. They'd both been studying at the library late one evening toward the end of their programs when she'd noticed him watching her. As uncomfortable as his unwavering glance had made her feel, she held his gaze. That was all the encouragement that Nicolas had needed; he grabbed his books and made his way to her. His swagger was confident and purposeful. His eyes never left hers, causing her heart to beat faster. She looked away, trying to calm this unexpected flutter in her stomach.

"Hi. Nicolas Brinkton," he said extending his hand. "Sorry for staring, but you looked so beautiful and engrossed in your books that I couldn't help myself from thinking that I should meet you."

All the Evil Scatters

She laughed to hide her nervousness and played along. "If I'd known I would have saved you a seat," she smiled and took his outstretched hand. "Melissa Hargrove."

He held her hand for a few moments longer than necessary. She pulled it free, but as she did, his thumb caressed her wrist and at that moment she knew that she would love him forever.

They'd hit it off from the start. They talked about everything — school, the future, a family. No topic seemed out of reach that night. Nothing was too personal or off-limits. It was as if they'd known each other forever.

Evenings spent at campus pubs became customary. She never paid attention to how much Nicolas drank until they'd been together for about a year. They would go out for drinks; he'd out-drink her by a ratio of five glasses to her one. She noticed how he'd polish off a bottle or two of wine in one sitting. In those early days, she'd written it off to the stress of job hunting after graduation and the untimely death of his sister to leukemia earlier that year. But his drinking continued even after they'd moved into a rental in the Annex. She ignored the signs because there were so many good days: making love, sometimes twice a day; surprise gifts for no reason at all; his charismatic smile that could light up any room that he walked into; and, he treated her with kindness and unwavering love.

She was hired by the police force as a forensic identification officer; Nicolas eventually got a position at the University, teaching criminology. Over the next few years, his drinking binges increased; he often drank 40 ounces of vodka within a couple of days. He became belligerent and aggressive. He never hit her, but he came close once, putting his fist through the wall, narrowly missing her face. He had been mortified and apologetic about his behaviour and swore to lay off the booze. Things improved and appeared to have returned to normal, but his sobriety lasted only a few weeks before he started again.

"You have to stop drinking, Nicolas," she told him one night. "It's killing you and it's killing us!"

"I don't wanna stop drinking," he slurred and took a swig from a bottle of Vodka. "You should try it sometime. Let loose, babe. Come on. Here," he said, offering her the bottle.

She smacked his arm and the bottle fell from his hand, shattering on the linoleum floor.

All the Evil Scatters

"You're such a bitch!" He raised his fist and she protectively guarded her face with her hands.

"You touch me and I'll have you charged with assault."

"Do it! I dare you."

"Don't push me, Nicolas!" She said and then changed her tactic. "Honey. Why can't you see that you have a problem and that it's affecting you? Us! I don't know if I can continue like this."

"Me neither. I'm outta here!" With that, he grabbed his jacket and walked out of the apartment.

She flinched as the door slammed behind him. She sat down and cupped her face in her hands.

Later that night, when she heard him stumbling into their bedroom, knocking things over in the dark, she pretended to sleep, wondering which bar he'd been at. She said nothing when he bumped his way into their bed, turned away from her and fell asleep.

They didn't speak about that night or the ones that followed. She spent more time at the office and he spent more time at the bar. They were civil with each other and managed to co-exist in their apartment. Some days were better than others. But when something went wrong at the university or something happened that he couldn't handle, it triggered a drinking binge. It was during those times that Melissa contemplated life without Nicolas. But guilt over leaving the love of her life and the life they'd planned together overcame her doubts. She stayed with him, hopeful that things would change.

She often wondered what would have happened if she had left him in those early years. Could she have prevented the events that changed their lives forever?

Nicolas grew up witnessing his father's physical assaults on his mother. His father never hit him, but neither his mother nor his older sister, Emily, had fared as well. On many occasions, his old man came home drunk and demanding. Several times he beat his mother to within inches of her life. Emily left home as soon as she was 16 and made a life for herself by cleaning hotel rooms, finishing off high school and then getting a degree in nursing.

Nicolas often wondered why he'd been spared from his father's fist. Melissa recalled how Nicolas had told her how close he'd come to hurting his father. "I grabbed a knife and aimed it at his carotid artery. God help me. I wanted to kill him!" Nicolas had said, realizing what he had been about to do and dropped the knife to the floor vowing to be everything that his father never was. Those words still bring chills down her spine. Nicolas was 16 years old. *Hard to beat the cycle of alcoholism and violence,* she thought. *Why am I thinking about this now?*

She noticed the blue light blinking on her cell and reached for it. It was a call from her brother, Ari. He seemed to have it all — his wife, Wendy, two kids, Jonathan and Dana and a job as the crime editor of one of the daily newspapers. His voice message was brief but hinted at the recent homicides. He was looking for the story behind the crime, just as she was. She smiled. The love for her older brother filled her heart like nothing else these days; he was the only family she had after their parents were killed in a car crash.

41

I drive out of the city streets, onto the highway and then onto a winding country road. I cast furtive glances from one to the other to confirm that they are still breathing — their breath is shallow, but it's there. I suppose opposites attract. Was that what had attracted my Parents to one another? Or was it a base need in their genetic makeup to inflict pain and suffering on me?

I look over at the small woman, bird-like in appearance with a thick plume of grey hair atop her head. The man named, Wallace, lies slumped over on his stomach in the back seat. I can't see his face, but that's temporary.

"So, you thought you would help the blind, huh?" I yell at them, the inflection in my voice sounding like Him, and then it shifts, sounding more like Her.

"Shit. Shit. Shit." I know even before looking in the back of the car that it was not there. In my haste to get them into the car, I had left the cane behind. I can't worry about that now. I know I was wearing gloves. Surely, I hadn't left any prints on it? "Think. Think. Think." I was certain that I'd never handled the cane with my bare hands. But still. Doubt consumes me. Once again, I question my plan. Should I have planned it out more? But her eyes. Surely I must ensure she hurts no one else.

I reach over to Her and I am pleased to see the slightest movement of Her lips. She was trying to say something. Maybe She was trying to curse me with Her evil eye. Was She trying to beg me to forgive Her for what She had

All the Evil Scatters

done? For running away? "Any eye is an evil eye That looks in on to a mood apart." I quote Robert Frost. She watches me, unable to speak. "Don't look at me!" I say and pull Her lids over Her evil eyes. Her blue stare disappears and I am safe.

"Of course, you think you're better than I am," I turn to the back of the car. "You always did. You never stopped to ask how I felt. Only how I made You feel. Tonight You will be pleased with what I have in store for both of You," And then to Her, I say, "You were just as complicit! You could have saved me. You didn't. And for that, You will pay."

I drive in silence for a few minutes and then say, "It's really good to have You both with me again. It's how it should have been. Right, Mother? Right, Father?"

It takes a long time to get out of the city, the streets are a mess — potholes, black ice, poor traffic management, and the general ineptitude of drivers. I finally relax as I leave Toronto and ease the car onto the country roads. An occasional skunk or fox darts out onto the road that I swerve to avoid.

I round the bend with ease and race down the deserted side road which leads to the farmhouse; the gravel pings and bounces off my car like a pebble storm.

I reverse the Oldsmobile into the carport, edging it close to the entrance which leads to the basement. I get out and hastily unlock the door.

I return to the car, open the door and pull on Wallace. "God, you're heavy!" I say. He makes the slightest movement. I pull him from under his arms, but his body resists my efforts and I land square on my ass. I wince from the effort, but rise with renewed determination, pulling, lifting and dragging his body out of the car until it falls to the ground. I drag him by the arms, down two steps toward the basement door which leads to my workroom, and push him inside. I take a moment to rest before rolling him onto the clean tarp. I turn him so that I can see His reactions, slight as they might be. I want to see His horror, and finally His understanding.

"Wallace," I look at him with the interest of a cat waiting to pounce. "Is your brain telling you to get up? Is your body not complying? Are you wondering what I'm going to do to you?" I smile, noting the faint movement of his lips. "You're mine now, Wallace. Relax. Enjoy the comfort of knowing that all will be revealed. Let me get your lovely wife." I swore he moved to

All the Evil Scatters

stop me. "What's the point, Wallace? You and I both know you aren't going anywhere tonight. Or any other night for that matter."

I return to the car and edge the woman out of the passenger side. I'm gentler with her. Not sure why as I explore her face. For a moment my conviction to kill her wavers. I recall the hug she'd given me earlier. How comforted I felt. I shake my head to rid myself of my reluctance, get behind her, put my arms around her waist, lift her over my shoulders and take her inside. "Don't worry. Wallace awaits." I laugh and position them side-by-side.

I remove my clothes and stand naked in front of them. I cross myself three times and chant, "Jesus Christ is victorious, and all the evil scatters by Him." When I'm done, I cross myself three times and mock-spit, *ftou, ftou, ftou*. "Take a good look at what You did to me," I say, turning to face the mirror. "I know I'm not magnificent to behold, but my work is. You will soon see that."

I reach into the closet and pull out my freshly laundered paramedic's uniform; a good soaking in bleach has turned the once sand-coloured outfit to a yellowy-white, eradicating all signs of the siblings. I press record on my video camera. I want to relive every moment later when the night falls and I cannot sleep.

"Since you left me, Mother," I say. "You shall go first. Father will watch. I suppose I can give you a detailed account of what you can expect from me."

"Father will go last, bearing witness to my plan from start to finish. You will have the benefit of seeing how the world will be rid of your evil." I walk over to the back of the room and pull the curtain, which I've washed in bleach, revealing the stainless steel table with its myriad of medical instruments which I'd stolen from the hospitals. For good measure, I've added an assortment of knives from the kitchen and tools purchased at Home Hardware. *Homeowners helping homeowners with expert advice* is their motto. I chuckle.

I angle their bodies giving them a better view of me in action; their eyes are wide open. I chant, cross my chest, and mock spit several times. Wallace blinks, trying to stop his flow of tears; she has none — she's strong, uncompromising. It will be a shame. "Gabriel! You're wavering again. Stop it!"

All the Evil Scatters

I pick up the needle prepared with catgut and move toward the woman.

I stop at the sound of a grunt coming from Wallace. "Did I hear a protest? Do you want to save Mother? I guess that is the gentlemanly thing to do, isn't it? Or are you a coward? You're willing to go first so You won't have to see what happens to Her."

"Sorry. I can't change my plan. Mother goes first." A tear trickles down his temple. "There. There. All will be fine. Stop crying. It'll be over soon. Sit back and enjoy the moment. My moment. Before I stop Your evil."

I note the slight movement of Her index finger. Accusing me. "You have no idea what I'm capable of do You? All You need to know is that this is the end for You. How does it feel to be helpless? Unable to take control of Your life?" I can almost hear the word, *Monster,* cutting through her taped lips."

The *record* button flashes. In my best directorial voice say, "Take two."

I lean in toward the woman and move the needle close to her eye, cinch the upper and lower lids and pierce through them. Blood replaces her tears, a soupy mix. Her screams are silent, her body writhes in protest. When Her eyes are sealed and are no longer a threat, I grab the noose and slip it around her neck. She stops moving. I know that she has lost consciousness.

I want to crush her windpipe; take away Her last breath. I squeeze until I hear the crack of bone, almost like the sound of a chicken's neck snapping. She gurgles out Her last rattled breath.

I wait a few minutes before I feel for Her pulse. There is none. The evil has been vanquished. I rise, cross myself three times and mock spit, *ftou, ftou, ftou,* in her direction.

I look over at Father; His eyes are closed. I poke His side with my foot; His eyelids slowly lift. "I want you alert! You're my witness. See my work and know that You too will get what you deserve."

I unbelt His pants, the fabric coarse as my hands work down his legs. His polo shirt was blue like the sky, blue like Mother's evil eyes. His shirt comes off easily, catching on his head, before releasing it and His nakedness. He's disgusting to look at — rolls of fat embrace his belly, just like Him. And to make things worse, he's soiled himself — a mixture of urine and shit. "You're disgusting! Now I have to clean you up, get you ready.

"Do you remember Father? I had tried so hard not to pee, but my bladder gave in, no matter how hard I tried. You punished me for that —

All the Evil Scatters

locked me up, making me sit in my dirty clothes, waiting for You to come and forgive me for my weakness."

I see from the glassy look in His eyes that He has slipped into a world where sanity meets insanity. "What a surprise, Father. The fear return to His eyes, but quickly disappears, replaced by defiance.

I remove the noose from her neck and then fasten it around his neck. I squeeze the knot tight.

When I'm certain that he is dead, I grab the scalpel and say, "Now the final monster will be gone," echoing His words before He castrated me. "Jesus Christ is victorious, and all the evil scatters by Him. Jesus Christ is victorious, and all the evil scatters by Him. Jesus Christ is victorious, and all the evil scatters by Him. *ftou, ftou, ftou.*"

I make my first incision.

*

"My work is done," I say to the silent room. "Their evil is scattered." I pull the tape out of the machine and label it, *Mother and Father, #2.*

42

Far off in the distance, Melissa heard her cell phone. She opened her eyes; it was still slightly dark. She groaned at the time display: 7:02 a.m. She answered the phone and said, "I'm sorry I'm running late." She scrambled to her feet.

"That's okay. You'll need your beauty sleep…" RJ's voice drifted.

"What's going on? Do we have a break in the case?"

"We found two more bodies. Similar MO. I'm on my way to the scene. Get yourself ready and meet me there."

Ping. The crime scene address had arrived on her phone.

*

Melissa, RJ, Paul, and Greg looked upon two naked bodies, embracing each other, like their first two victims.

Melissa took photos of the bodies from several angles, and when she was done, she worked with RJ, Paul, and Greg to turn over the body as carefully as they could. Although they were prepared for what they would find, nothing could once again prepare them for the atrocity before them. They inhaled and then exhaled as if sharing the same breath. Melissa clenched her mouth, trying to stop the bile from rising — it was an older female.

RJ put his hand on her shoulder.

"I'm...I'm fine," she said, her voice quivering as her brain tried to understand man's darkest nature and his ability to inflict pain on others without mercy.

"Now this, once again, is the most horrific display of human depravity that I've ever seen," RJ said.

"Me too," Paul said.

"Ditto," Greg confirmed and took out the crime tape from the toolbox and worked with Paul to cordon off the perimeter of the scene.

"Monster!" Melissa said, surveying the bodies, all the while taking short breaths to steady her nerves. "There's no mistaking the similarity in the way the bodies are arranged and mutilated — a replica of our previous two victims. Except that there are differences between these victims and the other two."

"They're older. The positioning of the bodies, the method of castration, and the female's sutured eyes are the work of the same killer. Dare I say that we may be dealing with a serial killer?"

The words "serial killer" pinged through RJ's head as if a bell had gone off, "Okay asshole, *why* the fuck are you doing this?"

Melissa had come across serial murders before, mainly through case file studies over the years — some well-known cases such as Ted Bundy, Jack the Ripper, Son of Sam. The Golden State Killer was identified in 2018, decades after he'd murdered and raped dozens of people. More recently the serial killer, Bruce McArthur killed minority gay men and had gone undetected for years. Her only hands-on introduction to serial killings had been in Iowa, five years ago. She'd worked very closely on the case because two of the victims were Canadian. They caught the killer by matching DNA found at one of the scenes to DNA found in the data bank. That killer had been sloppy. This case was different — no DNA had been left behind.

"No ID," RJ said. "What do these two victims have in common with the siblings? Could it be they're also siblings?"

"We won't know if there's a biological link until we run their DNA."

"These victims are older. Usually, serial killers have a type, don't they?" RJ said.

All the Evil Scatters

"It's plausible that he's trying to figure it out still. Hasn't yet developed a *type*," Melissa said.
"Let's see if our killer left something for us — a calling card," RJ said.
"Another charm?" Melissa said.
"*If* it belonged to the perp. The dog could have picked it up from anywhere."
"Is there a note like with the other victims?" Melissa said.
"Good point," RJ said and looked at the victim's hands, shifted his gaze to their feet, and, there it was, a piece of paper, folded and tucked between the man's toes. RJ pinched it with his tweezers, unfolded it, and read:
There's more to come!
"I'm gonna get you. Son of a...!" RJ said, holding back the word.
Melissa handed RJ a plastic evidence bag and watched him slip the note into it and then drop it in the box.
RJ pulled out a cigarette and put it in his mouth; he didn't light it. He glanced around to confirm that no one could see him and reached into his pocket, pulled out his flask, took a quick drink, and put it back before he knelt beside her and said, "Let's do this."
"We have lots to do," Melissa said. "Tara's counting on us."
"As are the victims, their families and, God forbid, any future victims," RJ said. "We will be their voice because we're all they have,"
The evidence box was quickly filled with plastic bags that contained every item of interest.
"RJ? Look at this," Melissa said and pointed to the back of the man's neck, close to the crease of the left ear — a tattoo, the size of a child's palm depicting a scorpion.
He knelt beside her and followed her gloved finger pointing to the scorpion tattoo.
He pulled out a right-angle ruler and placed it against the man's stone-cold neck; Melissa photographed it.
"Might be something. Possible lead to uncovering their identity."
Greg and Paul were gathering evidence a few feet away.
Melissa waved them over. "What's up, Mel?"
"See this tattoo?"
"Uh, yeah. Want us to track it down?" Paul said.

All the Evil Scatters

"It's a long shot; tat parlours are everywhere," Greg said. "Send me the photos and we'll get on it as soon as we're done here."

43

The following morning, Melissa reviewed her messages, noticing that several were from her brother, Ari. She'd read his articles — he and all the other media outlets were making the link that the two cases were related and that a potential serial killer was at work.

She tapped Ari's number on her phone and waited for him to pick up.

"Mel!" A voice boomed on the other end of the phone. "How's it going, sis? What more can you tell me about these two cases? The public has the right to know." There was no doubting the frustration in his voice.

She adored her older brother. He had always been there for her, except, as the story goes, that one time when he had tried to choke her with her pacifier. It was lucky that their mother had arrived in time to pull it out of her mouth. There had been no further incidents. Melissa was a baby and didn't remember the event, but later, as the story was retold, she understood that her older brother had been jealous of her and overly possessive of their parents. She never held it against him; he had been only six years old. But that was a long time ago. Their relationship now was one of love and mutual respect. She knew he would always be by her side whenever she needed his support. They often joked about the pacifier incident, *if you don't put a lid on it, I'll pacify you!*

"You know I can't say much more than what's in our press release. We've yet to identify the victims," Melissa said.

"It's a serial killer, isn't it?" Ari said. "Do you think he'll strike again?"

She knew that it was a strong possibility but sighed and said, "Let's hope not. That's all I can say for now, Ari…" her voice trailed off.

"Are you alright? This kind of stuff can do a number on your psyche."

"Under the circumstances with little sleep and little information, I'm okay. These types of cases are never easy. Don't worry. How are you? Wendy? The boys? All well in that perfect little world of yours?"

"Great. Couldn't be better. We miss you. You haven't been by for weeks. Your nephews are asking for you. I think one of them is going to follow in your footsteps, oh Great One!"

All the Evil Scatters

"Give it up," she laughed. "You're no slouch yourself."

"I don't know. I could be better, um, more persuasive with my little sister…"

"You'll have to wait for the next release, along with everyone else," Melissa said.

"Sis. I gotta go. A couple of reporters are breathing down my neck. Editor duty calls. Come visit. Call when you have more info! Kisses."

"Soon," she said, knowing that *soon* was a pipe dream since they were as far away from closing in on the perpetrator as it was to find the proverbial needle in the haystack.

44

Another grey day dawned upon the city, the sub-zero temperatures made it feel like January rather than April. The weather was as unpredictable as the criminals that Melissa and RJ chased.

About ten police officers shuffled into the briefing room, their mood sombre. At the front of the room were Melissa, RJ, Paul, and Greg. They were gathered around the evidence board where Heather had tacked up the new information. There were close-up photos of the four victims from several angles, including the positioning of the bodies, the castration of the males and the sutured eyes of the females. Some images zoomed in on the continuous suturing pattern and closeups of the victims' necks showing tracks of scars left behind by a rope that was used to strangle them. Pushpins on a map showed where the bodies had been found: one in the East end, near the Scarborough Bluffs; the other close to the University of Toronto.

Along the bottom of the board was a rough timeline of the known whereabouts of the victims. The last time the young adults had been seen alive was around midnight at *Victor's* bar over a week ago. Their bodies had been found at approximately 7 a.m. Their estimated time of death was between 2 and 4 a.m. The elderly victims had been found around 6 a.m. the day before.

RJ and Melissa turned to face the group and nodded to Tara, who was looking on from the back of the room.

Tara cleared her throat and began, "Thanks everyone for your work. We all know there's much more to do — we barely have anything tangible. It's

All the Evil Scatters

been a week. I know how hard you've all been working, but we must work smarter and faster to catch this killer. That's why I've asked you to drop everything that you're doing."

There was nodding around the room, signifying that it was their duty to catch the killer.

Tara continued, "For you, all other cases are secondary. This case is our number one priority. Let's say it has become my crusade to catch him before he strikes again. You are all aware of the McArthur case. We don't need another stain on the department. Melissa and RJ? Please walk us through your findings."

"Here's what we know," Melissa said, taking command of the room. "We have two sets of victims with about a forty-year age difference between them. Fifteen kilometres separate the two crime scenes."

"Here and here," RJ said pointing at the map on the evidence board.

"We don't know if the perp is from Toronto," Melissa said. "Or whether he performs his heinous acts somewhere else."

"Quite the feat under either scenario," RJ said.

"What we know from the lack of blood spatter and the condition of the bodies is that the victims were killed elsewhere. As you know, the siblings' bodies were found in a laneway; the other two were found in a shrub, fairly visible to anyone passing by. Both locations are secondary crime scenes."

"Where do you think the killer took his victims?" Heather said.

"Good question," Melissa said. "It's a big city. Lots of places to hide. There's a high probability that all four victims were killed at the same location. A location where the killer feels comfortable and won't be disturbed."

"Is the killer targeting couples or pairs of people?" Heather said.

"We don't know for sure, but it's a possibility we're considering," Melissa said, locking eyes with the impressive young officer who was quick to offer possible theories. She made a mental note to seek her out and offer her a more significant role in the investigation.

"Any familial connection between the older victims?" Heather fired another question.

"There's no biological connection between the older couple, so for now we're thinking that the older couple might be husband and wife, or friends, or

All the Evil Scatters

maybe they were on a date," Melissa said. "We're running prints and DNA through our systems, both here and in the US, for possible identification."

"Do you think they knew their killer?" Heather said, monopolizing the floor.

Good questions, Melissa thought and then said, "We're working with the theory that the victims did not know their killer. Most serial killings suggest that the victims never knew their perpetrator."

"At this point, we're thinking they're stranger killings," RJ said.

"We're also looking at missing persons' reports across the country. Someone must have missed these people," Melissa said. "There's no evidence that they were either homeless since there were no nutritional deficiencies or that they were victims of street violence."

"Let's turn to the crimes themselves," RJ said. "We know that the bodies were mutilated posthumously, except for the eyes. Sadly the perp stitched the females' eyes shut while they were still alive."

"How did they die?" An officer from the back of the room said.

"Frank?" RJ said looking to the coroner for a response.

Frank was a burly man in his mid-40s, balding with a beard that compensated for the lack of hair on his head; he weaved his way from the back of the room to the front, never once lifting his focus from the notepaper he was holding. His hands shook as he rifled through the various documents; he was more comfortable with cadavers than a live audience. He coughed and said, "All four victims died of asphyxia. There were visible contusions around the neck. Such markings are consistent with strangulation."

"How do you think they were lured or incapacitated?" Heather said.

"The killer somehow made them feel comfortable, taking them easily into his confidence. Perhaps, in the case of our first two victims, he had something they wanted — drugs. In the second case, we think that he somehow gained their confidence," RJ said.

"Ted Bundy," Melissa said, "one of the most charismatic serial killers in history used plaster of Paris on his forearm and approached women in parking lots seeking their help. The unsuspecting women were then taken to isolated places where he mutilated, raped them, and then had sex with their corpses."

"Do you think our killer is like Bundy?" Heather said.

All the Evil Scatters

"There was no evidence of rape or necrocoitus," Frank said. "Only the mutilations."

The room went quiet; Melissa heard the ebb and flow of the officers' breath as if they collectively shared the same set of lungs. "We know from other serial killings, that people are willing to lend a helping hand to someone in presumed need. This would not be out of the realm of possibilities in this case."

"How could these two adults, in their mid to late 60s, fall prey to the killer?" Tara said.

"Perhaps something about the killer made them feel safe. Serial killers are often charming, outgoing, and seemingly well-adjusted on the surface," RJ said. "His victims trusted him. In the case of the younger victims, we found recreational drugs and cannabis in their systems. For the older couple maybe he asked for their help."

"Don't killers typically choose victims that are similar in profile, appearance, age, etc?" Heather said. "Why these people? They all seem so different."

"His choice of victims appears to be inconsistent, but we believe that there is a common thread between the four victims; we don't know what that is yet. We have to assume that whatever it is, it's significant to the killer," RJ said.

"The age difference could represent different periods in the killer's life," Melissa said. "The older victims could be stand-ins for his parents; the younger ones might remind him of someone close to him — friends, siblings, someone significant in his life who may have contributed to his trauma."

"Any distinguishing marks or features?"

"There was a small tattoo on the older man's neck, near the ear, depicting a scorpion. Any luck on that Paul?"

Paul shook his head and said, "There are at least a few dozen tat parlours in this city."

"I bet it's a booming business," RJ said. "Anything else, Frank?"

"Toxicology shows that the younger victims had been drinking," Frank said, rifling nervously through the lab results. "A high level of ketamine was also found in their bloodstream. That combination rendered them malleable. Ketamine is an anesthetic. A controlled substance."

All the Evil Scatters

"We believe that the ketamine was used to debilitate the victims," RJ said. "This would render them incapable of defending themselves. We know that the serial killer, H.H. Holmes was a Chicago pharmacist — he knocked out his victims by using illuminating gas which he'd piped through his building. The building was also referred to as the "murder castle". He tortured, killed, and then burned his victims in the building's furnace."

"We're not ruling out that he could be a vet, a pharmacist, a doctor, a nurse, lab tech — someone who has training in surgical or medical procedure," Melissa said.

"Do we know of cases where serial killers were in the medical profession or had access to medical equipment and medication?" Someone asked.

"Harry Shipman, also known as Dr. Death, may have killed over 200 patients," RJ said. "And you've all heard of Jack the Ripper?" RJ looked around the room. Everyone nodded. "He was never caught. But because of his skill with a scalpel, authorities presumed that he was a surgeon or even a butcher."

"And not only that," Melissa added. "he mocked the police by sending letters describing his murderous acts."

"Our guy left a couple of notes, didn't he?" Heather said and pointed to the whiteboard where the magnified images of the notes left at each scene were displayed.

Melissa nodded and said, "We've sent them to the lab for fingerprints."

"What does he use for the suturing?" Heather said and wandered over to the crime board to examine the photos.

"He uses catgut," Melissa said.

"How does our perp get catgut? I thought synthetics are more common these days?" Heather said.

Clever girl, Melissa thought. "Correct. That fact alone is helpful. Frank? Can you tell us anything more about this?"

"Catgut is readily available online," Frank said, "but its use today is mainly for stringed instruments, like a violin or a guitar; it's typically made from sheep or goat intestines. In this case, our perpetrator uses catgut made of hog intestines. It's handmade. You can tell this from the asymmetry in the material."

"The psycho uses Arnold Ziffel catgut," RJ said.

All the Evil Scatters

"Making catgut is a lengthy process, requiring time and patience to get it fine enough for suturing. He would have to clean it, removing any fat, steep it in water, followed by steeping in potassium hydroxide, which works like a detergent or soap," Frank said.

"That in itself is telling. He knows exactly what he's doing," Melissa said. "Frank, tell us about the suturing pattern,"

"In this case the sutures are continuous, using a single, short, locking stitch involving the full thickness of the skin," Frank said. "The same catgut was used in both crimes."

"Why do you think he kills them?" Heather said.

"Motive is a critical piece to unlocking this crime," Melissa said. "In these sorts of crimes we need to know what motivates the criminal to act in the way that he does. We know it's about power and control. Most crimes are. We also need to determine what psychological trauma the killer experienced in their life, probably at a young age at the hands of a ruthless parent or someone in a position of authority. Perhaps our killer was abused as a child, either sexually, or physically, or both."

"Why do you think he sutures female eyes? Castrates the men?"

"Could be about regaining control. Perhaps the killer feels emasculated. Perhaps metaphorically. Perhaps literally. We're trying to better understand why performs these specific procedures on them: the castration while the male is dead; the suturing of the eyes while the female is still alive.

"Why did he start killing now?" Heather said.

"Perhaps he witnessed or went through something so horrific that he disassociated himself from that event, shutting his mind to it creating, if you will, an alternate reality where he could distance himself from the trauma. Something happened to him recently, bringing him face-to-face with that event."

"Such as?" Heather said.

"The death of a parent or spouse or partner may have triggered his psychosis. Or, he didn't get the attention he craved either at home or work, making him feel powerless, angry, and resentful. He's acting out his power struggle in these murders," Melissa said. "Perhaps he felt cast aside as a child. Maybe he had to compete with his siblings for their parents' affection."

"Or, as with many serial killers," RJ said. "they take their time to perfect their craft. First, they experiment with small animals, cats, and dogs but his desire to practice on humans overcomes him and he reaches a tipping point."

"The young couple may not be his first victims," Melissa said. "But we can't say for sure that he's killed before because there have been no similar murders on any database."

"We wonder if he had daddy or mommy issues or both, given that we have two murdered sets," RJ said. "His father may have been a passive figure in his life, or he had deserted him and the mother at a very young age. On the other hand, he was likely the victim of child abuse — perhaps at the hands of a person in authority like a parent, teacher, or relative."

"Some significant event occurred recently that pushed him over the edge," Melissa said. "His world is now out of control. We speculate that these killings are his way to regain a semblance of control — the murders are likely the only part of his life that he can control. In these murders, he's likely killing the person or persons who caused him pain. He sews the females' eyes and castrates the males. The eyes were sewn shut while the female victim was still alive; the male was mutilated post-mortem. He's telling us something. These actions are significant to them. These are likely the clues to his motivation — emasculation of the male that was a threat to him; sewing the eyes shut could be that he was protecting the female in his life from what was about to happen to the male?"

"Do you think he acted alone? Girlfriend? Buddy? Or even a brother? Sounds like a lot of work for one person," Tara said.

"Hard to imagine one person controlling, killing, and moving two bodies. We've contemplated that there could be two of them working together. It's been done before," Melissa said.

"For those of us who were around, we can't forget the Bernardo-Homolka case of the 1990s," RJ said. "Homolka's plea bargain with crown attorneys for the exchange of information was called *a deal with the devil."*

"Weren't there a couple of cousins in the 60s in LA who killed together?" Heather said.

"The Hillside Strangler," Melissa said.

"But it can be a woman too, right?" Heather said.

"Definitely. Look no further than nurse Elizabeth Tracy Mae Wettlaufer who murdered eight seniors over nine years in Southwestern Ontario before being captured in 2016," RJ said. "Or nurse, Jane Toppan, who injected

All the Evil Scatters

poison into her victims, killing about thirty-one of them at the turn of the last century."

"We know that the first set of victims were at *Victor's* bar," Melissa said. "The manager told us that the two had been there the night they were killed. She also told us that she saw the young woman talking to someone — this is a person of interest."

"That sketch," Heather pointed to the whiteboard. "It's pretty vague."

"Agreed. But note that he is of small stature which leads us to believe that if there are two killers, this one might be the killer's accomplice," RJ said.

"Could it be a woman, like Homolka? She lured the victims to the waiting Bernardo. The young girls felt safe with her," Tara said.

"Possibly," Melissa said. "Given the height and stature of our person of interest, it could be a woman."

"What about this charm?" Heather said, pointing to the charm of an eye pooped out by the dog.

"Not sure. Could have come from anywhere," Melissa said.

"Any further questions?" RJ said and looked around the room. Silence answered him.

"Great work everyone," Tara said. "Melissa, RJ and the rest of the team. You have my full support. I don't have to tell you how important it is to keep these details confidential. The media is already making assumptions despite our tempered press releases and conferences. They've even dubbed the killer, *The Suturer*. Let me be clear. You are not to refer to the killer as *The Suturer* or as a serial killer. We have enough sensationalism around this case already. Thanks all," Tara said and exited.

The room grew heavy with unanswered questions. Some officers moved to the whiteboard, took photos, and jotted down notes. Other officers talked amongst themselves, all aware of the stakes.

45

"I'm thinking that he's probably out there right now, cruising, looking for his next victims makes me feel helpless," RJ said.

"We're doing all we can to uncover the victims' identities. Everyone is working around the clock. We'll find him." Melissa tried to assuage RJ, knowing how impatient he could get. *Who could blame him?* She thought, *after what happened to Ryan.* She sensed that this case probably reminded him of the futility of never finding his son's killer.

"We need something new to catapult us forward," RJ said and banged his fist on the wall.

"We have an artist's rendition based on the witnesses from the bar."

"A facsimile of a black hoodie that's in every store on the planet. What do we know about the tattoo?" RJ said.

"Nothing," Melissa said. "I wonder why there are no missing persons' reports that match our two sets of victims?"

"It is odd," RJ said. "Doesn't anyone miss them for crying out loud?"

Both looked up from the monitor as Greg entered the room.

The look on his face told them that something was up with the case.

"What's going on?" RJ said.

"I think the perp left you a message on one of our landlines, RJ."

"Ah shit," RJ said. "Game on. Forward the message will ya."

"Already done," Greg said.

Tara appeared in the doorway and stood by RJ.

"Did you identify the number?" RJ said.

Greg shook his head. "Probably a burner."

RJ called his voice mail and tapped on the speaker symbol. The voice came through high-pitched and garbled as if the caller were in a vacuum.

"Hello Officer Otombo," said the muffled voice, each word spoken as if the caller wanted every one to count. "This is your killer, the one the media has dubbed, *The Suturer*. How mundane. Not very original. I had hoped for something a bit more exotic. Something more applicable to my craft. What do you think? Have you come up with your usual profile story: bad childhood, horrible upbringing, a product of my environment? Are you wondering who I am? Of course, you are. *And I looked, and behold a pale horse: and his name that sat on him was Death, and Hell followed with him. And power was given*

All the Evil Scatters

unto them over the fourth part of the earth, to kill with sword, and with hunger, and with death, and with the beasts of the earth." There was what sounded like a chuckle and then silence.

"Is he quoting from the Book of Revelations?" RJ said.

"A religious fanatic?" Melissa asked of no one in particular. "But why did he call you?"

"He probably saw me on the news," RJ said.

"Was there anything familiar about his voice? Did you recognize him?" Tara said.

"No. You heard it, the voice was muffled," RJ said and pounded his hand on the desk. "He made sure to disguise it. There was nothing familiar about it."

"There was a feminine quality to the voice," Melissa said. "Could it be that our theory, that a man and a woman are working together, is correct?"

"Could be," RJ said. "Would make it easier to lure the victims. People often feel safer around women. You know, woman as nurturer and caregiver."

"This leads us back to our theory that there are two of them working together, and given the stature of the person of interest at the bar, perhaps it was a woman who was chatting with the female victim, even though both the restaurant manager and server thought it was a male," Melissa said.

"Could this be related to an old case of yours, RJ?" Tara said.

"I'll do some digging. See if something stands out," RJ said.

"Let's hope we find them before they strike again," Melissa said.

"Do you think he…they are crazy enough to kill again?" Tara said.

"He killed four people within a short time," Melissa said. "Strong possibility."

"Bastard," RJ said. "He's…they're playing with us, leaving no clues except some catgut."

The room cleared out; RJ and Mel were alone once again.

"He has thrown down the gauntlet, challenging us to find him. He's playing a fuckin' game." RJ paused to take a breath. He knew he was being emotional and that he had to stay calm — their killer or killers may be preparing to kill again. "We should probably have someone take a closer look at my past cases to see if there's anything that stands out."

"There has to be a connection to you somehow. There's a reason he called you."

All the Evil Scatters

*

An hour later, RJ returned in an agitated state, his eyes embers of anger and said to Melissa, "We've got nothing. Zip, zero nada. No one recognized the tat — probably not done in Toronto. From the fading of the ink and the stretching of the skin, Frank says that he thinks that the tattoo was inked about thirty years ago.

"If only we could figure out who they are," Melissa said, scrutinizing the photos of the four victims as if their identity would leap out of the photo.

"Let's see if we get a hit on one of our systems," RJ said.

"I'll check in on Paul on my way out. I suggest you go spend some time with Carla. Tell me, does she still wait up for you?"

"Sure," RJ said and looked into the distance.

Mel looked at him quizzically and said, "Everything okay at home?"

"Um, yeah. Why wouldn't they be?"

"I'm here if you need to talk," Melissa said.

They walked through the office which was half-filled with intense chatter among some of the task force members; others tapped their fingers on keyboards, rummaging through the internet for any activity that might relate to the homicides. Some of the desks were empty because their occupants were following up on leads.

"And to further complicate things," RJ said, "we found nothing on the CCTVs. Ain't that lucky for us."

"Again, why hasn't anyone reported them missing?" Melissa said.

"I was wondering the same. Most parents would be all over this, demanding answers if their children go missing. God knows I did when Ryan disappeared."

"You were probably a wrecking ball let loose at a construction site."

RJ smiled ruefully, his eyes welling, but he caught himself. *Even after all these years, the thought of what happened to Ryan still trips me up,* he thought. "They don't seem like street kids. Could be their parents are so busy in their entitled lives that they haven't missed them."

"Perhaps they were students at U of T?"

"It is exam time come to think of it. No scheduled classes. Lots of kids go into study mode and disappear from their parents' radar."

All the Evil Scatters

They gathered their notes and photos. It would be another long night pouring over the evidence. They were all on this 24/7. There would be no real rest until they caught their serial killer.

46

"We've identified the siblings," Melissa said as RJ entered the room with a box of deli sandwiches and drinks from Kaplansky's.

RJ noted Mel's look of apprehension and said, "That's good news. Isn't it? Finally, something to work with, right?"

She took a deep breath and exhaled slowly, easing the tension from her body. "You know how it is. As soon as there's a name, you begin to piece their life together. A life that is no more; young lives in this case. They didn't have much opportunity to live, love, laugh, or make mistakes. Except perhaps in this instance — trusting someone that they shouldn't have. A waste."

"Who are they?"

She sighed and continued. "We got a hit on the girl — her name is Penelope Smikowsky. She has a brother, Boris. She's 20, he's 21; it confirms the coroner's findings about their age."

"It won't be easy to tell their parents that both their kids are dead," RJ said, pulled out a cigarette, and placed it between his lips. "Why did it take so long to track her down if she has a record?"

"She was a young offender, 13 to be exact, when she was busted for possession of marijuana."

"Her records were sealed?"

"And lucky for us, her records had not yet been destroyed."

"Any other offences?" RJ said.

"No."

"Where are they from?"

"The parents live in Waterloo. Barring any traffic jams, we can be there in a couple of hours. I've had a cruiser brought around for us."

"What else do we know?" RJ prodded as they walked toward the cruiser.

"Seems to be a typical suburban family. Both parents work at the University of Waterloo. Professors. Good pedigree. Seem to be pillars of the community, you might say."

All the Evil Scatters

RJ smiled, his cigarette dangling from his lips and said, "Leave the cliches to me."

"Waterloo Regional has dispatched a cruiser to keep eyes on the Smikowskys until we get there."

Melissa and RJ made their way to the parking lot, got into the cruiser and settled in for the drive along the Gardiner Expressway West.

47

RJ stopped their cruiser beside the two officers parked beyond the wall of cypress trees which bordered the Smikowsky residence. The Smikowskys lived in a house on a street composed of cookie cutter 1950's ranch-style bungalows.

"Officers. Are the Smikowskys inside?" RJ said

"Mr. Smikowsky drove off about an hour ago, but he's back inside," the female officer said.

"Where did he go?"

"I followed him while Joseph stayed behind to keep an eye on the house. The man drove to the Loblaws and came back with a bag of groceries."

"What about the woman?"

"Never left."

"Thanks for your help," RJ said. "We'll take it from here." He waved two fingers in the air, signifying a thank you and good-bye at the same time.

RJ parked the car. They got out and walked along the sidewalk and up the driveway to the front door.

Melissa took a deep breath and rang the doorbell. The door swung open almost immediately as if the occupants of the house had anticipated their arrival.

"Mr. and Mrs. Smikowsky?" Melissa said, noting that the woman was several inches taller than her burly husband. On closer scrutiny, Melissa could see that her grey hair made her look older than she was; the man's jet-black hair was the pepper to her salt.

"I'm Harry and this is my wife, Olga. Can we help you?" Harry's eyes sparkled as he greeted them.

All the Evil Scatters

"Sir. Ma'am. We're from the Toronto City Police Force. I'm Staff Sergeant Hargrove and this is my partner, Staff Sergeant Otombo."
"You're a long way from home," Olga said.
"May we come inside?" RJ said.
Olga opened the door wide.
Harry stood awkwardly beside his wife, then stepped aside and said, "Come in."
"Mr. and Mrs. Smikowsky," Melissa began, searching for the right words. "There's no easy way to tell you this."
"Tell us what," Olga said, her face had no expression.
"You may want to sit down," Melissa said.
They followed the Smikowskys, their movements slow like in a movie scene, into their living room which was cozy and filled with well-worn furnishings. Melissa's eyes were drawn to the fireplace mantle where framed photographs of their children, easily recognizable as their young victims, were on display.
RJ followed her look and his eyes landed on a picture of a happier time for the young man and woman. They were probably about 7 and 8, the world yet to be discovered; their forever smiles held the exuberant innocence of youth.
Harry and Olga positioned themselves on the edge of the sofa, ready to rise if necessary and looked expectantly at RJ and Melissa.
"You may have seen the news about the recent homicides in Toronto," RJ said.
"No. We don't believe in television," Harry said.
"Internet? Social media?" Melissa said.
"Not into that nonsense," Olga said.
RJ knew that this wasn't going to be easy. It never was. "We're going to have to rip the bandaid off," he said, "and tell it to you straight. Over a week ago we found two bodies — they are those of your son and daughter."
"That's rubbish," Olga said matter-of-factly as she searched RJ and Melissa's faces for the truth. "You got it wrong."
Harry patted his hand on his wife's knee.
"There's no easy way to convey this information to you, but my partner is correct, the bodies of your children were found a week ago in Toronto."
Melissa glanced at the photos on the mantle and drew a deep breath.

All the Evil Scatters

"No! No! No! That's not them," Olga said. "It's preposterous."

"You've got it wrong," Harry added.

RJ cleared his throat and said, "I wish it were a mistake, sir, ma'am." His voice held the truth that the couple did not want to believe. He moved over to the mantle and removed one of the picture frames of their kids and said, "Are these your children?"

Harry nodded.

"We've run their DNA and found your daughter's sealed criminal record. There is no mistake. I'm sorry," Melissa said and handed them the photoshopped images of Boris and Penelope. "Are these your children?"

"My kids don't look like that. They're lifeless. They look dead." Olga stood her ground, dropping the pictures on the floor dismissively.

Why don't we give you some time? We'll step outside," Melissa said, seeing the stunned looks on their faces. *It will take a while, perhaps never, for them to comprehend the magnitude of what happened to their children.*

*

When Melissa and RJ returned inside, they noted the resignation on Harry's face, the last glimmer of hope in his eyes had faded to a blank stare. He was slumped into the back of the couch and repeatedly said, "No! No! No!" He then reached down and snatched up the photos that his wife had dropped to the floor and said, "These are our kids, Penelope and Boris," Harry said whispering each of his children's names as if by saying them loudly it would confirm what he already knew in his heart. That his children were dead. "Pl...Please tell us what happened."

"You're wrong, Harry," Olga said and rose from the couch as if she'd already had enough of this distasteful conversation.

"Olga. Honey. Please sit down and hear them out. If it's a mistake, we'll get to the bottom of it. Come."

Olga grudgingly sat back down and waited; she had an impatient look on her face as if she had more pressing things to get to.

"Mr. and Mrs. Smikowsky," Melissa said, "I know that these are not the kind of pictures that any parent wants to see of their child but I have no other to show you."

"Please tell us what you know," Harry said.

Melissa gave them as much information as she could.

All the Evil Scatters

"I knew Toronto was trouble," Harry said. "But you can't stop kids from living. They'll do it behind your back anyway. But they were together so we knew they'd be safe."

"Our children are alright, Harry. This is all a big misunderstanding," Olga said.

"Olga. Honey. We have to face the tru—"

"This is all wrong!" Olga said.

"I can only try to understand the unimaginable pain that you're feeling," Melissa said. "No one deserves this. Certainly not your children, and certainly not you. I'm sorry we have no answers for you —"

"They're not dead. You've made a mistake."

"Olga? Why would the police make up such a story?"

"I dunno," she said, her lips quivering. She looked up at her husband and nodded, acceptance slowly sinking in.

"We're going to get the son-of-a-bitch," RJ spat out. Melissa looked at him as if to say *don't make promises you can't keep*. She didn't want to give the Smikowskys any false hope.

"We will do all that we can to find who did this," Melissa said.

"We hope that now that we have identified your children," RJ said, "we'll be able to trace their steps; this could go a long way to identifying their killer. If you can give us any information on what they were doing in Toronto. Who they might have been meeting? Any boyfriend or girlfriend for either of them?"

"She and Boris left last Saturday on the GO train to Toronto," Olga said.

"Do you know what they were going to do in Toronto?" Melissa said.

"Visiting a friend, Donald Spielman. It was his birthday. Donald moved to the city last fall," Olga said. "I'm sure they're all together. I'm gonna call him. He'll know where they are." She reached for her cell.

"Mrs. Smikowsky. Please don't do that," Melissa said.

"Tell us about Donald Spielman," RJ said.

"Did something happen to Donald?" Harry said.

"Not that we know of, but we'll check in on him."

"Who did this to my children?" Harry said. "This is a nightmare. Please tell us that this is some kind of a joke?"

All the Evil Scatters

Melissa watched as the sun made its nightly journey toward the horizon, and as it did it cast short shadows onto the framed photos that adorned the mantle. Olga walked over to where the mottled light danced upon the pictures of her two children. She looked at them, willing them to leap out from the photos and stand next to her as if nothing had happened. Melissa saw Olga turn toward the door and knew exactly what Olga was thinking: that she wanted her children to walk through it, full of life and energy. Then she turned back to face the mantle.

"I told you we should have followed up with the police!" Olga said fidgeting with something on the edge of the mantle.

"You mean you spoke about this to the police?" RJ said.

"Yes. Four days ago."

Melissa noted on her phone that she'd need to follow up with the local police force.

Harry rose and walked over to his wife. He put his hand around her shoulders and whispered in her ear. Her shaking eased off, but then started all over again. They stared silently at the photos, the only sound other than Olga's sobbing was the whirring of the refrigerator. He picked up a picture frame and stared at the images of his children.

"This picture was taken shortly after Boris's high school graduation," Harry said. "Look at the hope and promise of a wonderful future — university, marriage, children." He turned to face Melissa and RJ, fists clenched at his side. Anger had trumped his grief, if only temporarily. "Why would anyone want to kill them? Boris and Penelope never hurt anyone. They were good kids except for, um, you know, Penelope's lack of judgment a few years ago. Couldn't he see that before killing them?" He pounded his fist on the mantle, knocking some of the frames on the floor. The glass shattered.

RJ picked up the frame, cleared the glass and said, "May I take this photo?"

"Of course," Harry said. "Anything you need. They're a year apart. We had them close so that they would be good company for each other — and they were."

Olga rushed out of the room.

Melissa followed her.

"I know what you're going through —," RJ began.

"How can you possibly know what we're going through?"

All the Evil Scatters

"I lost my son, Ryan, 18 years ago. He was taken from us when he was only eight."

Harry looked at him, a look of understanding passed between them. Melissa and Olga returned.

Olga returned with a broom and dustpan and cleaned up the broken glass. She bent down and with her free hand wiped the remaining glass from the photo, nicking her finger in the process. She watched the blood drip to the floor as if mesmerized.

Harry opened a drawer, grabbed a band-aid, and gently wrapped it around the cut.

"Could you both please come back and sit with us? We have a few more questions about their trip to Toronto," Melissa said.

RJ began, "You mentioned earlier that they were visiting their friend, Donald Spielman. Can you tell us more about him?"

"D…Donald is their childhood friend — the three of them were like siblings. He transferred from Waterloo to the University of Toronto. He was celebrating his twenty-first birthday last Saturday. The kids thought that they would go and spend the weekend there. They booked a hotel, I think it's the Inn on Jarvis. Downtown," Harry said and looked to Olga who nodded.

Melissa and RJ knew the area: high crime rate; the infamous Filmore's; and, recent high-rise developments to gentrify the area.

"I still don't believe any of this," Olga said.

"Th..th…this was going to be a big adventure for them," Harry said.

"Would you happen to have a number for Donald?" Melissa said.

"Of course," Olga said as if Donald was the key to this nightmare. She pulled out her cell phone, looked up his contact information and handed it to Melissa. "I'm sure he'll tell you that they're all together sightseeing. The kids always wanted to go to the CN Tower. Didn't they Harry?"

Harry looked dismayed but said nothing.

"We'll find who did this to them," Melissa said as she jotted down Donald's information. She was never one to make promises. But she needed to offer them some solace, a glimmer of hope that they would catch whoever killed their kids.

"Take me to see my babies," Olga said and stood up with determination; she grabbed her purse and exited the house.

All the Evil Scatters

Melissa, RJ, and Harry looked at each other and followed Olga into the night.

*

Melissa and RJ watched as Olga Smikowsky looked at her children, disbelief still clouding her face. But slowly, as if a light went on, her shoulders sagged and she hugged first her son and then her daughter and repeated, "Why?" Her heart-wrenching sobs filled the room.

Harry stood to the side of the room, unable to look at the two corpses that were once full of life. His wife's sobbing moved him to action. He went to her, and as she hugged her daughter, he said, "Let's go, Olga."

Reluctantly, Olga let her husband guide her out the door.

48

How wonderful to live in a time of instant gratification. I pour over the newspapers; the Toronto dailies and the national papers have covered my work! *My work. Front-page news.* "How great am I?" I say to the empty room. "Do You see that Father? Too bad I didn't let You live to see my triumphs."

Two photographs of the main profilers, Melissa Hargrove and RJ Otombo are below the story. She's pretty, in a Jessica Chastain kind of way. She looks decisive and in control. Her patrician nose is perfectly centred on her face; her red hair is secured into a ponytail, luxurious and thick like a horse's mane. I try to examine her partner's face, but it's angled, not giving me a clear view of his face. From what I can tell his jawline shows determination. Determination to catch me, I'm sure. There's something about that cop that makes me want to show him that I'm better than he is. That he will never find me.

Perhaps the TV coverage will give me a clearer image of him. He intrigues me. I laugh and turn on the old-fashioned television that was similar to the one we had back then. It was a new century and Father had one of those outdated clunkers. My tube TV was hard to come by. I had begged the owner, who rents props to movie production crews, to sell it to me.

I played around with the antenna's ears to get as good a reception as possible. I only get staticky images on CBC; no matter how I try to adjust the antenna, the vertical lines distort the images, but I get the general gist: that most of the facts are wrong and work to my advantage. I need to know all of the details that they have on me to ensure that I elude capture. Forever. I make a mental note to leave another message. "RJ Otombo," I say out loud, "your name rolls comfortably off my lips, familiar, like an old friend, I imagine. I never had any friends. I want to tell you how wrong you've gotten it. That I, and only I, am responsible. How dare you think that I am weak and in need of an assistant? Who am I? Dr. Frankenstein and his hapless assistant, Fritz? What an insult. I'll show you."

I peek through the window to the gravel road and recall how I drove Wallace and his wife to my house. That night, I was haunted by my thoughts and by the past. A past that I am vanquishing little by little.

49

"We'll have to split up," RJ said. "Why don't I talk to the friend, Donald Spielman?"

"Take Greg with you," Melissa said. "Paul and I will go to the hotel and check out the room where the siblings stayed. Perhaps they left something behind. It's a long shot because the room has probably been cleaned out and rented to other tourists by now."

"Maybe they left something behind?" RJ said.

"Let's meet up at Fran's Diner in a few hours and go over what we've uncovered," Melissa said.

*

RJ and Greg weaved their way across College Street, entering through the main gates of the University of Toronto which led to King's College Circle. RJ lit a cigarette and said, "Did you know that the University's sprawling grounds take up 180 acres of land?"

Greg shook his head.

"It's dotted with different architectural styles," RJ said, happy to share his knowledge of the city's structures. "There's the Brutalist Robarts library, the Romanesque Victoria University and the Neo-classical Convocation Hall."

"Even the Gothic Revival Hart House," Greg said, smiling pleased with himself that he could add to RJ's knowledge of the campus architecture.

All the Evil Scatters

RJ glanced around, people, young and old, scurried to get to class; some had earbuds affixed to their ears like appendages, listening to music or maybe a podcast; others were engaged in joyful banter.

They worked their way to Bloor Street to an off-campus residence on Madison Avenue where Donald Spielman rented a room in one of the old Victorian mansions. RJ remembered the suicide chicken wings at the *Helion Pub* that he and Carla had enjoyed back in the day.

As they made their way to Donald's place he noted the non-homogenous mix of people: the well-to-do, the ne'er do wells, the students, the homeless, the tourists, and those who came to enjoy the inexpensive eateries. All classes, all races, converging into one pulsating fervour of activity.

"Are you here you son-of-a-bitch?" RJ said out loud as if the killer was close by.

A woman walking in front of them turned, gave them a disgusted look and went on her way.

RJ chuckled.

The woman picked up her pace.

They found the brownstone, went up the steps and entered the foyer. Greg pushed buzzer #2, Donald's place.

RJ noted that there were six residences in total — he took out his cell phone and snapped photos of the names on the other buzzers. *Might come in handy, you never know,* he thought.

"Who is it," a baritone male voice said.

"It's Staff Sergeant Otombo and Sergeant Monaghan from the Toronto City Police Force. Can we speak with you for a few minutes, Mr. Spielman?"

"I'm a bit busy right now. Can you come back later?"

RJ and Greg exchanged looks. *It isn't often that people refuse to see the police unless they have something to hide,* RJ thought.

"It's about your friends, the Smikowskys."

There was a long pause before he said, "What about them? They're not here."

"We need a few minutes. It's urgent."

"Okay," Donald said and opened the door. The oak floors creaked, showing off their age, as they entered Donald's apartment.

All the Evil Scatters

A young man, looking much younger than his 21 years, opened the door. He was about 5'8" with a slender, some might say skinny, physique.

RJ arched his eyebrows. *Isn't this interesting? Donald fits the description that Jan gave us of the person who was seen chatting with Penelope. But what does it mean, if anything? Could he be their person of interest? Was it a friendship gone terribly wrong?*

RJ handed him his business card and entered the room. Greg followed. He glanced around for signs that the Smikowskys had been there and said, "I'm kinda thirsty. Glass of water?"

Donald walked over to the bar fridge, located under the counter, bent down and pulled out two plastic water bottles.

RJ looked around to see if there was any evidence of foul play. Everything seemed to be in the same messy order that it has always been in — he too had once been a student.

"Here you go, officers."

RJ took the bottle from Donald's shaking hand. *He's nervous about something. Did he have anything to do with his friends' deaths?*

"Why are you nervous, Mr. Spielman?"

Donald looked at RJ and said, "Not every day that cops come calling. What's this about?"

RJ moved a few books from a chair onto the floor and said, "Let's have a seat."

Donald hesitated, but the stern look on RJ's face made him sit down as if he were a puppet moving to the whim of his master.

RJ found another chair, flipped it around and positioned it directly in front of Donald; he sat down, leaned his stomach against the chair's back and draped his legs on either side of it. He folded his arms across the top of the chair, propped his head on them and looked dead on at Donald. He wanted to see every drop of sweat, every movement, every shift of his eyes when he questioned him.

"I know it's scary to see a cop, but I'm not here to bust you for pot — not my thing. We're here to tell you about Boris and Penelope."

"What's going on with them? Did Penelope get in trouble again? Did she bring Boris down with her? Ahhh. Shit. And you think I had something to do with her misguided antics."

All the Evil Scatters

"Let's hold that thought for a moment. What I'm going to tell you is more heinous than a drug bust."

RJ noted Donald's shoulders stiffening.

"Have you seen the news lately?"

Donald shrugged his shoulders and said, "Yeah. Why?"

"Did you hear about the two young victims that we found in an alley last week?"

Donald shifted in his seat and said, "Yeah. Are you...? What are you saying?"

"Your friends are dead, Mr. Spielman." RJ could see that Donald was visibly shaken. Even most actors couldn't fake unrehearsed shock.

"I had no idea that it was Pen and Bo on the news," Donald said, obviously distraught.

"Your friends came to visit you and now they're dead."

Donald looked at RJ, his mouth agape. "Holy shit. Do you think I had something to do with this? You're off-base man."

RJ arched his brows and said, "Most people now would say: *OMG. That's horrible. What happened to them?* But not you. Are you hiding something?"

"Of course not! It's horrible dude. They're my friends. Tell me what happened."

"I'll tell you what happened — someone murdered your friends," RJ said watching every quiver on Donald's face, every muscle, looking for signs of guilt.

"You mean someone killed them?"

"That's what I said."

Donald looked over to where Greg was rummaging through his things and said, "Can the cop stop snooping around? Aren't there laws against that?"

RJ motioned for Greg to stop, but not before Greg bent over a stack of books and picked up something. He turned it around for RJ.

RJ saw the unmistakable image of a hand-drawn eye.

"Where did you get this?" RJ asked Donald.

"I dunno. I've never seen it before."

"How did it get here? Walk in all by itself?"

"I swear I don't know. But then people bring their shit here all the time. They think my place is a waste disposal area."

All the Evil Scatters

"I wonder why they'd think that, Mr. Spielman?" RJ said shaking his head as he scanned the room that looked like the aftermath of a tornado.

"Can we take it with us, if that's alright with you?" Greg said.

Donald nodded.

They watched Greg put it in a plastic evidence bag and seal it shut. Greg moved over to the window and faced them.

"Thanks for cooperating Mr. Spielman. I want you to tell me about the time you spent with your friends. Where you went? What you did? Who was with you? I'll need all of the names. All of it. Tell me everything you remember from the moment you saw them. I want you to retrace all your steps."

"If I had known that you wanted all these details, I'd have taken notes."

"Look," RJ said rising slightly from his chair to show Donald who was in charge. "Your friends are dead and you're cracking jokes. What's wrong with you kids these days?"

"I'm sorry. I meant no disrespect. It's hard, you know. They're my friends. I've known them most of my life."

"Okay then. Help me. Answer my questions. And remember, if you lie to me about anything I'll haul your ass down to the station and have you charged for possession of cannabis — we still arrest people for that you know."

"I'll tell you everything I remember. But can you tell me what happened to them?"

"You first. And then I'll decide if there will be any quid pro quo."

"Can I grab a water?"

RJ nodded.

When Donald returned to his seat, he began. "I met Pen and Boris at Union Station. You know it's hard for first-timers in the Six. We walked over to their hotel —"

"Which hotel?"

"Inn on Jarvis. Near Dundas Street."

"Go on."

"The hotel is cheap. Nothing fancy. I'm not allowed to have sleepovers here. Strict landlord rules. One misstep and you're out. Then where will I go? There are no places to rent for cheap. Otherwise, I would have let them stay. If I had let them stay do you think they would be alive now?"

All the Evil Scatters

"Stick to the story."

"Checked in. Went to the room. Didn't stay long. Pen and Boris were hungry so we grabbed a bite. I took them to the *Helion Pub* — great wings and close to home and the party."

"Where was the party?"

"A couple of blocks from here. On Bernie."

"I'll need the exact address and the party host's name."

"Sure. I'll text it to you."

"Pen and paper is fine," RJ shook his head, reached into his pocket and handed him his notepad and pen. Donald jotted down the address and a name. RJ glanced at it: Kayla Latournee, 53 Bernie Ave.

"What did you do after the *Helion Pub*?"

"We went to Kayla's party."

"How many people were at the party?"

"Couple of dozen."

"Did you know everyone?"

"Pretty much."

"What does that mean?"

"You never know everyone at a party."

"There were strangers?"

"To me, yeah. But not to Kayla. She knows a lot of people."

"Okay. Did anyone look suspicious in any way?"

"Like how?"

"Oh you know, standing around, not engaging with anyone, seemingly out of place? Did someone pay close attention to either Penelope or Boris?"

Donald scratched his head and said, "Well, now that I think of it — there was this girl. She started coming on to Boris and he seemed to enjoy her company. They left the party and reemerged a bit later." Donald gave RJ a meaningful look.

RJ arched his eyebrows. "And Penelope? Where was she?"

"Dancing. Drinking. Having fun."

"What were you doing?"

"Same."

"How long did they stay at the party?"

"Till about 10:30."

"Isn't that a bit early to leave a party?"

Donald shrugged his shoulders, "Guess they wanted to explore the city."

"And you, as a good friend, let them go off on their own?"

"I guess I should have gone with them," Donald said.

"Did they happen to mention where they were going?"

"*Victor's* on Bloor."

"Do you go to *Victor's* often?" RJ said.

"No."

"Did you join them there?"

"No."

"Why not?"

Donald squirmed in his seat.

RJ turned his face and focused his eyes on the couch that was covered with blankets, books and other things he didn't want to think about. "Why did they leave the party? I want the truth."

"Be...be...because I came on to Pen. I've loved her for so long and she didn't feel the same way."

RJ cocked his head with interest. Unrequited love. *Was Penelope's rejection strong enough for him to want to kill the object of his affection in such a gruesome way?*

"That's it for now," RJ said. "If you remember anything else, call me."

RJ and Greg exited Donald's apartment.

RJ turned to Greg and said, "Let's put a tail on him."

*

RJ knocked on Kayla Latournee's door. A woman in her thirties, with long, curly black hair, wearing Lululemons and a poncho, circa 1972, opened the door and said, "Yes?"

"It's Staff Sergeant Otombo and Sergeant Monaghan. Are you Ms. Latournee?"

The woman nodded.

"May we speak with you for a moment?" RJ said and handed her his card.

She glanced at it but didn't take it. "About?"

"The party you threw on Saturday."

"What about it?"

"May we come in?"

All the Evil Scatters

She let them enter and closed the door. They stood in the foyer.

"What's this about?"

"Two of the people who were at your party were found dead the next morning."

She looked at him confused. He could see from her expression that she was trying to process what she'd heard. "Wh…what? Who?" She said and moved into the living room where she plopped herself on the Victorian-style couch.

"Penelope and Boris Smikowsky."

"Who…? I don't know who they are."

"Friends of Donald's. From Waterloo. Ring a bell?"

"Oh yeah. Pen and Bo. Sorry to hear that. Nice kids. But why are you here? Were they driving drunk? That's not on me."

"No. It wasn't a car accident. They were murdered."

"You're kidding?"

RJ's eyes bored down at her.

"Of course you're not. I'm sorry. This is crazy," Kayla said.

"Was Donald at the party all night?"

"I think so," Kayla said.

"*Think* is not going to cut it. I need you to be sure."

"I didn't have eyes on him all night. But I know he left here around 2 a.m."

"Are you sure?"

Kayla nodded, "Wait a minute. Do you think he killed them? I can't believe that of Donald. He's a kind, gentle soul. Won't hurt a fly."

"Thanks for the endorsement," RJ said.

Kayla cocked her eyebrows and said, "They were friends. Childhood friends. That's messed up."

"Did he behave oddly in any way?"

"No. But…I think Boris and Donald had a heated exchange. And then Pen and Boris left."

"Did you hear what they were arguing about?"

She shook her head.

"I'll need the names and numbers of everyone who came to your party."

She rose from the couch, got her phone and started jotting down the names and numbers of everyone who had attended the party and handed the piece of paper to RJ.

"Thank you Ms. Latournee. You've been a great help. Sorry to have disturbed you."

"Officer. Can you tell me what happened to those kids?"

"All I can say is that they met an untimely and horrific death."

"Ooooh," she said.

They said goodbye and went to interview a couple of the people from her party that were on Kayla's list and were in the area. They added nothing to the story they already had, including what a nice guy Donald was.

No one could confirm that Donald had been there all night.

50

RJ sat at the booth located in the farthest corner of Fran's Diner. He had ordered the rib special, a limited-time menu item. Comfort food accompanied by a large cup of coffee. He might even spring for a slice of their lemon meringue pie. He waved Melissa over to him when he saw her.

"What a day it's been," Melissa said as she sat in the booth facing RJ. "I'm hungry, but can't eat. I'm sleepy, but can't stop going until we find out who's doing this."

"Me too," RJ said and motioned to the server. "What did you find at the hotel?"

Melissa ordered a cup of coffee and then said, "Nothing. Got their belongings to return to their parents."

The server brought her coffee and set it on the table accompanied by a small white bowl filled with miniature cups of milk and cream.

RJ picked up a napkin to wipe off his sauce-slathered fingers, tossed it into the plate of half-finished ribs and pulled up a photo of the hand-drawn image.

"Did you find this at Spielman's place?" And when RJ nodded, she said. "This can't be a coincidence."

All the Evil Scatters

"He's the same stature as the person described by Jan. He didn't seem too disturbed about his friends' deaths and he was cracking jokes. Who does that when their supposed best friends had been killed?"

"What did he say about the drawing?"

"He never saw it before," RJ scoffed. "In my world, things don't walk into my house by themselves. Could be a person of interest."

"Did you put eyes on him?" Melissa said.

"Yup."

"Great. Let's see where he goes, who he talks to and what he does."

"I'm convinced that if Donald is our man, then he wasn't acting alone. You should have seen him — skin and bones. A push of my hand against his chest and he would have fallen. Okay. I'm exaggerating, but you get it."

"He might be the best lead we've got."

They left the diner, slightly more optimistic than they were when they had started their day.

51

While RJ filed the paperwork to search Donald's apartment, Mel returned to the office, exhausted and on edge. No other case had kept her this wired. The dark circles under her eyes held the truth about the stress of the past week. She looked over the sketch of the hooded person of interest. *It could be anyone,* she thought. *It's the garment of choice for young and old alike.*

She laid out the photos of the charm and the image of the eye. *This must be related. If so, what does it mean?* Greg and Paul had re-examined the evidence bags for the two elderly victims and found nothing resembling an eye.

They had looked into Donald's background — there was no evidence of any training or knowledge of medical procedures and equipment or pharmacology. He was an artist. *Of course these days anything could be found on the internet — ask Google.* She typed in *self-taught surgery procedures* and wasn't surprised to discover that it was extremely difficult to learn to make proper incisions without formal training in anatomy, pathology, physiology, or biochemistry, to name a few, and only in extreme circumstances and out of necessity, people could learn to operate. There were rare instances where someone performed minor surgeries on themselves. *I'll wait for Frank's autopsy report. For now, I'm going with the theory that the killer had an assistant who was well-versed in surgical procedure and suturing. Was Donald the assistant, a sheep following the direction of its shepherd?*

*

The phone rang. Melissa saw the name, Frank Williams, Chief Coroner of Ontario, appear on her screen. She tapped on it and said, "Hey Frank. What do you have for me?"

"Hi, Mel. I need to send you some photos that you'll find of interest. I found something near the base of the scorpion tattoo. I thought it might be important to the case."

"What did you find?"

"Well, it was hard to discern because it was so close to the tattoo. But on further examination, the tattoo ink and the ink from the eye are different from one another."

"Did you say eye?"

"Yes."

"Send those photos right away, please."

"Already done."

Melissa looked at the photo on her cell. Once again there it was, the eye staring back at her. Only now it was embedded into the scorpion design. "How did I miss this?"

"It's hard to detect because of the intricacy of the tattoo, but the shades of ink were different on closer examination — it's hand-inked, likely made around the time of the victims' murders."

"Thanks, Frank," Melissa said and clicked off. She picked up her cell and tapped on a number.

"RJ? It's Mel. Frank found another eye symbol on the older couple."

"Another charm?"

"No. It was drawn into the scorpion tattoo."

RJ whistled. "This links our two cases! The eye is his calling card! I'm coming right up."

*

All the Evil Scatters

As RJ entered her office, Mel's cell went off; her display said: *Greg*. She tapped her phone. "Hey Greg. RJ is with me. I'm putting you on speaker."

"Tell us you've found something on this eye thing," RJ said.

"It's not just an eye. I think it's the evil eye which dates back to ancient Greece, to at least the sixth century BC. It's found on all kinds of artifacts from that time period."

"Do you think we're looking at someone who's Greek?"

"Can't quite say. These charms or talismans are found everywhere from Africa to Europe to South America. The evil eye is a symbol of superstition for many cultures."

"Now we're getting into voodoo."

Melissa gave RJ a look and he raised his hands apologetically.

"The Greeks wear trinkets or charms to ward off the eye of someone who, when they look at you, can cause harm. There are ceremonies or incantations practiced by elder Greeks, even today, to ward off the evil eye. I'll shoot you over a YouTube video."

"Thanks, Greg. Keep working the angle and let us know if you come up with anything else," Melissa said and hung up.

"Maybe we need to look at Donald from a different angle," RJ said.

"What are you thinking?"

"Let's see if there are any books on the occult or superstition at his place."

"Good point."

"I'll follow up on that damn warrant," RJ said. "We need an expert on this voodoo stuff."

"There must be someone in the police force who can help," Melissa said.

"Worth looking into. Maybe at the university?"

"Maybe…"

"Here's what doesn't make sense about Donald," RJ said. "Could he have left the party, committed his killings and returned? Unlikely. But if he had an accomplice, a phone call to him when the siblings left was all he needed. And there's his alibi."

Melissa nodded, "All roads lead to Donald, yet…" her voice trailed.

"What?"

All the Evil Scatters

"It's too easy," Melissa said, the last word hanging in the air as they pondered about the victims, about Donald, about the evil eye.

52

It was late and a few stars that weren't obscured by the city lights shimmered in the night sky.

People milled about, carefully avoiding each other as they scrambled home, or to a bar, or a restaurant. RJ needed time to think. To clear his head. This case was getting to him. It was hitting too close to home. He pulled out his cigarette, used his Ronson lighter, a gift from his late father, and headed east on College Street, past Yonge Street toward Carlton Avenue. Yonge Street is famed to be the world's longest street and divides the City of Toronto between the East and the West. The area was a mix of residential and office buildings, retail stores, and homeless people.

RJ puffed on his cigarette. A photo of a missing boy on the street pole reminded him of his and the community's efforts to find his son, Ryan. If he were still alive he'd be 26 years old. *How would you have turned out, Ryan? Would you have become a lawyer? Doctor? Artist? You were pretty creative. Perhaps an architect or a builder.*

He recalled Carla's frantic call that sweltering June day toward the end of the school year. "Ryan hasn't come home from school! His friends had waited for him but left when he hadn't shown up. Hadn't we agreed with the other parents that the kids would go to and from school together? Hadn't we?" She sobbed into the phone.

RJ never forgot the precise time she'd called. 7:03 was forever embedded in his mind along with all the memories from that night.

"Now Carla, he's probably at some friend's place — someone we don't know."

"You know it's not like him. He loves his buddies," she cried into the phone. "How can you be so calm?"

RJ had to remain calm. He didn't want to further alarm her. He saw it every day — children gone missing. Some were found sans harm, but many were never found; still, others were found dead or irreparably damaged psychologically and physically. Of course, Ryan was fine. He was a smart kid. He'd probably gone off somewhere and lost track of time.

All the Evil Scatters

"I'll be right home. In the meantime gather the numbers of his teachers, friends and their parents. I want to speak to every one of them."

"Oh RJ, you're scaring me."

"Carla. I promise I'll find him. Plus, I'm connected with the police. I have an in, right?"

He could tell from her breathing that she'd calmed down slightly. "I know. Find him RJ. Pleeeeease."

RJ bolted into action. He went straight to Tara, who was his Staff Sergeant at the time, and told her what happened.

"Whatever you need. You've got it. I'll send someone to the school and find out if anyone saw him after class. You go home and start making those calls."

As soon as RJ entered the front door, he saw Carla's red, puffy eyes, her hands tucked inside the sleeves of her sweater; she leaned against his chest and sobbed. It was nine o'clock. More than five hours since anyone had seen Ryan.

"Shh. Shh. Come on honey. Let's have a seat. I'll make you some tea."

"I don't want tea! I want my son!"

"Okay. Okay," RJ said holding his hands up in acquiescence.

"Did you speak to Tara?" Carla said.

"I did. She's throwing everything she's got on it."

"She's a good person. I'm thankful that she's on our side."

RJ nodded and said, "Give me those numbers and I'll start calling."

"Do you think I didn't call them? I'm a cop's wife after all," she said and stared at him willing him to challenge her.

"Okay then. We'll drive around the neighbourhood, his school. Everywhere we can think of."

"What if he's hurt and he can't get home," Carla said. "I can feel him. He needs us. It's dark and my boy doesn't like the dark."

"We'll find him."

"Promise?"

"I love our son too. I will stop at nothing to get him home by bedtime."

Carla nodded and wiped her eyes.

RJ felt as guilty now as he had back then. Back then when the promise he had made to his wife never materialized. The "what ifs" had replayed in his mind endlessly like an old movie reel, and continued to this day. The guilt from his failure never dissipated. He had failed everyone: his wife, himself and most of all, his son. This case brought back all the memories which welled beneath the surface like bubbling lava ready to spew.

53

A drizzle had started, tapping on Melissa's head as she walked home. She shivered, the dampness finding its way underneath her jacket. People scurried to take cover in their apartment buildings or into restaurants or bars. In a flash, the streets were deserted. Mel zipped up her windbreaker and picked up her pace.

Sensing that someone was behind her, she turned to look. It was a couple of teenagers looking for shelter from the rain. She watched them run into one of the pubs.

She shook her head and thought, *what I need is a good night's sleep — all the caffeine is making me jittery.* Her police training had taught her to be aware of her surroundings at all times. She couldn't shake the feeling that someone was following her. Was she being paranoid after long days of hunting down a killer? She glanced over her shoulder once again, but there was no one behind her, only the rain tapping lightly on the pavement. Melissa quickened her pace as she walked in the direction of her apartment.

Stop it, Mel! You're being paranoid — this case has you riled up. Don't go looking for killers in the shadows. Plus you don't fit his MO — you're alone, she scolded herself.

It seemed that the slightest sound spooked her, so unlike her, but she chalked it up to the stress of the case, the lack of sleep and too much caffeine. The combination made her edgy.

Melissa had decided to walk the four kilometres from her work to her home. She needed to go over the evidence in her head. They had lots of information but not enough to point them toward their killer. The female victims had their eyes sewn shut; the males had been castrated. Why? What had happened to the killer — had he been mutilated and is now exacting his revenge on the person who had terrorized him? Was it his father? Mother? Someone close to him?

All the Evil Scatters

She'd gone over all the evidence, filled out paperwork and worked with the communications department to prepare press release after press release hoping to identify the older couple.

They had decided not to release the sketch of the person wearing a hoodie — one could hardly call that a likeness of anyone. It was too obscure. The public would have a field day with it; calls from hundreds of people would be received saying that they'd seen the hooded person.

Again, she thought she heard footsteps behind her. There was no one. Her instinct told her that someone was lurking in the shadows on this wet spring night. She felt for her gun, knowing that she would use it without hesitation. But she didn't want to go there. She picked up her pace none-the-less, thanking her daily exercise routine for giving her the extra boost of energy that she would otherwise not have if she only walked from the apartment to the office and back every day.

There it was — the faint pitter-patter on the pavement. It was not the rain. Now she was certain that someone was following her. Following her very closely. She unfastened the strap which secured her gun firmly in its holster. She clasped her fingers over the revolver as she had been trained. She would be ready to pull it out in an instant. She had many years of training, but no occasion to use her weapon. She would not hesitate to use it tonight if she had to.

Unmistakably, the steps were getting closer and closer. She rounded her finger over the trigger, heart pounding against her chest and turned around to face her assailant. As she turned, she loosened her grip on the revolver, surprised to see him after all these years. She stared into the brown eyes, the cut above his lip, a skiing accident in the Laurentians when he was a teenager, the way his hair fell on his brow. The man she had once known so well. The man who was responsible for the nightmare in her life. Melissa's surprise turned to anger, "What the HELL are you doing here, Nicolas?"

"Waiting for the courage to speak to you."

"I almost shot you!"

"But you didn't."

Melissa clipped her holster, making sure that her handgun was safely back where it belonged. And then as she remembered what he had done, her fury toward him bubbled over and she said, "How dare you show your face here!"

All the Evil Scatters

"I've been wanting to see you. To explain."

"Explain what? That you killed my parents?"

"It was an accident. I would never have intentionally hurt them."

"But it was intentional for you to be in a drunken stupor, drive recklessly and kill the two most important people in my life."

"I'm sorry, Mel. I know that's not enough, and that I can't bring them back. But I've changed."

"If there's anything that I've learned from my job is that people don't change. They become chameleons adapting to their environment, their true nature beneath the surface."

"I spent three years in jail and five years atoning for what I did to your parents. I want to…to…to somehow atone to you, if you'll let me."

"You skulked about in the rain like a lunatic?"

"I figured if I came to your office, you wouldn't see me."

"And now you've seen me, Nicolas. Good-bye."

"Please let me make amends."

"What do you want me to say? That I forgive you? That all is well? You KILLED my parents! I will never forgive you. Go repent to your priest."

"I understand. I'm sorry I've bothered you. I regret what happened —"

"What happened? You KILLED them." Years of pent-up anger came to the surface and Melissa let loose everything that she'd held inside for such a long time. "That accident didn't *happen*. You chose to get into the car, drive intoxicated, and slam your car into the oncoming traffic, killing them instantly! Do you understand that those images will remain ingrained in my brain forever?"

"If there was a way I could take away the pain —"

"There isn't. You can't bring them back."

They stood quietly, each living with their regrets as the rain fell heavily upon them.

"I wish I had died with them," Nicolas said.

"You should have died. Not them!" She immediately regretted what she'd said, but it gave her satisfaction to see the hurt in his eyes. "Go. We have nothing to say!"

"If I could have a few more minutes, I'll never bother you again."

"What do you want to say, Nicolas?" She said.

All the Evil Scatters

"Let me tell you what's in my heart. I want to tell you how sorry I am about everything — our fights, my lies, my drinking. And, more importantly, your parents. Everything. I need to make amends — part of the AA philosophy. I had hoped that with time your pain would have subsided. I know now that I was wrong."

"I'm glad you're better and that you're atoning for what you've done. But no. I can't forgive or forget."

He touched her arm gently, but she pulled it away. "I'm sorry Mel. I know the hurt I caused you and Ari is unforgivable, but I need to make you understand. That night I hit rock bottom. I'm a different man now. I want you to know that I loved your parents an…an… and, that I loved you too."

"That's not love, Nicolas. That's regret!"

"I regret everything."

"I want you to go." She said, pointing in the direction from where he'd come. "Go now!" She saw the pleading look in his eyes and she knew that he was crying, his tears mixing with the raindrops. She looked down as he pressed a soggy card into her hand.

When his tall figure disappeared down the street, she found a bench and sat on it, oblivious to the beat of the rain. *Why now Nicolas?*

54

"Morning, Mel," RJ said as he hovered over her desk; she was reviewing the case file.

He looked quizzically at her face, her eyes told him that something was off. "What's going on, Mel? You look spooked. I know this case is tough, but you look different, almost like…" his voice trailed off.

She told him what happened with Nicolas the other night.

"That son-of-a-bitch. How could he ever think that you'd forgive him?"

"Alcoholics Anonymous. He said. Atonement."

"Not sure if that stuff works."

"Maybe it does or maybe it doesn't. But I have an idea."

"You want me to pay him a visit?"

"No," Melissa said, the brightness returning to her eyes.

"Then what?"

"I was thinking about it after our encounter. Maybe there was a reason he came into my life. A sign. Perhaps there's a way that he can help with the investigation."

"You're kidding, right?"

"He's a forensic anthropologist. His dissertation was on superstitions and ancient cultures."

"Meaning?"

"He may have insights about the evil eye and its significance for the killer. It would strictly be on a need-to-know basis."

"You can't be serious. He killed your parents."

"Look at it as his way to repent."

"How do you think Ari will react to having him around?"

"I hadn't thought of that. I'll speak to him. The last thing I want is for Ari to run into Nicolas without any warning."

"And it will make things worse for you if he's kicking around here. Are you prepared for that?"

"I don't want to be angry anymore, RJ. I realized when I saw him the other night that I let sadness and anger consume me, making me stay in the past. Perhaps I need to forgive him."

RJ pondered that. He too was living in the past. He knew it intellectually. Emotionally, he could not let it go. "If you think it's a good idea and that he might be able to help, then fine. But I'll be watching him. If I see him causing you pain, I'll haul his ass outta here so fast, he won't know what hit him."

She laughed. "You're a great friend, RJ. Thank you."

They were interrupted by the ringing phone.

"Hi, Greg," Melissa said and put him on speaker.

"I might have some good news," Greg said.

"We're listening," Melissa said.

"There's a man here filling out a missing person's report on his parents. From what he's said it sure sounds like it could be the older victims," Greg said.

"What's his name?" RJ said.

"Brent Lawson. He's a physician."

*

Melissa and RJ sat across from Brent Lawson.

All the Evil Scatters

RJ assessed Brent Lawson's small, dishevelled physique. Brent saw him looking and tucked his shirt into his pants; he patted down his clothes, trying to ease out the wrinkles that were in desperate need of an iron. His clothes looked as if he hadn't changed them in days. Maybe he had rolled out of bed. At first glance, the man looked to be about 20 years old, but he was in all likelihood in his forties.

Melissa introduced herself. RJ followed suit.

"Mr. Lawson?" She extended her hand and felt the limpness in his handshake as if he were afraid to touch her. "We understand that your parents are missing?" Melissa scanned the report, noting that there were indeed some unmistakable similarities between what she was reading and the two elderly victims. Certainly, the age was right and his father had a scorpion tattoo. But Melissa was more interested in what was not in the report and why it had taken him so long to report that his parents were missing.

"Would you mind if we record our conversation?" Melissa said and sat beside Brent who gave them his consent.

Greg adjusted the camera.

RJ took the chair directly opposite Brent Lawson.

"We're ready," Greg said, the camera now positioned and ready to go. He tapped a button and nodded.

Melissa: Interview with Mr. Brent Lawson 10:29 a.m. Greg Monaghan, RJ Otombo, and Melissa Hargrove of the Toronto City Police Force are in attendance. Mr. Lawson. Please tell us why you think your parents might be missing.
BRENT: Well.... My parents are nowhere to be found. I've looked everywhere, called everyone. You're my last resort.
MELISSA: You indicated in your report that your parents' names are Rita and Wallace Lawson.
BRENT: Yes.

All the Evil Scatters

MELISSA: You say in your report that you haven't seen your parents in over a week. Can you tell us why you think your parents are missing? Do you see your parents often?
BRENT: Once a month. We'd made plans to meet for dinner last Tuesday night.
MELISSA: Where? Was there a reservation?
BRENT: At Canoe. I have a standing reservation.
MELISSA: That's a fancy restaurant, Mr. Lawson. It says here that you're a doctor.
BRENT: Yes
RJ: What kind of a doctor?
BRENT: Obstetric and gynecological surgeon.
RJ: Tell us about Tuesday's dinner.
BRENT: We get together on the first Tuesday of each month. I waited for them at the restaurant for over an hour.
MELISSA: Then what happened?
BRENT: I ordered a bison tartare with pickled chanterelles, cherries, Ontario lamb, salted coffee crumble and some wine.
RJ: Fancy. Did you not call your parents during your dinner?
BRENT: Of course, I did. Many times. There was no answer.
MELISSA: Then what happened?
BRENT: I got a call from the hospital that I was needed in surgery. I paid my bill and left.
RJ: And you didn't think anything was wrong, until now?
BRENT: I was in surgery. When I was done, I went to lie down and fell asleep. When I woke up, I called their friends. No one had seen or heard from them. I...I started to worry. I went to their

home and let myself in. Their bed was made — Mom is very meticulous about that.

MELISSA: Thank you. Mr. Lawson? Why didn't you check on your parents after you left the restaurant?

BRENT: I told you. I had to go to the hospital. I figured they'd get in touch with me sooner or later. I never thought I wouldn't be able to find them. I've racked my brains trying to find them. But I got nothing. Now, I'm looking for your help.

RJ: You look like you haven't changed clothing or showered for days.

BRENT: Believe me, when you're the on-call surgeon your wardrobe and appearance are the least of your worries. We're talking about life and death situations here.

RJ: We certainly are.

BRENT: What do you mean by that?

MELISSA: We have a few more questions, Mr. Lawson. Please tell us where you searched and who else you contacted about your parents. Don't omit anything. Every detail is important.

BRENT: After I left their house, I, um, I looked for their car in the garage. It wasn't there. I started to worry. I thought perhaps they'd been in a car accident and couldn't call me. My thoughts raced. I called the hospitals. Nothing. Not a trace. I called the police to see if there had been any accidents. Nothing.

MELISSA: What kind of car do they drive? Can you give us the plate number?

BRENT: Sure I'll jot it down

MELISSA: Please add the make, year and colour of their car.

BRENT: Here you go.

All the Evil Scatters

MELISSA: Do you recognize the people in the photos?
BRENT: Where did you get these pictures? Is this some kind of a joke? What's going on here?
MELISSA: Please sit down and take a good look. Are these your parents, Mr. Lawson?
RJ: You're a doctor. You must stare at death every day.
BRENT: My parents are dead? Why didn't you tell me from the beginning?
MELISSA: We had to be certain that we were talking about the same two people. I'm sorry.
BRENT: I see.
MELISSA: Mr. Lawson. We deeply regret that we didn't tell you earlier, but we needed to be certain that these were your parents.
BRENT: What happened to them? Car accident? What?
MELISSA: They were killed sometime between Tuesday evening and early Wednesday morning. The coroner puts their death at around 3 a.m.
BRENT: Killed? What do you mean killed? Was it a robbery? No. No! Does this have anything to do with the recent murders on the news? Oh my God. It does. I see it in your eyes. I can't believe this. Why?
MELISSA: That's what we're trying to figure out. Did your parents have any enemies?
BRENT: No way. They were sweet and kind, to a fault. Always willing to help.
RJ: What we'll tell you next stays between us. This is an active investigation and we want no leaks to the media. Do you understand?

All the Evil Scatters

MELISSA: When we found your parents, they were completely naked. There was no identification.
BRENT: Naked? Sick bastard. Were they, uhh? Was my mother raped?
RJ: Neither one was sexually assaulted, but there is a sexual component to their deaths. Here are some photos.
BRENT: Oh my God. This is a nightmare. Who would be so sick to do this?
MELISSA: We're going to find out, Mr. Lawson.
BRENT: Were they alive when, um, when...?
MELISSA: I have to say that sadly, your mother's eyes were sewn shut while she was still alive. They died from hypoxia. We know that the castration was done posthumously.
BRENT: This is a nightmare.
MELISSA: We understand that this is difficult, but can you answer a few more questions?
BRENT: Whatever you need.
RJ: Can you tell us about your parents' financial situation?
BRENT: You think this was motivated by money?
MELISSA: We need to look at every angle. The information will help us.
BRENT: Of course. They own their house. They drive one car, the Intrepid. They have a cottage in Haliburton, inherited from mom's parents. They have a few investments. I guess you could say they're financially secure.
RJ: You could stand to benefit from their death.

All the Evil Scatters

BRENT: That's preposterous. I'm a doctor! I have my own money. I'll give you access to my financial records. And anything else that you need. I have nothing to hide.
MELISSA: That would be great. Thank you. We'll do whatever we can to find out who did this to your parents. One more thing. Can we have your permission to post any recent photos of your parents in the hope that somebody saw something?
BRENT: I have one in my wallet. We took it last month to replace one that I'd lost.

Melissa took the photo and turned to Greg, signalling him to stop the tape. "Could you please grab Mr. Lawson a coffee and some food, Greg? Whatever he wants."

Brent Lawson ran his fingers through his greasy hair. "I don't want to eat or drink. What I need is a shower. Badly."

After Greg left with Brent Lawson, RJ got right to the point, "This is not our guy. He was a bit edgy and defensive, at times. But my money is still on Donald."

"When we showed Lawson the pictures of his mother's eyes sewn shut and his father's castration," Melissa began, "his gag reflex was real. I thought he was going to heave right then and there."

"He's a surgeon. He certainly has the kind of knowledge that our killer seems to have," RJ said.

"Good point. We'll know for sure when we look into his background."

"For a doctor he sure was squeamish."

"Seeing your parents like that would make anyone's stomach turn. Even a surgeon's." She looked out the window and recalled her visceral reaction to the news of her parents' death. "As much as I would like all the pieces of the puzzle to come together, he doesn't fit the profile. He seemed truly distraught and confused. Now, what about the car?"

RJ looked at Brent's scrawl: *Intrepid. 2017. Dark blue.* "Let's keep an open mind and get some warrants issued. We need to be clean on this. We can't assume anything. Let's eliminate him as a suspect. We'll have Greg

All the Evil Scatters

review his financials and make sure that no skeletons are dangling inside his proverbial closet."

"At least now we know the identity of all four victims: Wallace and Rita Lawson; Boris and Penelope Smikowsky," Melissa said.

"I'll call the hospital and see how long his sleepover lasted," RJ said.

"I'll work with the comms department and get photos of our four victims on the air," Melissa said.

55

I read the article with interest.

Toronto. Police have now confirmed that last week's murders of an elderly married couple, Rita and Wallace Lawson and siblings, Penelope and Boris Smikowsky, are the work of the same killer, a serial killer, also dubbed as *The Suturer*. They believe that couples are being targeted and are of significance to the killer. Police will not confirm, but sources say that they have a person of interest who they would like to question. This person is not a suspect but may have information related to the two cases. Police are asking that this person present him or herself to the police as soon as possible.

Police have now released photos of the four victims in the hope that someone saw something. Anyone with information is asked to contact the police.

"There they are," I say, looking at their images in the newspaper. All four had been very much alive in those photos, their evil staring back at me, taunting me. I know they can't hurt me or anyone else.

I gently fold the paper, taking great care not to make creases on any of the words. I want to be able to read the article in the years to come. I wonder who the person of interest might be. I highly doubt they figured out it was me. They have no idea who I am. They won't know until I'm ready. As for the name they've given me, *The Suturer*. What a joke.

All the Evil Scatters

56

Melissa looked out onto College Park at the Winner's retail store which had replaced the once iconic Eaton's department store and said, "I have to do this. I need to shed the past." She reached for the phone, dialled and when the call was answered on the other end, she said, "Nicolas?"

She heard him pause.

"Hey, Mel. I didn't think I'd ever hear from you. Are you okay?"

"Yes."

"You don't know how sorry I am about all of this. I know that *I'm sorry* is the most overused phrase in the English language, but I truly am sorry," Nicolas said.

"Maybe this was a mistake. I should let you go."

"Don't go. You had a reason for calling. What was it?"

Melissa breathed in and closed her eyes as she exhaled. "I called you because... First of all, it's not about you being sorry, or about me forgiving you, or about regrets, or anything like that. It's not even a social call."

"Why did you call?"

"You said you want to atone for what you did to my family?"

"What do you need? You know I'll do anything for you."

"I'm sure you've read the news about, dare I say, *The Suturer*?"

"What does this have to do with me?"

"We need your help. We can use your expertise."

"I'm not sure how I can help."

"Wasn't your thesis on superstition in ancient cultures?"

"Yes, it was. Go on."

"Not over the phone. I need you to come to the station and meet with us."

"I'm on my way. And, Mel? You won't regret this. I promise."

57

RJ brushed off the light dusting of snow on the car with his sleeve and looked at the Intrepid's license plate. "This is it," he said.

Melissa walked around the car. "No apparent signs of a struggle." She peered through the driver side window while RJ inspected it from the passenger side. "I can't see anything out of place inside." She put on a latex glove and pulled on the door handle. "It's locked."

RJ looked around him and said, "I see a camera over there." He motioned with his finger and Melissa spotted the camera near the ATM and nodded.

"I'll ask Heather to get the footage for the last week or so. Maybe there will be something," Melissa said.

"I hope so," RJ said glancing around him to see if there might be some CCTVs. He spotted a camera at the end of the street. *Was it positioned close enough to capture the victims and/or their killer?* "He has to slip up at some point. Let's hope we'll catch a break."

"We'll have to bring it in for prints and trace evidence. If this is where the killer met his victims then maybe he left something behind." RJ tugged at the door handle. "Where's that locksmith?"

"Why don't we walk around the area and see if there's anything out of place? The restaurant is a couple of blocks from here."

"Why would they park so far from the restaurant?" RJ said

"It was the only available spot?" Melissa said. "They wanted to stretch their legs?"

"Let's check out Lawson's reservation."

"Greg cleared his financials," Melissa said.

*

The restaurant manager, Ken Brigham, confirmed that Brent Lawson was a regular and that he had been there for a while on the evening in question until he'd received a call and left.

"Anything odd about Mr. Lawson that night?" RJ said.

"Mr. Lawson is a nice man. Gentleman. Great tipper. He often comes in with his parents."

"How often?"

"Once a month. Like clockwork."

"When they're all dining together, what's the mood like?"

"They're always so animated. Talking and laughing. They seemed to be a very happy family."

"I guess he wasn't animated the night in question."

"He was alone," Ken said.

"Of course," RJ said. "Anything else?"

"Nothing jumps out," Ken said.

"Did he talk to anyone in the restaurant?" Melissa said.

"He greeted a few of our regular patrons. That's it," Ken said.

"Did anyone seem out of place?"

"Not that I recall."

"One last question. Did the elder Lawsons show up for dinner that night?"

Ken shook his head.

*

By the time they returned to the Intrepid, the car had been unlocked and the locksmith was waiting for them inside his van.

"Thanks, Tony," Melissa said. "I appreciate you staying with the car. We don't want any trespassers."

"Or carjackers," RJ added.

"No problem," Tony said and drove off.

They searched inside the car. There didn't seem to be anything amiss. The Intrepid was spotless.

"Our killer didn't do anything here. He must have intercepted them en route to the restaurant. Let's go back and retrace their steps. Maybe we'll find something," Melissa said.

"Worth a shot."

They walked the route that they thought the Lawsons had taken to the restaurant. They looked under garbage bins, around grates, the manholes, and the entrances to the buildings.

"Nothing here," Melissa said. "Let's head — "

"Wait a minute," RJ said, stooping to pick up something that was lodged between where the sidewalk abutted the street. He picked it up, shaking off the snow.

"It's a blind person's cane," Melissa said. "Why is it here?"

All the Evil Scatters

"Wouldn't the person know it's missing?" RJ said. "How would they get home without it?"

"Someone who has a visual impairment would never abandon his or her cane," Melissa said. "I don't recall that Brent said anything about one of his parents being visually impaired."

"Unless that someone didn't need it," RJ finished her sentence.

"That's sloppy if it belongs to the killer," RJ said. "Let's go with the theory that it belongs to our killer. Why would he leave it behind?"

"Maybe he got caught up in the moment and dropped it."

"Another stupid criminal?" RJ said and laughed.

"Let's take it to the lab and have it dusted for prints," Melissa said.

58

Melissa and Sofia, the communications director, were huddled at a desk reviewing the story that would be released at 2 p.m. that afternoon.

"Here are the photos of the siblings and the Lawsons, the Intrepid, and where we found it," Melissa said. "Someone has to recognize or remember something.

"I'll release it via our comms channels which will go live on CP24, Twitter, Facebook, etcetera. It'll likely be in print in tomorrow's dailies," Sofia said.

Melissa thanked Sofia and then turned her thoughts to another time, the night of her parents' accident.

She'd been waiting at the theatre for her parents and Nicolas to arrive for the stage production of *Rock of Ages*. As she alternated between calls to her parents and Nicolas, she paced the lobby of the Royal Alexandra Theatre before returning to the street to see if she could spot them. She hoped that they were looking for a parking spot, often difficult to come by during theatre nights. Soon it would be curtain time. It wasn't like them, or him for that matter, to be late. Nicolas had his flaws, but poor time management was not one of them.

She'd waited until intermission and hailed a taxi back to her apartment. She called everyone she could think of. And as she wondered what had happened to the three most important people in her life, there was a knock on

All the Evil Scatters

her door. Her eyes lit up with relief but were soon replaced with dread as she opened the door and saw RJ. The grim look on his face made her shudder, the tears that had been threatening to escape, flowed down her cheeks.

"Let's go inside. Okay, Mel?"

She collapsed into his chest. This was a scene in which she'd been on the other side many times. She had never imagined that one day she'd be on the receiving end.

Melissa sat expressionless at the kitchen counter while RJ made coffee. He placed a mug in front of her and took a sip from his.

She finally mustered the courage to ask, "What happened?"

"Your parents were killed in a car crash earlier this evening; they died instantly. The Jaws of Life were used to extricate their bodies from the wreckage."

The cop in her asked, "What time?"

"Seven thirty-eight p.m."

"On their way to the theatre."

RJ nodded.

"Nicolas was supposed to have been with them. Where's Nicolas? Is he…?" Her voice trailed off in horror as the thought of losing all three of them in one fell swoop was too devastating to say out loud.

RJ took a deep breath, pulled out a pack of cigarettes and slowly removed one from the pack and placed it between his lips. He promptly put it back inside and went around the counter to where Melissa was sitting and put his arms around her and said, "Nicolas is alive."

"Thank God. I have to go to him. Do you have the person who did this?"

RJ nodded.

"I want to interview him. I want to know what happened."

"Mel? What I'm about to tell you —"

"Tell me what?"

RJ held her in place and tilted her chin upwards to face him. "There's no easy way to say this —"

"Nicolas is badly injured. How serious?"

"Nicolas is fine, at least physically. The person we have in custody is, um, Nicolas; his blood alcohol level was five times the legal limit."

All the Evil Scatters

"Nicolas? What? Oh my — " she said, moved over to the sink, stopped and turned on the tap. The water fell into the sink, fast and loud, drops jumping onto the counter, muffling everything that RJ was saying.

"We've charged him with driving under the influence and criminal negligence causing death."

"This has to be a mistake." Even as she spoke, she knew that this wasn't a mistake.

"I'm sorry, Mel."

"You're telling me that he got into the car drunk? After he'd told me he stopped drinking and swore that he was done with it? I should never have let him bring them to the theatre. I knew that he wouldn't keep his promise to get help!" She said and turned to RJ. "Where is he?"

"He's in custody, Mel."

"When I see him, he's going to wish he was dead."

"Let's take a few breaths. Sit down. Come —"

"I don't want to sit down. That son of a bitch killed my parents. I want to see my parents."

"Of course, you or Ari or both will need to identify them —"

"Does Ari know? I have to call him."

"One of our officers is with him now. I can take you to him if you don't want to be alone. You can lean on each other."

Melissa gazed into the distance and said, "Take me to my parents, and then I want to see their killer."

"You're a cop. And this is personal. I don't have to tell you that the answer to the latter is no."

"Please?" She needed him to understand that she had to confront the man who killed her parents. The man she had loved. The man who had broken his promises time and time again. The man she had believed in.

"You can see him in the courtroom tomorrow," RJ said. "I know it's going to be beyond difficult for you and Ari, but I'm here for both of you. The entire force is."

Melissa had stayed away from the courtroom the following day. She'd later learned from Ari that Nicolas had pleaded guilty and when sentenced, he could face up to seven years in prison. She never saw him again until the other night.

59

There was a knock on Melissa's door, Greg entered and said, "I have the CCTV footage near the Lawsons' car."

"Tell me what you found," she said. RJ walked in behind him.

"We got quite a bit of footage on that night," Greg said. "It's hard to make out the faces sometimes, but it's clear enough to see who it is. This puts our victims with their possible killer. Let's have a look at the video."

The three of them huddled in front of the computer screen. Greg pressed play. They watched the Lawsons get out of their car — at that point, it was only the two of them. They began walking toward the restaurant, following the exact path that RJ and Melissa had taken the other day. Another camera picked them up talking to a man with a hoodie, who appeared to be holding onto something that looked like a cane.

"Could that be the cane we found!" RJ said.

"They don't appear too concerned. They're chatting like old friends," Melissa said.

"That could be our guy — he's wearing a hoodie. Perhaps glasses, but I can't be sure," Greg said.

"Okay. They walk together. Then, the hooded guy and Wallace Lawson walk off together, leaving Mrs. Lawson standing alone on the street, clutching at her throat," RJ said.

"And then suddenly, she hurries away, out of the camera's range. That's the last we see of them," Greg said.

"I wonder if the cane we found belongs to the other person in these images?" Melissa said.

"That could be our killer," RJ said.

"We can't see much of his face, except that he closely resembles our person of interest: height's about the same, as is his stature and the often imitated hoodie," Melissa said.

"Sure shows that whoever left the cane behind didn't need it," RJ said.

"He likely used a cane to gain the Lawsons' sympathy. Maybe he asked them for help. They seemed to go along willingly. They don't appear to have been forced to do anything," Melissa said.

All the Evil Scatters

"Too bad we don't have anything after Mrs. Lawson darts in the direction of her husband," RJ said.

"Do you think she saw something happening to her husband and ran to his rescue?" Greg said.

"Could be," Melissa said. "What about the cane? Any prints?"

"We should have something soon," Greg said. "When Paul and I saw the footage, he went immediately to the lab to hurry them along."

They turned at the sound of a knock on the door; Paul entered with an excited look on his face and said, "I have two pieces of good news for you."

"Spit them out," RJ said impatiently.

"The lab found a print on the cane that matches that of Wallace Lawson," Paul said.

"Circumstantially, it puts the cane in the hands of, or at least near, our person of interest. Wallace Lawson was not blind and the hooded person was holding a cane," Melissa said.

"The SOB must have lured them by feigning that he was blind," RJ said.

"Any other prints?" Melissa said.

Greg shook his head.

"No other prints suggest that they had been wiped away, or the cane was handled by someone wearing gloves," Melissa said.

"Our conniving killer had planned it. There's premeditation," RJ said.

"Why leave it behind?" Melissa said. "Did he want us to find it?"

"Playing his fuckin' head games like with his notes and messages."

"You said two pieces of good news?" Melissa said.

"There's a Lee Chen," Paul said. "He saw the Twitter feed with the photos of our victims and thinks he may have seen the Lawsons on the night in question. He recognized the woman."

*

The camera was set up for the interview by the time RJ and Melissa entered the room.

A tall, gangly man, with razor-straight hair, sat at the small table with his hands clasped upon it.

"Mr. Chen," Melissa said. "Thank you for taking time away from work today. Do you feel comfortable being taped? It's for the record."

All the Evil Scatters

"It didn't happen if there's no photo or video right?" He laughed and raised his two hands apologetically.
Greg pressed *record*.

MELISSA: 4:17 p.m. We are interviewing Mr. Lee Chen regarding Wallace and Rita Lawson. Staff Sergeant Otombo, Sergeants O'Brien and Monaghan, and myself, Melissa Hargrove are present in the interview room. Thank you for coming, Mr. Chen.
LEE: Thanks for seeing me. How come there are so many of you?
MELISSA: Routine. From time to time, one of my colleagues may wish to ask you a question. Is that all right with you?
LEE: Yes.
MELISSA: Mr. Chen. We want you to tell us what you think you saw involving Mr. and Mrs. Lawson on the night in question.
LEE: I was on my way home from work when I noticed a man coaxing an elderly woman, the one in the news, into the passenger seat. I asked if he needed help.
MELISSA: What did he say?
LEE: He said, something like Mom's tired, and dad, well, he's tied one on as usual.
MELISSA: What happened next?
LEE: He seemed embarrassed by his parents.
MELISSA: How tall was he?
LEE: He was no more than five-eight. Slender.
RJ: Any distinguishing features?
LEE: He had a scar on his right temple.
MELISSA: Can you describe it to us?

All the Evil Scatters

LEE: It was maybe a half-inch long, maybe longer, starting at his brow, angling toward his temple. I couldn't see much of it because he wore sunglasses.
RJ: Sunglasses?
LEE: Yeah. I thought it was odd since it was after 8, the sun long gone.
RJ: Other than the woman, was anyone else in the car with him?
LEE: A man lying face down in the back seat.
MELISSA: Was he alive?
LEE: I'm not sure. At the time it never even crossed my mind.
MELISSA: What about the woman?
LEE: I think so. She was lolling about in the passenger seat, half asleep — her eyes twitching, moving as if she were dreaming in a REM state.
MELISSA: And you didn't think it strange that there was a man face down in the back of a car and a woman, barely awake?
LEE: Hey look. It was a long day at the office. I offered my help. What else could I have done?
RJ: Anything else?
LEE: I asked again if he needed my help and he said something like, always happens after we go out for dinner. Too many carbs, and then he chuckled and said, thanks so much for offering to help. Then I left.
MELISSA: Did you ever see any of them again since that night?
LEE: Not until I saw the photo of the woman. I couldn't tell if that was the same man in the back seat.
MELISSA: Tell us about the car, Mr. Lee. Did you get a plate? Model? Make? Colour?

All the Evil Scatters

LEE: It was a dark Oldsmobile. Blue or black. No, not black. Blue. I didn't think to look at the plate. I'm sorry.
MELISSA: You've been very helpful. One more question. Was the man carrying a cane?
LEE: Like a walking cane?
RJ: More like one of those white canes that someone who is blind uses.
LEE: I didn't see a cane.
MELISSA: Thank you. Would you work with our sketch artist?
LEE: Of course. I hope you find him.
MELISSA: Thank you for your time. Sergeant Monaghan will take you back downstairs.

*

"His description is consistent with that of Jan, the Manager at *Victor's*," Paul said.

"Matches the height and his physique," Melissa said.

"I dunno. He matches Donald's physical description, but...," RJ said. Melissa took a sip from her coffee cup.

"Nary a blemish on the soft-as-a-baby's-bottom complexion," RJ said. Greg nodded. "Maybe we missed it?"

"Or maybe Lee Chen was wrong. It was dark; he was tired," RJ said.

Heather, the rookie, entered the room waving a piece of paper in front of them. She put it before Melissa and pointed at the image on it.

The four of them looked at the artist's rendition of their suspect as provided by Lee Chen which now included the scar. They looked at one another and nodded. They were thinking the same thing: *the pieces were coming together and they were pointing directly at Donald Spielman.*

"Let's bring Mr. Spielman in for questioning," Melissa said.

All the Evil Scatters

60

I examine the charm and place it in Mother's palm, closing her fingers around it. She opens Her hand, the charm slips out and rolls onto the floor, finding its way to a small crevice. It stops and stares at me, accusatorially, its black centre, a menace from the past. My fingers automatically make the sign of the cross, the familiar prayer rising to my lips: "Jesus Christ is victorious, and all the evil scatters by Him. Jesus Christ is victorious, and all the evil scatters by Him. Jesus Christ is victorious, and all the evil scatters by Him *ftou, ftou, ftou*"

I reach for it and clutch it tightly in my palm, but it has a life of its own. It's hot against my hand.

"You understand nothing of what this means! Now wrap Your hand around it and close it tight. In Your hand, it protects me from the atrocities that You intend to inflict upon me. I must save the world from You."

This time She obeys my command and clasps the charm in Her hand, shielding it from me. A heavy sigh escapes me. I am safe.

Her eyes fix on mine, the fear evident.

I knew when I saw her eyes, blue like a summer sky, glance at me before entering the restaurant with her husband. She was evil and had to be dealt with. Moments later, she came out alone and went to a car and retrieved a bag with something in it. She returned to the restaurant and they came out holding hands. Her husband was holding a bag, filled with their lunch. I noted which car she'd opened, and when no one was around, I went to it, pulled the door handle, and luck was on my side — she'd left the driver's side open. I slipped in. No one saw me.

She screams, but the gag swallows Her cry for help.

"You are evil. Just as much as He is. Neither one of you will ever harm me again," I whisper in Her ear.

I reach for my needle threaded with catgut.

She opens then closes her eyes aware that her life is about to end.

I cross myself and say: "Jesus Christ is victorious, and all the evil scatters by Him. Jesus Christ is victorious, and all the evil scatters by Him. Jesus Christ is victorious, and all the evil scatters by Him." I mock spit, *ftou, ftou, ftou.* I repeat the words and cross my fingers against her chest before piercing the needle through Her lids.

All the Evil Scatters

Her screams are muffled by the duct tape; her body convulses beneath me.

"You're not going to leave me again, Mother! Jesus Christ is victorious, and all the evil scatters by Him. *ftou, ftou, ftou.*"

*

I turn off the recorder, remove the videotape, label it, *Mother and Father #3,* and prop it on the shelf with the others. I move over to the closet, pick up the old piece of glass and cut through the lines of rough skin on my upper arm. The blood escapes, freeing me, releasing me from the pain.

61

RJ stood near the door, his eyes focused on Donald. *If Spielmans's nervous, he sure is keeping it under wraps,* he thought. RJ was disappointed that their warrant to search Spielman's apartment had yielded nothing that could tie him to the case. They didn't find any books or paraphernalia on superstition or the occult.

Greg prepared the camera and set it in front of Donald.

"You're going to tape me?" Donald said in a high-pitched voice.

"There's no mistaking what you say and how you say it," RJ said and turned to Greg, "Ready?"

Greg nodded and clicked on the camera.

MELISSA: 1:29 p.m. We are interviewing Mr. Donald Spielman. Staff Sergeant RJ Otombo, Sergeant Greg Monaghan and Melissa Hargrove are present. Thank you for coming, Mr. Spielman.
DONALD: Did I have a choice?
MELISSA: We appreciate your cooperation. We have some follow-up questions for you. Can we get you something to drink?
DONALD: A tequila shot would be great.
RJ: You're quite the comedian.
MELISSA: Staff Sergeant Otombo will grab us some water.
DONALD: I don't like that guy.

All the Evil Scatters

MELISSA: This isn't a popularity contest, Mr. Spielman. We're doing our job to find out who killed your friends. Don't you want to know?
DONALD: Of course I do. Thanks for the water, man.
RJ: Officer Otombo, "man".
MELISSA: Okay. Now that we're all settled in, let's get back to why we're here. Mr. Spielman, please tell us about the time when you met Penelope and Boris at Union Station and what happened after that.
DONALD: I met them around 6 p.m.
MELISSA: What happened next?
DONALD: We walked over to the hotel, The Inn on Jarvis, as I told your officer.
MELISSA: What did you do there?
DONALD: They checked in and we went to their room.
MELISSA: Did anyone else meet you there?
DONALD: No. Only the three of us. Hanging out. It's been a while since we'd seen each other.
MELISSA: What did you discuss?
DONALD: I don't know. School, life, you know. Whatevs.
RJ: Any talk about getting some drugs or anything like that? Why are you squirming Donald?
DONALD: Well, I, um, hooked them up with some dope. That's all, man...officer. I don't do that other shit. That's for losers.
RJ: How long did you stay at the hotel?
DONALD: Not long. Half an hour. Maybe an hour.
MELISSA: Then what?

All the Evil Scatters

DONALD: We went to the Helion Pub and hung out there for a while before going to the party. We were a bit hungry from firing up a couple of Js.
MELISSA: What time was that?
DONALD: About eight.
MELISSA: Did you meet anyone else there?
DONALD: Ran into a few friends. There's always someone there from school.
MELISSA: Did anyone take a particular interest in either Boris or Penelope?
DONALD: Yeah. Couple of guys hit on Pen. She was a looker.
RJ: Did that make you jealous?
DONALD: Yeah. I mean no. Well, yes. I told you before that I had a thing for her. Always did.
RJ: And it bothered you that she paid attention to them and not you?
DONALD: That's cool. Free country and all that, you know.
RJ: No I don't. Tell me about it.
DONALD: People do whatever they want.
MELISSA: What time did you leave the pub?
DONALD: Must have been around nine or so when we finished up and went to Kayla's party.
RJ: And that's when you hit on Penelope and she rejected you, right?
DONALD: Yeah.
RJ: What time did you and Penelope have your fight?
DONALD: We didn't fight.

All the Evil Scatters

RJ: Okay. You disagreed. Irreconcilable differences, as they say. Time?
DONALD: 10:30, I think.
RJ: What time did they leave?
DONALD: Soon after that.
MELISSA: What time did you leave the party?
DONALD: Around 2:00 a.m.
MELISSA: Are you sure, Mr. Spielman?
DONALD: I'm sure.
RJ: This is your chance to come clean with us.
DONALD: I'm telling you all I know. I went home and fell asleep. What more do you want me to tell you?
RJ: The truth, Mr. Spielman. You said you didn't go to Victor's. I'll ask you again — are you sure you didn't go?
DONALD: Uhh, no. I told you before.
RJ: You're lying. The bar manager, at Victor's, saw you talking to Penelope Smikowsky around 11:30 p.m. Cat got your tongue?
DONALD: All right. I was there. I just wanted to talk to her. I didn't like the way things ended. But I didn't kill her or Boris.
MELISSA: You were one of the last people to see them alive. You're nodding Mr. Spielman.
DONALD: I guess so. I dunno. When I left them, they were still alive.
MELISSA: When was that?
DONALD: Around midnight.
RJ: Humour me for a minute, Mr. Spielman. If it wasn't you then think about who might have done this to your friends.
DONALD: How would I know?

RJ: I'll ask you again. Did you see anyone suspicious on the night in question?
DONALD: I can't recall. Wait. Wait a minute. I saw somebody lurking in the bushes near my apartment.
RJ: What was he doing?
DONALD: He was searching for his phone. He was dressed in black and his hoodie covered most of his face.
RJ: A hoodie exactly like yours? How convenient. Did you see his face?
DONALD: No. He was buried in the bushes looking for his phone.
RJ: And you didn't think that it was important to tell us earlier?
DONALD: I just remembered it, man. I mean, sir. Officer.
MELISSA: Please take a look at this sketch. Do you recognize the man in it?
DONALD: This is bogus.
RJ: That's you. You recognize yourself, don't you?
DONALD: I don't know where you came up with that, but it's not me.
RJ: Let me tell you how this went down. You were one of the last people to see them alive. You came on to Penelope. She rejected you. You argued. Then you followed them to Victor's and she rejected you once again. You got mad. I get it. Love sucks sometimes.
DONALD: No. No. I didn't. You're making things up. I love, loved, Penelope.
RJ: Then why did you do it?
DONALD: I didn't do anything to her. I loved her. I did. I would never hurt her or Boris. They were my best friends.

All the Evil Scatters

MELISSA: Let's try a different approach. Please take a moment to gather your thoughts, Mr. Spielman. What can you tell us about Wallace and Rita Lawson?
DONALD: Who?
RJ: Mr. and Mrs. Lawson, dipshit. The elderly couple that you killed.
DONALD: I have no idea who you're talking about.
RJ: Maybe this will refresh your memory. Don't push the photos away, Mr. Spielman. Take a good look at them.
DONALD: I don't. Didn't. Why are you doing this to me?
RJ: Tell us who you're working with. What's his name? Tell us and maybe the Crown will consider the fact that you helped.
DONALD: I'm not working with anyone!
RJ: You're working alone?
DONALD: No. I'm not. You're trying to confuse me.
RJ: We know there are two of you. Give us his name.
DONALD: There's no one. Not me and no partner.
MELISSA: Okay. Let's try this, Mr. Spielman. What can you tell us about the drawing of the eye that we found at your place?
DONALD: That piece of garbage that you took? I've no idea. It's not mine. Never seen it before. I don't know where it came from.
RJ: Very convenient that you don't know anything about anything. And that you see people lurking in the bushes.
DONALD: I saw him. And I keep telling you: I had nothing to do with any of this!

    Melissa clicked off the camera and said, "Mr. Spielman. We're going to hold you here for 24 hours."
    "Are you arresting me?"

All the Evil Scatters

"We have the discretion to detain you; we'll let you know if charges will be laid."

"Charges?"

"Yes, Mr. Spielman," RJ said. "Make it easy on yourself and confess."

"I told you. I didn't kill them. I don't know who gave you that sketch, but I tell you. I. Didn't. Do. It!"

"That's what they all say. The evidence says otherwise," RJ said.

Melissa opened the door to the interview room and said, "Greg? We're going to hold Mr. Spielman until we can get him before a judge tomorrow."

"I tell you," Donald said, now hysterical. "You've got it all wrong! My father will sue your asses. He's a lawyer you know!"

Melissa and RJ looked at each other. Once the lawyers got involved, then their man would be off-limits.

"I'll take him to lockup," Greg said.

"You can't do that. I have rights! I need to call my father."

"We'll get you a phone. Call your daddy lawyer," RJ said.

"This is bull crap."

"If you change your mind about telling us the truth, we'll be right here, waiting with bated breath," RJ said.

"I didn't do anything to them. They're... were my friends." Donald wiped the snot and tears with the back of his hand, put his head on the table and clasped his hands over it. His shoulders heaved up and down.

The guilty ones always do. Tears on demand, RJ thought.

"He was surprised when we asked him about the Lawsons. I saw no recognition in his eyes," Melissa said.

"There has to be a connection between Donald and the Lawsons," RJ said. "And when we find it, we're going to nail him to the wall."

"He has no scar," Melissa said.

"Chen, our witness, could have gotten it wrong. He was tired."

"He seemed pretty certain."

"Explain this. How is it that Spielman suddenly saw someone in the bushes, matching the description that we have?"

"I know that it seemed like an afterthought, but what if he saw someone? Don't we owe it to the victims to check it out?" Melissa said.

"I'll prove to you that Spielman is our guy. I'll ask Paul to look for any fibres, DNA, anything in and around the bushes at his place."

All the Evil Scatters

"Let's bring Lee Chen in as soon as we can and see if he can identify Donald in a line-up," Melissa said.

*

Melissa, RJ, and Lee Chen stood behind the one-way mirror that gave them a clear view of six men of varying heights and statures, wearing a hoodie or a baseball cap and sunglasses, standing in front of a wall with lines running across it. Numbers denoting the height of each man flanked the wall on either side like etchings on a wall where a parent might record their child's height over time. Each man held a number from one to six against his chest.

The three of them watched each man step forward, turn to one side and then to the other. When all of the men had repeated the same movements, Melissa turned to Lee and said, "Is the man you saw with the Lawsons on the night in question behind the mirror?"

"That's him," Chen said, quickly pointing to the fourth man in the line-up.

"For the record, please state the number of the man that you recognize," Melissa said.

"Number four."

"Thank you, Mr. Chen," Melissa said. "You've been a great help."

Melissa and RJ looked at one another and escorted Lee Chen out of the room.

62

Melissa, RJ, Tara, and Crown attorney Andreas Doros, sat in the interview room while Donald's father, Jacob Spielman, paced around the room.

"I want answers! I jumped on the first flight out of Montreal to be here," Jacob Spielman said, banging his fist on the table. "Where is my son?"

"We appreciate the speed at which you got here. We'll let you see him after we tell you why he's here," Andreas said.

"He told me why on the phone. Those two kids were his friends. We've known them all their lives. I know their parents, for Christ's sake."

"Mr. Spielman. Please calm down," Andreas said. "We'll tell you everything we have on him."

"I'm listening," Jacob said. A sudden calm replaced his anger.

All the Evil Scatters

These lawyers can turn their emotions on and off, like actors, RJ thought and looked intently at Donald's father.

"We have evidence that suggests that your son was involved in two sets of murders," Andreas said.

"That's preposterous!" Jacob said, rose to his feet and paced about the room. Melissa could see the battle raging in Jacob. As a father he can't accept that his son may be involved; as a lawyer, he'd probably seen his seemingly innocent clients turn out to be the bad guys.

"We have a sketch from an eyewitness that places Donald with the second set of victims, the Lawsons, on the night they disappeared. Donald was also picked out from a police line-up. Your son was also the last to see the Smikowsky's alive — he admitted to having been at the same bar shortly before their disappearance."

"Circumstantial!" Jacob said, his eyes boring down on Andreas.

"We also feel that your son might be working with someone. The skill and strength required to commit these murders appear to be the work of more than one person," Melissa said. Can you think of why your son might want to do this?"

"You're joking, right?"

"We also found the same symbol. It's not unusual for killers to leave a calling card at the scene of the crime," Andreas said. "We found it in your son's apartment."

"What symbol is that, Dan Brown?" Jacob's smile did not reach his eyes.

"It's what we Greeks call the evil eye," Andreas said.

"Great. And my people call it the *ayin ha'ra*. It's all superstitious hoo-ha that my bubby extolled ever since I can remember. Surely, you don't believe in that?"

"There is a connection, Jacob," Andreas continued. "And your son is in the centre of it. You must see that this can't be a coincidence."

"You said earlier that your witness found a charm that a dog pooped for Christ's sake," Jacob said. "He could have found it anywhere. You can't say that it's connected. Chain of evidence. Have you heard of that?"

"Okay, maybe we don't have a direct link, but even still, how can you refute that the charm or images of the evil eye have appeared in both crime scenes, including your son's place."

All the Evil Scatters

Can't be easy to have your son accused of being a cold-blooded murderer, RJ thought observing Jacob's lips firmly pressed together, nostrils flaring.

"I'll have this and everything else tossed if you go any further," Jacob said.

"And he lied to us. When the police questioned him the first time, he denied having gone to *Victor's*," Andreas said. "When we told him that there were witnesses who had placed him at the bar, talking to Penelope, he caved. Why would he lie?"

Jacob slammed the palms of both hands on the table and spat out, "Did you find any physical evidence? DNA? Fingerprints connecting him to the murders? Weapons? Anything other than this flimsy evidence? I expected more from you, Mr. Crown Attorney," he said and turned contemptuously at Tara, then RJ, then Melissa and continued. "I will shut this all down. Your so-called eyewitness — it was late and dark. He was tired and going home from work. Many holes in your theory. What does he have to gain from all this? What's the connection between the victims and my son? I repeat, it's all theory and conjecture."

"Your son admitted to being at the last known place where his friends were seen alive," Andreas said. "He admitted to having argued with Penelope and that he was in love with her."

"Lots of people get rejected and don't kill. They move on."

"Some do," Andreas's words hung in the air like heavy rain clouds ready to burst upon them.

"Find the real killer or killers and release Donald. He is not a killer. He is not working with anyone else."

"We're going to charge your son, Mr. Spielman," Andreas said. "For the murders of Penelope and Boris Smikowsky and Wallace and Rita Lawson."

"That's preposterous! I will have all of your heads."

The five of them turned in unison at the sound of a knock on the door. Greg entered and said, "Can I see you in the other room?"

"We'll be right back, Jacob," Andreas said.

"What's up Greg?" RJ said when the door to the interview room banged shut behind them.

"We have two more victims. Their lividity shows they've been dead for about six hours."

"And Donald was here with us during that time," Melissa said. "How could he have been in two places at the same time?"

"Or did Donald's accomplice act alone this time, giving him the perfect alibi?" RJ posited.

"Do you think we can release Donald? Watch him and see where he goes, who he sees, what he does?" Melissa said.

"I can do that since you only held him in custody with no formal charges," Andreas said. "I'll tell the father that he can take his son home."

All the Evil Scatters

PART 3

63

"Who found the bodies?" Melissa said as she and RJ examined the corpses of their new victims, a man, and a woman, with similar mutilations to those of the Smikowskys and the Lawsons.

Frank was bent over the bodies conducting a preliminary assessment.

"The two joggers over there," Heather said, gesturing with her head toward two young women in their jogging clothes.

"Let them go home, but ask them to be prepared to make a formal statement down at the station," RJ said.

For the third time in less than a month, Melissa gathered evidence within the perimeter of where the bodies were found in their death embrace. The bodies were on full display, in the open, in the Dallington Park Ravine where someone was sure to stumble upon their bodies.

"The finesse in the cutting of the skin and the suturing appear to be the work of the same perp or perps," Frank said.

"Can you tell how long the bodies have been here? Time of death?" Melissa said.

"Given their lividity, they've been dead for about seven hours. Give or take," Frank said.

"We may have to dismiss Donald as a suspect," Melissa said.

"Now hold on. We still think there are two, right?" RJ said.

Melissa finger-combed her hair away from her forehead and focused on the ground. "These deaths give Donald the perfect alibi — he was sleeping at the police station," she said.

"I'll confirm everything back at the lab," Frank said. "But these victims are in their early to mid-forties."

"What do the male-female killings represent to the killer?" RJ said. "Who do they represent?"

"Reenacting his past? Is it about his parents? Some other figure or figures in his life?" Melissa said, turning as the paramedics hoisted the trollies carrying the bodies onto the ambulance.

Something tiny dropped to the ground.

It appeared to have come from the female victim's hand. She kneeled and picked it up with a pair of tweezers. She examined a charm similar in shape and size to the one they'd found with the siblings, the one that the dog had pooped. *Now we can rule it out as a random trinket.* She placed it in a plastic evidence bag.

"Whatcha got?" RJ said.

"There's no doubt that the evil eye is the centrepiece of the killer's motivation," Melissa said.

Through the plastic, RJ could see the blue, black and white charm — the evil eye.

*

"I think you need to see this," Heather said, bursting into the briefing room with her usual enthusiasm. She handed Melissa a file.

Melissa scanned it and said, "It's a Missing Person's Report."

"What's it say?" RJ asked Heather.

"Last night, Eric and Cassie Olsen, aged 9 and 12 respectively, called 911 and reported that their parents hadn't come home from work yesterday," Heather said. "I wanted you to see it right away in case there was a connection to the bodies we uncovered at Dallington."

"You might be right," Melissa said. "Description seems to match that of the couple in the ravine."

"Where are the kids now?" RJ said.

"They're with social services," Heather said. "The social worker gave us this picture of the family."

Mel and RJ looked at the photo and nodded, unable to deny the fact that the couple they found in the ravine was the Olsens.

"Any next of kin?" Melissa said.

"There is a maternal grandmother, Rhonda Peterson. She lives alone in the Deer Park area."

"Let's go," RJ said.

*

RJ and Melissa approached a woman who was stooped over a flower bed, muttering to herself and digging in the front garden of her 1930s two-story house.

"Mrs. Peterson?"

The woman turned and looked up at them and said. "Hello. Do I know you?" She rose, dusted off the front of her pants, and ran her fingers through her short silver-grey hair. She was about 70 years old and she appeared to be in excellent physical shape.

"We're police officers, ma'am. From the Toronto Police," RJ said and showed her his identification. Melissa followed suit.

Mrs. Peterson rose with a steady elegance. A stray wisp of hair escaped her coiffed head; she tucked it behind her ear. Her eyes twinkled as she said in a breathy voice, "To what do I owe the pleasure?"

"Is there somewhere we can sit?"

"A social visit? By the police? What's this all about?"

"We're not here for a social visit, ma'am," Melissa said.

"You're not? Then why are you here? I live alone. My sweet, Emery. God rest his soul, used to turn the soil over for me. He died from pancreatic cancer you know. Horrible pain. Horrible death. Now I have to do it myself. Keeps me young," she smiled showing perfect teeth. "Helps me remember him. Who are you again?"

"We're the police, Mrs. Peterson," Melissa said, exchanging a look with RJ.

"Of course. You're here for a visit."

"Can we sit down, Mrs. Peterson?" RJ said.

"Call me, Rhonda. Mrs. Peterson makes me sound so old, like my mother-in-law. I'll be celebrating my 40th birthday in a few weeks."

Melissa and RJ exchanged puzzled looks, noting that Mrs. Peterson was almost twice that age. They followed her around the front yard, down the length of a terra cotta driveway leading to a garden table with four chairs. RJ rearranged the chairs so that he and Melissa faced Mrs. Peterson.

Rhonda looked up expectantly. "Now where did Emery put my glasses."

"Rhonda? Mrs. Peterson?" Melissa said and patted the older woman's hand. "My friend and I are going to admire your beautiful garden."

"I have a beautiful garden, don't I?"

"You sure do. We'll be right back," RJ said.

"I don't like this. I think she has some cognitive impairment," Melissa said.

"I don't know if we should say anything to her," RJ said. "I'm not sure if she'll be able to fully comprehend the magnitude of what we are about to tell her."

All the Evil Scatters

"You're right. But we have to. She is listed as Abigail's next of kin."

"Abby? Where's Abby?" Rhonda called out. "She's always late coming home from school. Always getting into trouble. Emery won't be happy about it. He thinks she has too much freedom. I disagree. Don't you, uh, Mr. and Mrs? I'm sorry I didn't catch your names."

"Mrs. Peterson? Do you have any family that we can contact?"

"My sister," Rhonda said. "She was always the smart one. The pretty one. She's a fashion photographer."

"Where does your sister live?"

"Right next door," Rhonda said and scurried to the fence and yelled, "Frankie. I have company and they want to meet you."

"Be right there," a voice sounded from behind the fence.

A woman who resembled Rhonda in looks and grace, came through the fence door and said, "Hello? Can I help you?"

"Ma'am? Could we have a word with you?"

"Of course. You're police officers, aren't you? I saw your car out front."

"We're here to speak with your sister, but we don't think she's in a condition to understand what we have to tell her."

Frankie nodded in understanding and said, "Hi. I'm Frances Vereshagen. Everyone calls me Frankie," she said, extended her hand in greeting, and then continued, "My sister has Alzheimer's. Some days she's good, other days she's not. What do you need to discuss with her?"

"It's about her daughter, Abigail Olsen, and her husband, Christopher."

"Has something happened to Abigail? To Christopher?"

"Abby? Is that you?" Mrs. Peterson called from the table where she sat in eager anticipation.

"Mrs. Vereshagen. We're sorry we have to tell you this, but your niece, Abigail, and her husband, Christopher were found murdered in Dallington Park," Melissa said.

"What do you mean?" Frances said, shock registering on her face.

"Your niece's children, Eric and Cassie reported them missing last night. Their bodies were found this morning," RJ said. "They were murdered."

All the Evil Scatters

Frankie gasped; her hand went to her throat. "There must be some kind of a mistake. They were here the other day looking in on Rhonda. What happened to them?"

"We believe that it is the work of the same person who killed two other couples."

"Oh my, God. The one in the news? No! No! No. This can't be," Frankie said reaching for the gate to steady herself.

"We know it's hard to fathom, Mrs. Vereshagen, but we are certain," Melissa said.

"How can you be so sure?"

RJ pulled out photos of the dead couple.

Frankie's eyes expanded with horror; her lips formed a silent, "o".

"We're so sorry for your loss," Melissa said.

"Where are the children now? Have they been harmed?"

"The children are alright; they are with social services," Melissa said noting that Frances would have to take care of the children; Rhonda wasn't in any condition to do so.

"I must go to the children," Frankie said.

Melissa watched her pace back and forth, sorting out the news she'd received.

"They need to be with us now," Frankie said in a decisive, take-charge tone, assuring Melissa that the children would be in good hands.

"They have no one," Frankie continued. "Christopher has no family other than us. Poor children. Poor Rhonda. I don't know how I'll tell her. She's gotten worse in the past few months. My husband, Raspy, and I will take care of the children."

"You'll find a way to tell her. We'll have the children brought to you," Melissa said, pulled out her cell and tapped on it. When the person on the other end answered, Melissa said, "Heather. Please advise the social worker that the children need to be with their family and to bring them to the address that you have for Mrs. Peterson. Her sister, Frankie, will meet you there."

"Why would anyone want to kill them?" Frankie said.

"We're going to find out, ma'am," RJ said. "You can be sure of that."

"Mrs. Vereshagen," Melissa said. "Do you have a work address for your niece?"

"Of course. I'll text it to you. She and Christopher work at the same place," she said, her hand shaking as she looked at RJ's card that he'd given her. She scrolled through her contacts and within seconds, Mel heard RJ's phone buzz. The information had already arrived.

"They both worked at Scotiabank?" RJ said, looking at his phone.

"It's where they met and fell in love," Frances said. "I must find a way to tell Rhonda. Will she understand?"

"Is there any way we can help?"

"Thank you, but I have to do this when the time is right."

"One more thing before we go," Melissa said. "Will you be able to come to the morgue and identify your niece and her husband?"

"Right now?" Frankie said.

"No. Tomorrow. The next day. Whenever you feel ready. Perhaps bring your sister," Melissa said, reaching out and putting her hand on Frankie's shoulder. She felt the other woman's body tense as if she wasn't comfortable with human contact.

"Thank you," Frankie said, her eyes welling, threatening to spill over. "My husband Raspy and I will take good care of the children."

With a determined nod and turn of her head, she walked over to her sister, took her hand, and sat down beside her.

"Can this case get any more morose?" RJ said and pulled out a cigarette. He badly needed a drink but decided that now was not the time.

"Let's see if we can make it to their office before they shut down for the day," Melissa said.

"I'll call Abigail's boss, Michael Horvath. Make sure he's still at the office," RJ said.

64

Michael Horvath and two of his staff, Rebecca Farmer and Tomaz da Silva, sat around the small boardroom table listening to Melissa and RJ deliver the devastating news about their colleagues.

"This is tragic," Michael said. "They were a lovely couple. So in love. Who would want to kill them?"

"That's what we're here to find out," RJ said

All the Evil Scatters

"What can you tell us about the Olsens? Their habits? Anything unusual happen yesterday?" Melissa said.

Michael cleared his throat and said, "They drove in together daily, parked across the street and left together at the end of the day. Yesterday was no exception, as far as I know."

Melissa looked at the silent Tomaz, smiled encouragingly and said, "Is there anything that you can add, Mr. da Silva?"

Tomaz was a geeky-looking guy with horn-rimmed glasses; he shifted nervously in his seat, adjusted his eyeglasses, and shook his head.

"You have nothing to add? Correct?"

Tomaz nodded.

"Any changes in their behaviour in the past few days?" Melissa said, turning to Rebecca, who on several occasions had opened her mouth to speak, but held back.

"I didn't notice anything out of the ordinary," Rebecca said. "They left around 5:30, about the same time they leave every day. They have to pick up their kids from school. Eric and Cassie. Abigail's always showing photos of her kids. Cute kids. I feel terrible for them."

"Did they leave the office during the day?" Melissa said.

"At lunchtime, I think."

"Where did they go?" Melissa said.

"Probably *Morty's* down the street for take-out."

"Were they gone for long?" Melissa said.

"Don't think so. They came back and ate at their desks, working through their lunch hour to finish off a project they were working on."

RJ sensed that Rebecca knew everything that went on inside and outside that office. He walked over to the window that had an expansive view of the street below and the parking lot across the street and said, "Is that where the Olsens parked their car?"

"Yes," Rebecca said.

"Did you see them getting into the car?"

"Yes," she began, once again eager to tell her story. "I was getting ready to go and wanted to see if it was raining, according to the forecast. I keep my umbrella in my desk drawer. Always prepared for anything. You know how quickly the weather can turn at this time of year," she laughed, and then noting that no one else did, she continued. "The clouds were overcast, but no rain yet. I could feel it coming. It's—"

"What did you see when you looked out the window?" RJ said.

She cleared her throat. "I saw them get into their car. Christopher always drives. They have a nice Honda Civic. White. 2015 model. It's sleek and —"

"Were they alone?"

"I think so, but… but…"

"But what?" RJ said.

"I saw Abigail turn around and focus on the back seat. It looked as if she was nodding her head."

"You can see that far?" RJ said, scrunched his eyes, and tried to see inside the cars that were parked across the street.

"I have 20/20 vision thanks to my laser surgery."

RJ wondered how often she looked out the window with her perfect vision to spy on Abigail and Christopher and probably others.

"Why do you think she was looking toward the back seat?" RJ said.

"Can't be sure, but thought I saw some movement. I thought it odd at the time, but figured they'd picked up a friend."

"Did you see them with a friend before they got into the car?"

"No."

"Then why would you say that?" RJ said.

"Abigail focused her attention at the back of the car and nodded several times. If I were looking for something in the back seat, I would have gotten out and looked thoroughly for what I was after."

"I see," RJ said, tired of this woman's assumptions and so-called 20-20 vision. "Anything else?"

"After several minutes, she turned her head toward Chris before fully focusing on the road ahead."

"And then?"

"Chris pulled out onto the street and drove off."

"Thanks for your time, everyone. If you think of anything else, please give us a call. You have our numbers," RJ said then turned to Melissa. "Let's have a look at the parking lot."

*

"Open lot. Exposed to the street from three directions. Anyone can come and go unnoticed unless they don't pay for parking," Melissa said and read the parking lot sign: *This lot is being monitored 24 hours a day. Vehicles parked illegally will be towed at the owner's expense.* Melissa looked for cameras but didn't see any.

They explored the area where Rebecca had said that the car was parked. There was nothing out of the ordinary.

"We'll have to bring a team here. Maybe they'll find something," RJ said.

"Do you think someone was in the car waiting for them?" Melissa said.

"Possible. For someone who was going to see about the rain, she sure noticed a lot," RJ said.

"She said the Olsens' car was a Honda Civic, which checks out with their vehicle registration information. It's also one of the top ten cars reported stolen or broken into," Melissa said.

"Let's see if there are any other cameras. I think I see one across the street," RJ said.

65

Greg entered Melissa's office and said in a broadcaster-like voice, "You're not gonna believe this!"

"What?" Melissa said.

"We found blood behind the bushes near Spielman's house. Maybe it's related?"

"Seems like a long shot," Melissa said. "Is the blood recent?"

"According to Frank, that's a yes," Greg said. "There's no degradation of blood cells, leading him to believe that it's recent."

"Can we tell anything else from the blood?"

"He's AB negative."

Something niggled in the back of Melissa's mind. She reached for it, but couldn't quite make the association with the blood type.

"Something came to you, Mel?"

"I can't quite put my finger on it. Tell me more about this blood type."

"Only a small percentage of the population have AB-negative blood," Greg said.

All the Evil Scatters

"Which means it could help us narrow down suspects," Melissa said.
"It's something. May not tell us anything now, but it will when we catch the perp," Greg said.

*

Melissa typed a name into the DNA database. Within seconds, she had a hit — she'd been right. Nicolas's criminal record came up, as did his blood type, AB negative.

Interesting how you suddenly appeared in my life just as the murders started, Melissa thought. *Is atonement a ruse? Are you the second person of interest we're seeking? You're bigger and stronger and could certainly help move the bodies. I'll keep it to myself for now.*

66

Melissa, RJ, and Nicolas were in the station's boardroom table. Melissa's hand trembled as she went through the papers and photos in her file. *I have to stop thinking about what I suspect,* she thought as she observed Nicolas. By looking at him, nothing stood out. *Is it possible that he's somehow involved? And I brought him closer to it by inviting him to help. I can't believe it; he's not a killer.* He did *kill my parents.* She placed her hands on her lap to steady them and noted RJ's immovable stance, arms crossed against his chest, eyes fixed on Nicolas. She could tell that he was like a lion in the wild ready to attack its prey if provoked.

I can't have RJ suspect anything. I need more information on his whereabouts during the three homicides. For now, she wanted Nicolas close to her so that she could observe him. What would RJ say? *Keep your enemies closer.*

"Nicolas," Melissa began, "What can you tell us about the evil eye and how it relates to our killer?"

"The evil eye originates in ancient Greece. But it's not unique to that culture; the concentric design is also popular in the Middle East."

"Then we may be looking at someone with a Greek or middle eastern background?" RJ said.

"Not necessarily. Geopolitical movement over the centuries has brought this amulet to many parts of the world. Many cultures believe in the potency

All the Evil Scatters

of the eye and its ability to cast evil upon someone, someone who they envy, thus bringing bad luck on them."

"This doesn't help us, Nicolas," RJ said with disinterest and rose from his chair.

"Let's see what else he has for us, RJ," Melissa said, easing him back into his seat with her hand.

"There are different names for it: the Greeks call it *mati*; it's the *Nazar* amulet for many Asian cultures; in Hebrew, it's the *ayin ha'ra*; and, for Italians, it's the *malocchio*."

"Cut to the chase, Nic," RJ said.

"I think that your killer saw something in his female victims' eyes that he perceived to be harmful to him. Something that he feared and that by sewing their eyes shut he was defending himself from this perceived harm that they could inflict upon him. Psychologically, he was associating the victims with whoever traumatized him, exacting the abuse that he may have experienced, " Nicolas said. "The killer probably grew up in a religious, highly superstitious environment, probably made to pray to repent for his sins, and was physically punished to wash away his evil. As your evidence shows, the female victims had blue eyes. According to evil eye beliefs, the blue eye is the most potent in casting evil on someone."

Melissa sifted through her files for eye colour and found that the three females had blue eyes. Only one of the males had blue eyes, but his eyes weren't sewn shut. He must somehow relate to the blue eyes of the female victims.

"What does this mean?" RJ said.

"Whoever the person was that caused irreparable trauma may have had blue eyes," Nicolas said.

"He kills them because he feels threatened by what he sees in their eyes?" Melissa said. "By sewing their eyes shut, the victims can't harm him."

"Exactly," Nicolas said.

"Is he protecting himself by sewing them shut?" RJ said.

"He kills them to *ward off their evil*, shall I say?" Nicolas said.

"Anything else?" Melissa said.

"The philosopher, Plutarch, suggested that there was a scientific explanation — that the human eye could be powerful enough to release invisible rays of energy strong enough to kill children or small animals," Nicolas said.

"Right," RJ said. "I think I saw that in an episode of the *Outer Limits*. Sounds like sci-fi mumbo jumbo to me. We're done."

Nicolas ignored RJ and said, "Older generation Greeks believe in many superstitions compared to younger ones. These beliefs are passed from generation to generation. There are some interesting ones that I discovered through my research."

RJ sneezed a few times and said, "Damn allergies!"

Nicolas continued non-plussed, a smile forming on his lips, "Never directly give someone a knife if you want to remain friends, instead, place it on the table or counter and let them pick it up. If you say cheers to someone with a coffee, it will bring bad luck; say cheers with any other imbibe. And my personal favourite is that when you sneeze it means that someone is thinking of you."

"I guess a lot of criminals are thinking of me behind bars," RJ said.

"What about the castration?" Melissa said.

"The killer could have suffered extreme sexual trauma in his past, either at the hands of one or both of his parents or some other figure of authority. My bet is on the father; females are less likely to become sexual deviants. Maybe the killer underwent some form of physical castration? Or perhaps he feels metaphorically castrated and the murders are a symbolic reenactment or manifestation."

"Hadn't thought of that," RJ said and looked at Nicolas with reluctant interest. "If his parents did this to him, I want them to be punished just as much as their killer spawn."

"Anything else?" Melissa said.

"That's it for now," Nicolas said. "I want to thank you both for trusting me."

Interesting choice of words, Melissa thought, then said, "This is helpful. Gives us more insight into the killer's motivation."

The three stood up and, as Melissa gathered her papers, Donald's picture fell to the floor. She carefully watched for Nicolas's reaction as he picked it up. There was not a flinch of recognition on his face.

"Is this your suspect?" Nicolas said.

"Have you seen him before?"

All the Evil Scatters

"Me? No. Why?"

RJ cocked his head toward Melissa, eyebrows arching.

"Wasn't sure if we'd shown him to you before."

"I see. Do you have a few minutes to speak with me privately?" Nicolas said but his eyes were on RJ's face who glared at him as if he wanted to punch him.

"I'll be fine," she said lightly and touched RJ's arm reassuringly.

When the door closed behind RJ, Melissa said, "What's up?"

"I want to thank you for letting me work on this case," Nicolas began. "I will spend the rest of my life atoning for everything that I did to you and your family. Perhaps with time—"

"You're here because we need your expertise. Nothing more," she said and placed Donald's photo back in the file.

"I wanted you to know—"

"Tell me why you suddenly appeared in my life after all these years, Nicolas? Why now? What are you doing here?"

Nicolas's eyes betrayed his confusion. "What do you mean?"

"Your sudden appearance in my life is quite fortuitous."

"I told you I'm here to atone for what I did to you and your family. Are you saying I have ulterior motives?"

"Do you?"

"Absolutely not! My motives are pure. I want to make amends."

"You keep saying that but your timing is…"

"Is what?" Nicolas said searching her face for clues.

"Highly suspect. Your eagerness to work on the case. To get closer to me."

"I told you why I'm here. You asked me to work on the case, not the other way around."

"That's true. But we found a rare blood type at one of the crime scenes," she said and took a deep breath not once taking her eyes off his. "It matches yours, Nicolas. AB negative. Are you involved in the murders?"

"What are you saying? You suspect me?" He started laughing as if she'd cracked a joke, but when he saw the seriousness on her face, he was overtaken by concern. "You're serious. You've got to be fucking kidding me. I'm not the only one with this blood type." He paced around the room like a caged animal.

"But it's a rare blood type, and here you are."

"Still. That doesn't give you the right to question me like a common criminal. I've done my time for what I did to your parents."

"Try to see it from my perspective. You witnessed your mother and sister's abuse by your alcoholic father. I know how traumatic that was for you. You even told me that you wanted to kill him. I don't want to believe that you're involved, but you have to admit that your timing is very coincidental. To a cop —"

"You're unbelievable! And that makes me a murderer? How can you think that of me? But I guess you're a cop first, aren't you? Always interrogating me, like back then!"

Her head recoiled as if he'd slapped her. Had she done that to him? "I had to ask. Try to understand my position."

"Your position?" He said and pounded his fist on the table. When she didn't say anything, he continued, "How can you think that of me? I want to help you get this monster who killed these people. That monster is not me. I've done a lot of things that I'm not proud of. The biggest of which is killing your parents and what that did to you. I am not a serial killer! How can you think this of me?"

Melissa looked into his eyes and wanted to believe that he was telling the truth, but then he'd bold-faced lied to her about his drinking. "You're right. I'm sorry. I've been on edge. This case has gotten to me in more ways than you can imagine."

"I know I deserve your scrutiny and mistrust, but this? I've gotta go."

She saw the hurt on his face, the tightness of his lips, and the sad, humiliated look in his eyes before he walked out the door.

67

Melissa returned to the office the next day for a 6 a.m. meeting with RJ, Greg, Paul, and Heather. Tara arrived toting a box of savoury pies and said, "Thought I'd switch things up a bit." She grabbed one of the pies and bit into it. The others followed suit.

"Thanks. Beats the sugar rush from the doughnuts," Paul said.

Melissa went to the whiteboard and added the new dates and times for their latest victims. "Okay," she said. "Let's look at the timeline. We brought

All the Evil Scatters

Spielman in for questioning around 10 a.m. two days ago. We didn't release him until noon yesterday. That's 26 hours. During this time, the only person he contacted was his father. The Olsens left their office at 5:30 p.m. Their children reported them missing at seven that evening. Their bodies were found yesterday. Frank puts their death sometime between 2 a.m. and 4 a.m."

"And Donald was with us from the time of their disappearance to when the joggers found the bodies," RJ said.

"His father is going to enjoy throwing that in our face if we continue to pursue their son as a suspect. We have to tread carefully where Donald Spielman is concerned," Tara said.

"Especially if he's the second man, the follower, the pleaser," RJ said. "Our killer is brazen, strong, and patient: he breaks into cars during the day; and, lures victims by acting fake-blind."

"The killer also has a scar on his brow; Spielman doesn't have one," Melissa said.

"We can't rule out that our witness may have been mistaken about the scar — it was dark and the perp was wearing sunglasses," Tara added.

"We also want to show you the video that we obtained from the retailer across the street from the parking lot where the Olsens were last seen two days ago," Melissa said, tapped a couple of keys on her laptop and gave it to Greg who in turn brought up a video.

The images were unclear, the face not visible, but they could see someone attempting to open the driver's door of the Honda. The figure fit the general description of their person of interest. They couldn't see what he was doing. Moments later he opened the door, climbed in, and pulled the door closed.

"During the next five hours the person stays in the car," Greg said and pressed a button on the laptop, fast-forwarding through the next five hours of footage. "Believe me, we watched every second of it. He never left. I'll stop the footage at 5:32 p.m.," Greg said and pressed the play key. "As you can see, Abigail and Christopher Olsen got into their car. Watch what happens next."

Melissa, along with the rest of the team, watched Abigail turn her head toward the back of the car; she held the position for a couple of minutes as if she was talking to someone or perhaps looking for something. Christopher's face was not visible. He was holding on to the steering wheel. When she

All the Evil Scatters

finally turned around, she looked out the window, toward the sky and while they couldn't see her expression, they imagined what she might have been thinking. Her children. Her mother. Perhaps she was praying for a positive outcome. Did she take a final look at her office building across the street and wonder if it was the last time that she would see it?

"And there was no one else with him?" Tara said.

"No one. But we're still not ruling out that there might be two of them working together," Melissa said. "Perhaps he meets with the accomplice later to enact their macabre murder."

"I know I've been a fan of the theory about two killers, but after seeing this, I'm not sure," RJ said.

"We certainly have precedent, such as in the Zodiac murders in Northern California back in the 70s," Melissa said. "The killer targeted a couple picnicking at Lake Berryessa in Napa County. He made the woman tie the man and then the Zodiac tied her up."

"Wonder if, dare I say, *The Suturer,* threatened them with a knife or a gun?" Greg said.

"Perhaps he threatened their children. Maybe he told them if they didn't cooperate, he'd kill them," RJ said.

"But he didn't kill them there," Heather said.

"That's his M.O.," RJ said. "Nabs the pair, takes them somewhere and that's where he kills them."

"The *where* is the key," Tara said.

"It's a big city. He could be doing it anywhere," RJ said.

"Heather's been working on other CCTVs and cameras to see if we can piece together a possible route that the Olsens were forced to take," Melissa said and turned to Heather. "Do you have any information on the Honda's route?"

"I do," Heather said and turned to Greg who vacated his seat for her so that she could take control of the keyboard. She clicked on a few keys and brought up a series of clips. "I took the 45 minutes of footage from the various street cameras and condensed it into 2 minutes. After they left the parking lot, you can see the car turn onto Yonge Street. For the next 43 minutes, the vehicle makes its way through the rush hour traffic, which was surprisingly light that day."

"Do we know for sure that it's the Olsens' car?" Melissa said.

All the Evil Scatters

"The plate was clear enough to confirm that it belonged to the Olsens," Heather said and froze the frame, the licence plate visible.

"As you can see," Heather said, "the Honda ended up in the transit parking lot of the Finch subway station. It was around 6:30 p.m. and still lots of cars parked, but see here," she pointed to a corner of the screen.

"Is that the three of them getting out of the car?" Melissa said.

"I believe so," Heather said, clicked on a few keys, and pulled up a different video. "Here you can see the three of them exiting the car and walking away from the station, where…"

"Where what?" RJ said, his face flushed with impatience.

"Where another camera picks them up entering another vehicle on one of the streets adjacent to the parking lot."

"Tell me you got something on the other vehicle?"

Heather nodded and continued, "The vehicle looks like an Oldsmobile. Fuzzy footage given the location of the camera. We got partial plates. The three of them get in and drive off. That's the last trace of them."

"This is something. A partial plate on an Oldsmobile," RJ said.

"Didn't they stop making them in 2004?" Tara said. "Can't be that many on the street."

"It will take some time, but we can narrow it down."

"Find the car; we find where this monster lives," RJ said.

"Great work, Heather," Melissa said.

"It's gotta be our guy!" RJ said, rising excitedly from his seat, this time remaining standing. "Chen saw the Lawsons in an Oldsmobile. This can't be a coincidence."

"Now where does he take them?" Melissa said.

*

Hours later, the Olsens' Honda Civic was brought in for processing. It had been exactly where they had seen it in the video — the Finch subway station parking lot. A yellow ticket fluttered under the windshield wiper as if waving to them.

For the first time in weeks, RJ felt that they were closing in on the perpetrator. They had a good sense of the motive, a partial plate, the killer's vehicle, and video footage showing that the Lawsons and Olsens being abducted. But there was something about the case that bothered him. Why had the perp contacted him? Had he busted their killer before? He racked his brains, but nothing came to mind. He went to the file room and pulled out a box containing his case files and plopped it on his desk.

"Where do you take them? Who are you?" RJ said and flipped through some files.

He grabbed his cigarette pack and went out for a puff. He was about to light it when his cell phone went off.

"I hope it's good news, Greg," RJ said.

"I'm here at the Centre for Forensic Sciences processing the car. You won't believe what I found."

"What?"

"I found a message wedged between the front seats. I've texted you and Mel the image."

Ping. The text promptly arrived in RJ's inbox. He opened the image and looked at it. The message read:

> *Have you figured it out yet? There will be more until you figure it out.*

The evil eye was prominently drawn on the bottom, right-hand corner, like an artist's signature.

"Fuck! Fuck! Fuck! He's going to kill again." RJ said and pounded his fist against the wall, splitting the skin on his knuckles.

68

Toronto. In what has been an elusive case for the Toronto City Police Force, investigators have once again discovered the mutilated bodies of a man and a woman, identified as married couple Christopher and Abigail Olsen.

They were found in the Dallington Park Ravine in the City's west end. Police will not comment, but sources say that it is the work of the same killer, *The Suturer*.

There is no clear motive, but psychologist, Dean Ramsden, suggests that in such killings, the perpetrator often acts out traumatic events that occurred in their lives. Events that are very significant to the killer. Perhaps he was physically and/or sexually abused at the hands of someone in authority and is reenacting that trauma through

All the Evil Scatters

these murders. There are no suspects at this time, but a person of interest was questioned and later released.
The victims are survived by their son and daughter. Their names cannot be disclosed due to their age.
Police request that anyone with information contact them at the numbers provided.

I put down the newspaper and wonder who their person of interest might be. There are no details of my achievements. No matter. I know.

The video of that night is on a continuous loop: the Olsens, first the woman, she struggles, blood streaming down her cheeks, then the snap of her larynx. The man knows his fate as he thrashes about. I tighten the noose, cutting out the air, suffocating him, and stealing his last breath. My suturing skills are impeccable. My media name, *The Suturer*. Nice. I've changed my mind about it — it's not as pedestrian as I'd once thought. An apt description, but I am so much more.

I increase the volume on the video machine; my voice rises in concert, "Jesus Christ is victorious, and all the evil scatters by Him. Jesus Christ is victorious, and all the evil scatters by Him. Jesus Christ is victorious, and all the evil scatters by Him, *ftou, ftou, ftou."*

69

RJ feverishly sifted through the reams of paper on his desk. The light from the outdoors had disappeared, replaced by the darkness of night. He turned on the lamp which shone on the papers like a beacon. *Too bad it can't shed light on this case,* RJ thought. He'd decided to work from home so that he could be with Carla, maybe have a drink together later. He picked up the bottle of Scotch and refilled his glass.

There was a light tap on the door; he looked up as Carla entered and said, "RJ, we need to talk."

He put down his glass, the tone in her voice commanding him to pay attention. "What's wrong?"

"I don't know where to begin," she said.

RJ raised the glass, took a swig from it and said, "You can tell me anything."

All the Evil Scatters

"It's hard to say this. There's no easy way…"

"You're scaring me. Take a deep breath and tell me," RJ said concern clouding his face. He rose, walked over and reached out to her.

She pulled away and went over to the window, her back toward him, and, without turning around, she said, "I…I… I met somebody."

RJ gulped the contents of his glass, his hand shaking as he moved to refill it. This was not what he was expecting to hear. "You're…you're having an affair?"

"I said, *I met somebody*," she said and turned to face him.

"You met somebody? Is that code for sleeping with him?"

"I'm not sleeping with him. I wouldn't do that to you. We've met for coffee a few times."

RJ's bitter laugh filled the room. "And that's supposed to make me feel better? How could you do this to us? Our family?"

"Family? Us? What are you talking about, RJ? We haven't been a family since Ryan died. I never saw him grow up. He could've been something.."

"Don't do this. We can find our way back to each other."

"I've made my decision; I'm moving forward."

"Moving forward with another man?"

"I don't know," Carla said. "Maybe, maybe not. I don't know. All I know is that he makes me laugh. He makes me smile. We have common interests. And he has a normal job. I don't have any of that with you." Her chin jutted out stubbornly, her lips pursed in a tight line.

"Someone who gives you what I can't?" RJ scanned his wife's face. She was the same woman that he'd married but there was something different about her, something cold and distant. Had it been there for a long time and he'd never seen it? "Why?"

"I've been feeling lonely for a long time. I feel forgotten. Cast aside. Nothing is as important to you as chasing down criminals. Your focus is on your job, not me. You're up all night, you spend most of the day at work, and on the odd occasion you crawl into bed, you fail to notice me. If you dig deep you'll see that I'm right. This case has consumed you. I can't do this anymore RJ. I need to go."

"I'm sorry I never brought back our son, but I've always been here for you."

All the Evil Scatters

"That's not how I see it. You were so bent on finding our son's killer that you forgot about me. Sure we somehow found our way back to each other, but it was never the same. We became two different people. This case has made things very clear to me: the case will always be your first love. That's what drives you. The hunt. I can't do it anymore."

"I'll change. I promise."

Carla shook her head and said, "But you won't. And that's okay because your passion and drive are what make you who you are."

"This case will be over soon and I'm filing for retirement."

"It's too late. I'm sorry, RJ. Jake —."

"Is that his name?" RJ said and downed the rest of the Scotch.

"Yes. Jake and I want to see where it goes. I thought it only fair that I told you before we took it further."

"Well isn't that peachy? And oh, so considerate." RJ threw the glass against the wall. The glass flew outwards in large and small pieces before spreading out on the floor. He picked up his files and the half-empty bottle of Scotch and stumbled out the door.

*

Later that night, RJ woke up in a cold sweat, his heart beating hard against his chest. *Was I screaming?* he thought and looked around his office, remembering that he'd spent the night there after what Carla said to him. He recalled snippets of his dream: the killer, his face a blur, obscured by a hoodie; his son Ryan, smiling, laughing, and then his cold dead eyes staring back at him.

He rose, went to the restroom, took out his flask, and drank from it, the liquid coursing through his body, calming him.

He sneezed a couple of times, stared at himself in the mirror and said, "Who are you?"

70

RJ burst into Melissa's office like a maelstrom, knocking a picture frame from the wall. He straightened it and said, "I'm sorry."

"Want to talk about it?" Melissa had seen that look before, an impenetrable gaze, eyes void of their usual sparkle. She walked over to RJ,

All the Evil Scatters

put her hand on his shoulder, and said, "Sit down, RJ. We'll clean it up later. Talk to me."

He looked at her; there was no mistaking his tortured look, and then it was gone, replaced by the sparkle to which she was accustomed.

"It's all good."

"Okay. If there's something going on, you know you can tell me. And you look like hell. Are you wearing the same clothes as yesterday?"

RJ assessed whether or not to tell Melissa what was going on with him and then blurted out, "Carla left me. She finally saw through me."

"I'm sorry, RJ. Are you sure?"

"Her intentions were clear. She's having an affair. She wants to explore things with this Jake guy. Hasn't slept with him yet. She's right. I failed her. She needs to be with someone who gets her. Twenty-five years of marriage and I don't *get her*."

"The years must have been so hard for both of you. I can't imagine living with the loss of a child. I thought you had worked through it together?"

"I guess not, right?" He said. "The last 18 years, we've been immersed in our grief, losing sight of one another. Although her words were like a punch to the gut, I have to be honest and admit that there's truth to what she said. I failed her. Still, I want to fix it. She doesn't. She's leaving me."

"How can I help?"

"Bring back my wife, and... and my son!" RJ cradled his face in his hands, his shoulders heaved up and down.

Melissa moved closer and took a step back and wondered, *is that alcohol I smell on him?*

RJ raised his hand, stopping her, and went over to the window, "I remember what a gorgeous summer day it had been the day we had Ryan's ceremony," he said. "The sky was blue, like today, only it was August, not April. And like today, there wasn't a cloud to be found. If only I had acted sooner. If only I —"

"None of what happened to Ryan was your fault or Carla's."

"It was my fault."

"It wasn't your fault. How could you have stopped any of it? His disappearance? His death?"

"I could have done more. Left no stone unturned. If only..."

All the Evil Scatters

"Stop torturing yourself. A tragedy like this can tear families apart. Many don't make it as long as you have. I know I'm not a parent, but I also blame myself for what happened to my parents. If I hadn't suggested that Nicolas drive them to the theatre, maybe they'd be here today. And now, with Nicolas back in my life, I might have the opportunity to forgive myself and perhaps him."

"You're stronger than I will ever be."

"You're the strongest person I know. Forgive yourself."

"Sure doesn't feel like it."

"If you still love her, go to her. See if there's anything left."

"She's the love of my life."

*

She glanced at Greg's text; he'd been discreetly fact-checking Nicolas's movements for the last month or so. There were no signs that Nicolas was involved in the killings. When Nicolas left his apartment, he was either at the university teaching or at the library working on his research. His whereabouts had been accounted for.

Suddenly, as if she'd willed his presence, Nicolas burst into Mel's office and said, "What the fuck Mel? Why is your cop friend checking up on me?"

"I had asked him to check out a few things before we talked the other day. I'm sorry."

"This is unacceptable. This cop questioned my boss about my whereabouts. You're out of line. How could you?"

"I asked him to be discreet."

"Did you think it wouldn't get back to me? Did you ever stop to think about the kind of damage this line of questioning can do to me? Especially with my criminal record?"

"I'm sorry," she said in barely a whisper. She knew she'd messed up.

"You of all people must know that assumptions like these have sent innocent people to jail!"

Melissa nodded and shuffled a few papers on her desk, steadying her nerves.

"Does RJ know you suspect me?"

"No one knows."

"What about that cop who was spying on me?"

"I told Greg that I wanted to make sure that you weren't drinking. That I had a responsibility because you're helping us with the case."

"Better an alcoholic than a murderer," Nicolas said bitterly.

"Perhaps part of me wanted to know whether you were telling the truth about the drinking."

"Then why does RJ watch me like a hawk?"

"He's very protective of me. RJ is a good man. He was the one who told me about what happened to my parents. Since then, well, as I said, he's very protective."

"Unlike me," Nicolas scoffed. "I am a lot of things, but a killer? I know I was responsible for your parents' deaths, but I would never intentionally harm anyone."

"You're right. I'm sorry."

"I'll finish helping you with the case and then I'll be out of your life forever!"

He exited, leaving Melissa with thoughts of regret, betrayal, and a life that could never be unless she took her advice and forgave herself and Nicolas.

71

"You won't believe this," Heather said, entering Melissa's office.

She looked up and said, "Got something?"

"I located an Oldsmobile matching the partial licence plate that we got off the CCTV camera. It's registered to a man named, Gabriel Santis, a paramedic with the city of Toronto."

"A paramedic. Hmm. Someone with access to an entire slew of medication and medical equipment. It's consistent with our profile," Melissa said.

"Can't be a coincidence," Heather said.

"Let's see what else we can find out about Mr. Santis."

*

Several hours later, Heather reappeared at Melissa's door, looking as excited as a puppy discovering its world. "I'm not sure if it means anything, but as I looked for info on Gabriel Santis, I came across this article from over 10 years ago," she said and handed Melissa a printout.

All the Evil Scatters

RJ walked into the room and said, "I hear we might have something?" He hovered over the article with Melissa and read:

Orangeville. The remains of the victim found in the old Orchard House four days ago have been identified as those of Aidan Santis, a paramedic who had been injured on the job four months previously. Significant amounts of oxycodone were found in his bloodstream suggesting that he'd taken too much of the highly addictive and over-prescribed drug which rendered him incapable of escaping the flames that eventually consumed him. The cause of the fire is believed to have been started with kerosine fluid leading authorities to suspect that the Orangeville arsonist, who has plagued the area for over a year, may also be responsible for this fire.

Police are looking for Mr. Santis's wife, Eugenia, and their son, Gabriel. According to Mr. Santis's colleagues, he and his wife were separated. Aidan Santis lived alone. To date, authorities have been unable to locate Mr. Santis's next of kin.

"This can't be a coincidence," RJ said. "Are Gabriel and Aidan Santis related?"

"The mother and son were never found?" Melissa said.

"The police reports go on to say that only one body was recovered from the fire, " Heather said. "There's no evidence that the mother and son were in the house. They were never located."

"Could this Gabriel Santis be the missing son?" RJ said.

"Does he live alone? Are there any other Gabriel Santis's?"

"As far as I can tell he lives alone. Six others match that name, three live in British Columbia, and two in the Maritimes. None of them own an Oldsmobile. The sixth person is 86 years old and owns an unlicensed Oldsmobile. He lives in Manitoba."

"Could Gabriel Santis have stolen the car?"

"According to the owner's wife, the *car is safe and sound in the garage*," Heather said. "The car belongs to Gabriel Santis. He is the registered owner."

"What else do we know?" Melissa said.

All the Evil Scatters

"A man named Frederic Gauvin was charged with arson and was subsequently sentenced to manslaughter. He was a local arsonist who torched 10 properties including the one in which Mr. Santis perished. The other nine properties had been abandoned and no one was harmed."

"Seems open and shut," RJ said.

"Feasible, but—, " Heather paused.

"What are you thinking?" RJ said.

"I found out that while Mr. Gauvin admitted to nine of the fires, he claimed his innocence on the one involving Mr. Santis," Heather said. "He denied any involvement, but the evidence pointed to him for all of the fires. He was sentenced to 25 years with a possibility of parole. He has served almost 10 years of that sentence. I spoke to the officer on the case at the time and he confirmed that Gauvin has maintained his innocence throughout the years."

"Great work, Heather," Melissa said. "Let's find out whatever we can about Gabriel Santis. I think we need to question Mr. Gauvin, see if he knows anything."

"Anything else?" RJ said.

"That's it for now, but I'd like to do a deeper dive on tracking down the wife, see if there are any links to Gabriel Santis," Heather said.

"Let's visit Mr. Gauvin while the warrant to search the Santis residence in Orangeville is being processed. Although from the age of the crime, I doubt we'll find anything," Melissa said.

"There's something I need to take care of," RJ said. "Can you and Heather interview Gauvin?"

72

Melissa and Heather sat in an interview room at the maximum-security penitentiary where Frederic Gauvin was an inmate.

"Thank you for meeting with us Mr. Gauvin," Melissa said.

"Did I have a choice?"

"We want to hear your side of the story about what happened over 10 years ago to Mr. Santis."

"As I said back then. I had nothing to do with that. You got it all wrong!"

All the Evil Scatters

"But you did confess to nine other fires?"
"So? Did someone else die and you're looking to pin it on me?"
"Do you consent to our recording our conversation?"
"I got nothing to hide."
"Thank you. We can stop recording any time that you want."
Frederic nodded.
Heather turned on the cell's camera, propped it in her hand and sat beside Melissa.

MELISSA: Officer Heather Catsell and Staff Sergeant Melissa Hargrove are interviewing Mr. Frederic Gauvin, with his permission about his recollection of the fire at the Santis residence 10 years ago. Mr. Gauvin, please describe in detail what happened on the night in question.
FREDERIC: As I told them other cops, I was torching another place over 10 kilometres away. I got convicted for that too. I admitted to those fires. But not to the one where that man died.
MELISSA: Had you ever seen "that man" before or did you ever go to his house?
FREDERIC: I saw his photo in the paper a few days after the fire. I was at a diner reading the article when I saw it.
MELISSA: Sounds like you recognized him?
FREDERIC: Sorta.
MELISSA: Can you explain?
FREDERIC: I seen him at his house.
MELISSA: You had been to his house? The house to which you eventually set fire?
FREDERIC: No. No. That's not how it went down. I told this all to you before. This is stupid. Gua—

All the Evil Scatters

MELISSA: Please bear with us Mr. Gauvin. I assure you that we're not here to blame you for anything. You're already convicted for his death.
FREDERIC: I didn't set fire to that place. I killed nobody.
MELISSA: Help us understand. Tell me how you came to see him at his house.
FREDERIC: Alright, I never told this to anyone. Maybe I should have, but at the time I thought they'd pin it on me whether I said anything or not.
MELISSA: Do you want to tell us now?
FREDERIC: About a month before the fire, I was casing the area for abandoned structures. I came upon his house and saw him.
MELISSA: What was he doing?
FREDERIC: Digging, clearing the bush. You know farm stuff.
MELISSA: Did he see you?
FREDERIC: No.
MELISSA: Did you see anyone else with him?
FREDERIC: No.
MELISSA: And you didn't return later when you thought no one was home?
FREDERIC: No way. Once I see people, I move on. That wasn't my jam.
MELISSA: Torching abandoned buildings was?
FREDERIC: Yes sir. I mean, ma'am.
MELISSA: Anything else?
FREDERIC: That's all.

    Heather turned off the camera.
    "Thanks for your time," Melissa said.

All the Evil Scatters

"I got nothing but time," Frederic lamented, turned and followed the correctional officer out of the room.

"Can't help thinking that most criminals have a code of ethics," Melissa said. "As unethical as their crimes might be. His *jam,* as he said was torching abandoned and uninhabited buildings."

"If Gauvin has been telling the truth all these years, then he was convicted for a crime he didn't commit."

"If that's the case, then who set the fire?"

"Accelerant was found at the Santis home, in and around his bedroom where his body was recovered," Heather said. "This was the key piece of evidence in convicting Frederic Gauvin of Aidan Santis's death."

"No signs of the wife and son were ever found. Surely they would have had a claim to the property as it was owned outright by Aidan Santis. And now we have someone with the son's name, who owns a car that was seen during the abduction of the Olsens," Melissa said.

"Too many coincidences," Heather said.

"Does Gabriel live alone?"

"Yes."

"If this is the son, then where's the mother?"

"If you know the right people you can disappear forever."

"Or maybe she never left," Melissa said.

"There was no mention of another body or bodies found in the fire."

"Maybe they weren't looking in the right place."

"It merits looking into it further," Heather said.

"I'll see if I can get a warrant to search the Santis property, the grounds. Maybe the investigators missed something back then, especially if they weren't looking for it. After all, they attributed the fire to Frederic Gauvin. Case closed."

73

A convoy of police vehicles converged on the derelict Santis property. Only a skeleton of the house remained. Decaying pieces of wood jutted toward the sky, reaching out like disjointed fingers, black and rotting from the fire that had consumed everything in its path. Branches intertwined with weeds, shrubs, and ivy as if in a loving embrace.

All the Evil Scatters

Melissa and RJ exited their vehicles and waded their way through the overrun property, feet crunching on twigs and branches still sopping wet from last night's rain.

They observed the canine unit heading toward the east of the property with the Human Remains Detector dog, Sammy, which was ready to search and recover, assuming that there was anything to find.

Melissa and RJ worked their way toward the last known residence of Aidan Santis.

Clop. Clop. Clop.

Melissa stopped and touched the ground, clearing the debris with her gloved hand. She bent down and examined the concrete square slab. She rose and moved forward, discovering another, and then another along the path. "I think these slabs lead to what used to be the house."

"Wonder what secrets lay buried in the weeds?" RJ said, picking up a piece of decaying wood that crumbled, and fell to the ground. RJ nodded to where the remains of the Santis house beckoned. A sudden spurt of sneezes escaped RJ and said, "Damn allergies."

"Let's keep going," Melissa said. "There might still be —"

Sammy's incessant barking stopped them in their tracks. They looked in the direction of his yipping and headed toward it. On approach, they saw Sammy circling an area, overgrown with weeds, sniffing and yelping at the ground.

"I think there may be something here," said an officer, who seemed to be leading the hunt. "Let's get the ground-penetrating radar machine fired up!"

Another officer wheeled in what looked like a lawnmower and showed them how it worked. "The screen will relay images of anything found below ground."

"When will we know if there's anything here?" RJ said.

"If there's anything, we should get a signal fairly quickly," the officer said. "Think of it as a signal from a submarine pinging on a radar screen."

Melissa and RJ waited for the results as the GPR scanned the ground as if it were mowing the lawn.

"Yup," the lead officer said. "There's something here and here. Two sites where we've detected something. I'll show you."

All the Evil Scatters

Melissa and RJ looked at the digital images on the survey encoder. "Look," the officer said and pointed. "This denotes changes in the soil and from the speed at which the signal came back, whatever is buried there it's not too deep."

"Let's dig," the officer said to his team who commenced the slow and methodical task of breaking through the ground, hardened by the winter's cold, in search of what lay beneath the surface.

*

Melissa and RJ surveyed the metal table which held the human bones that had been recovered from the Santis residence and were neatly reformed into two separate skeletal shapes, one small and the other slightly bigger.

There was a rap on the door and Nicolas peeked in tentatively and said, "Should I come in?"

"You're on the case aren't you?" RJ said impatiently.

Nicolas nodded and walked over to the table without glancing at Melissa.

"Thank you for coming on such short notice, Nicolas," Melissa said and, when he remained focused on the bones, she looked away and met RJ's questioning look. She nodded signifying that he needn't worry.

"What can you tell us about the bodies, Frank?" RJ said.

"The bones are from two different human bodies," Frank said. "We have a rough idea of when they were buried and how old they were when they died, but we don't have *a who they are*. The smaller bones indicate that one is a young male, probably about 10 years of age. The other is an adult female, about forty."

"Can you tell how long they'd been buried there?" Melissa said.

"I would say that the young male has been buried for about 20 years. The female is more recent, she died approximately 10 to 15 years ago."

"Do we know the cause of death?"

"See this u-shaped bone, the hyoid on the female?" Frank pointed. "It's fractured and could be the result of being strangled."

"You mean someone might have done this to her and buried her in the yard?"

"How did the boy die?"

"Nicolas," Frank said. "Why don't you tell them what we discussed earlier."

All the Evil Scatters

"You met earlier?" Melissa said.

"There are indications of malnutrition in the abnormally formed bones. Also his teeth. See the X-ray," Nicolas pointed to a scan of the skull. "The teeth have decay that's different from the decay caused by the passage of time. See here and here — they're cracked. I can't say that he starved to death, but it might have sped it up. Could have been an infection of some sort."

"The article reporting Aidan Santis's death indicated that the mother and son were never found," Melissa said.

"Could these bodies be those of Eugenia and Gabriel Santis?" RJ said.

Melissa looked up at him and then at the two skeletons and said, "If that's the case, who killed them? And who is this Gabriel Santis who drove off with the Olsens?"

74

"We've identified through dental records that the skeletal remains are those of Eugenia and Gabriel Santis," Nicolas said. "Further research shows a thickening of the inner table of the frontal bone, the forehead, suggesting that the boy had been castrated.

"How do you know this?"

"There is a body of work that suggests that changes in the hormone levels from someone who has been castrated, like in that of Carlo Maria Broschi, an opera singer in the early 18th century, had been castrated as a boy because of his singing abilities. Analysis of his remains suggests that the thickening of the frontal bone was a strong indicator that the changes to his hormones led to changes in his bone structure."

"A eunuch?" RJ said. "You think this boy was castrated for his singing skills?"

"Not necessarily. There are other reasons for castration."

"Such as?" RJ said.

"I've seen this type of injury before in my research," Nicolas said. "There is documented evidence that young boys were castrated and then enslaved to keep them in check. Testosterone meant rebellion. Castration meant acquiescence. For example, during the Miao Rebellions against the

Ming dynasty, Chinese commanders castrated hundreds of Miao boys. Several hundred died because infection set in and poisoned their blood."

"If he was castrated, could he have died from it?"

"Possible if it went untreated. He could have died from sepsis."

"Someone tried to castrate him, but he was not treated properly and died?" RJ said.

"Strong possibility," Nicolas said.

*

"What do we have?" Tara said the excitement of knowing that the team was onto something was evident on her face.

"A plate that matches an Oldsmobile, registered to a Gabriel Santis," RJ began. "A 10-year-old case of arson and death, and the buried bodies of Eugenia and another Gabriel Santis near the site of the fire."

"My gut tells me that there's a connection between the serial killer, Aidan's death and the skeletal remains at the Santis property," RJ said.

"Any information on this Gabriel Santis?" Melissa said.

"Yes. We talked to his employer at the Toronto City Paramedic Service," Heather said. "He was recently reprimanded for performing an unauthorized procedure on a patient."

"What did he do?" RJ said.

"He stitched up a woman's hand."

"Don't paramedics do this?" RJ said.

"They do, but you have to be certified accordingly. Gabriel Santis did not have the necessary credentials," Heather said.

"Someone with access to medical equipment, someone who stitched another person, a possible stolen identity," Melissa said.

"Wasn't Aidan Santis a paramedic? Now, this Gabriel Santis is one too? That's one too many fuckin' coincidences," RJ said.

"And get this," Heather said. "His boss reported that he hadn't been at work for almost a month."

"That must have been his trigger," Melissa said. "Do we know where he worked before becoming a paramedic?"

"Yes," Heather said. "He worked at a restaurant as a dishwasher and then as a short-order cook. The owner died of a heart attack. There was no evidence of foul play, but…"

All the Evil Scatters

"Are you thinking that he could have been a victim of our killer?" RJ said.

"It's suspicious that he died when Santis was working there," Heather said.

"People die from heart attacks every day," RJ said dismissively.

"You're right," Heather said her face flushed with embarrassment

"Good thought Heather, but it doesn't match the killer's M.O.," Melissa said.

"And what about the arsonist?" Tara said. "Could he be telling the truth that he had nothing to do with the Santis fire?"

"At this point, it looks like he may have been telling the truth," Melissa said.

"Is there an address for that Oldsmobile?" RJ said.

"Yes. It's in Erin, Ontario," Heather said.

"I think we have enough to proceed," Tara said. "I'll start making calls and putting the paperwork together for the necessary warrants."

"Let me know when you have what we need and I'll meet you there," RJ said. "Right now, I need to be somewhere else," RJ said.

75

My hands shake as I read today's article on Father's death. An overwhelming sorrow overcomes me. I don't recall the last time I was so saddened by something, except for Cat, who had slinked off into the night and never returned. But this was different, it came from somewhere deep. Somewhere in my stomach. I clutch the newspaper, hoping to steady myself. "Jesus Christ is victorious, and all the evil scatters by Him," I repeat several times. The words calm me and I reread the article.

Orangeville. Earlier this week, police made a gruesome discovery at the residence of arson victim, Aidan Santis. The skeletal remains of Eugenia Santis and her son, Gabriel, were sniffed out by an HRD dog. The pair, thought to have left their homestead due to irreconcilable differences between the husband and wife, had never left. That was about five years before the fire. At the time, Aidan Santis, a paramedic

All the Evil Scatters

with the Orangeville EMS, had told colleagues that he and his wife had separated but that the son came to visit him from time to time.

It was previously determined that Santis's death was the work of the Orangeville Arsonist, Frederic Gauvin, who had torched nine uninhabited structures in the area, mainly barns. Mr. Gauvin was later convicted of manslaughter in the death of Mr. Santis based on the accelerant that had been used in the fire. Mr. Gauvin is serving time at the Millhaven Institution in Bath, Ontario. To this day, Mr. Gauvin has denied involvement in the Santis home fire. He admitted to setting fire to nine other structures in the area.

The investigation continues.

"I'm here! I'm not dead!" I yell at the TV screen.

"Don't you see? That's an impostor! I'm alive. I'm the only Gabriel Santis. How can there be two of us with the same name? Was there another one before me?"

And the woman, my mother, has been dead all these years. What happened to her? You lied to me Father. You did this! Oh, mother. I thought that all these years you had deserted me. That you'd left me to save yourself. Only you didn't. You were right there, decaying, the worms and bugs eating through your skin.

And the other Gabriel, the one with my name. Who was he? My brother? Did you inflict your evil on him? Why didn't you kill me too and bury me with them? If you had, I wouldn't have become a monster.

I grab a knife and cut through the skin on my forearm, releasing the pain. A pain that comes from deep inside me. The cut itself does not hurt. With each drop of blood, I release the horror that never ends.

"What have I done? What have You made me do? Jesus Christ is victorious, and all the evil scatters by Him. Jesus Christ is victorious, and all the evil scatters by Him. Jesus Christ is victorious, and all the evil scatters by Him, *ftou, ftou, ftou.*" I repeat the words and cross my fingers against my chest.

76

RJ rehearsed his speech as he drove to see Carla. Mel had been right. He had to try again.

"Before you go any further with this Jake guy," RJ recited as he eased the car onto their driveway. "I want you to give us one more chance. I will change. You'll see. I'll be home at a normal time. I'm retiring after this case is over. I know we can be all that we once were."

RJ got out of the car and hesitantly walked toward the front door.

He wanted to use his key but knocked instead. *The new me,* he thought. He was about to knock again when Carla opened the door. A man, with curly grey hair and hazel eyes, stood directly behind his wife.

"That was fast," RJ said, a voice full of sarcasm. "Jake I presume. You've already replaced me.

"RJ, I didn't want you to meet like this. I wasn't expecting you."

"Clearly!"

"Why are you here? Is everything alright?" Carla said.

"I came, um, I came to talk to you. But your mind seems made up."

"Can we talk about this later? Let's meet for coffee."

"No need. I should have never come back." RJ looked at her with regret and disappointment.

He turned around, went to his car and drove off.

77

As RJ drove out of the city, Melissa was reviewing the evidence — a daily habit for her these days, always searching for something that she'd missed. A few officers were at their desks. Tara was talking animatedly on the phone, likely getting all the i's dotted and the t's crossed for the Gabriel Santis warrant.

Beep.

She looked at the computer and saw the word: MATCH on the top of the screen. There was a hit for the blood found near Donald's home. She looked at the details of the blood sample they'd gotten in the bushes. "Oh my!" She gasped when the blood matched that of an old case. A case long-thought to have been closed. She ran the information again. The results were the same. In both instances the rare blood type, AB negative figured prominently.

"RJ. No!"

She jumped up and headed toward Tara's office.

*

"This is unimaginable. How could this be?" Tara said.

"That's what I thought, but I ran the search several times," Melissa said.

"Damn it! I couldn't find him at the station, so I left a message. Went to voice mail, I told him to meet us there, but not to approach the suspect if he got there before us."

"We got warrants for Santis?" Melissa said.

"Yes. Did you try calling RJ?"

"I keep getting his voicemail," Melissa said. "We need to reach him and tell him what we've discovered."

"I know," Tara said.

"I called Carla and she said that he'd been by their house earlier, but that he'd left in a hurry and that he was angry."

Tara reached for her phone and dialled. "Still no answer."

"RJ where are you?" Melissa said and left with the hope that she would arrive at the house before RJ did.

78

I feel restless, expectant like the sails of a boat being taken down in preparation for a looming storm. They are unconscious, seemingly asleep, as they lay on the tarp. That is the beauty of my always dependable ketamine. They, a boy and a girl, no more than nine years old had been easy to deceive, accepting my plea for help for my ailing dog. But that was before I found out that the Monster had killed my mother. Everything that I had done to those women was wrong. She had never done anything to me. She never left me. She had been with me all that time, buried in her shallow grave.

The kids are about the same age that I was when the Monster took over, bringing with Him the darkness that no evil eye could ever eradicate. Did mother know that He would kill her? I remember hearing the *che che* of the spade hitting the dirt that night long ago. Had that been the day she'd died? Could I have saved her? Was she already dead?

I put the evil eye charm atop the girl's forehead and say, "I will always protect you."

79

RJ didn't know how long he'd been wandering through the woods, an intricate mass of trails, north of Toronto. He needed to be as far away as possible from Carla, from the case, from everyone. He needed to make sense of how his life had taken such a turn. He shivered and looked around him. It had gotten cold, the darkness was closing in on him.

He remained seated on a fallen tree and drank from his flask. He lit a cigarette and looked at the ground littered with butts. RJ knew he shouldn't drink or smoke. But lately, it didn't seem to matter. "Oh, Ryan. Oh, Carla. I failed you both." He took another swig, but the flask was empty. He let it drop to the ground.

He looked around him, noticing that the light was quickly disappearing, collected his discarded cigarette butts, and put them in his pocket for later disposal. He inhaled the musty, dank air and began sneezing uncontrollably. "I wonder who's thinking of me now, Nicolas?"

RJ took the path leading to his car, his feet sloshing in the moist ground, the twigs clawing at him like fingers. He was oblivious to the cuts and scrapes on his face and hands.

Once inside the car, he looked in the mirror, barely recognizing himself. "I look like I'm a hundred years old."

He picked up his phone and saw several messages from Tara and Mel. There was one from Carla. An ember of hope lit his blurry eyes. *Maybe I made a mistake. Maybe I misunderstood. I'll go to her and we can work everything out.*

He noted that his phone battery was at one percent "Not now!" He played Tara's message. "RJ. We have warrants for Santis. His address is HWY 173 RR#2, in Erin. Wait for us there. Do not approach —".

"Not now!" RJ said as the screen on his phone went black. "Where's that charger?" He looked at the plug in his ashtray. Empty. "Shit!"

All the Evil Scatters

He put the car in drive and headed to the address that Tara had provided.

*

RJ was the first to arrive at Gabriel Santis's house. He parked his car out of range from the house, turned off his headlights, and waited. There was a solitary light coming from one of the windows near the back of the house. *Is he inside? Alone? With his co-conspirator? What harm can there be if I quietly search the grounds?* He could hear Melissa's warning as if she were right there beside him, "Don't you go in there alone, RJ. Wait for us."

He got out of the cruiser, treading lightly on the gravelly pavement leading to the house. He bent down and sniffed the ground, smelling the mix of stale gasoline and musty earth. He rose, straightened his body, and put his hand on his holster, unclasping it, ready to release the revolver in a split second. If this was their killer, RJ knew how important the moment of capturing him was for all of them: the victims, their families and the police force. He also knew that he should wait for everyone. *But what if he's in the process of another kill? I could save them.* RJ headed to the carport, noting that the grass had been disturbed, flattened as if something or someone had trod on it.

As he edged around the corner of the house; he saw it — the image of the evil eye painted on the gable above the door frame. He couldn't be sure of the colours, but its shape and features were unmistakable. A circle within a circle, the lighter colour looked like the sclera and the centre like an iris. The same as the images and charms found at the crime scenes. In this machination was it meant to keep evil out? Or did it signify the evil lurking inside?

RJ's doubts that their killer was beyond the door had disappeared.

80

I hear movement from downstairs, something falling. I take the narrow steps to where the kids I'd grabbed earlier were squirming and trying to free themselves. The ketamine had already worn off. Their eyes widen with fear at my appearance. I smile and approach, first the boy, administer a dose of the ketamine, and then the girl. They're both out in seconds. I want no more distractions. I return upstairs, grab my knife and, that's when I hear footfalls crunching on the pebbled driveway.

All the Evil Scatters

I peek outside. There's nothing. "Stop it, Gabriel," I say. "You're being paranoid!" I grab a glass of water and gulp it down, not stopping to take a breath and place it on the counter; the flimsy frame that holds a photo of smiling me, stares back. Was I ever that happy? I can almost smell the pine tree looming behind me, feel the prickly grass around my feet. I pick up the frame and one of the pieces of wood holding it together falls to the flo or. I notice something about the photo. Why hadn't I seen it before?

My hand shakes as I slowly remove the frame and the backing that holds it in place. I pull out the photo; it's folded.

I unfold it and reveal the image of a man standing beside me, smiling as if it were the happiest day of his life. It's him, a much younger version but still recognizable, the man on TV. I'd always sensed a familiarity, that somehow we were connected. My subconscious guided me, telling me to send him those messages. I reach for the memory, but it vanishes like a magician's first act,

My other life faded as time passed until it disappeared completely. It was as if a line in the sand had been drawn: before Him and Her and after Him and Her. He became my Father and she, my Mother. Eventually, I stopped thinking. Stopped remembering my other life which had vanished like a dream, there within my grasp, but unreachable. Until now. Snippets of memories come to me: a car driving along a winding road, branches scraping against its doors. A man and a woman arguing. I drifted in and out of consciousness. It was dark. I had been waiting outside the school. My friends were gone. I'm lost. They drive. I sleep. I have to get home.

Sleepy all the time. Darkness. The closet was small and filled with horrible smells. I slept there until He let me out. He hurt me. Punished me. Oh the hurt, the pain. I feel it along my body, the memories here with me, in the present. Time passed. My wounds healed and reopened at the next punishment. I drifted. I forgot everything, my friends. I waited for my food, obedient. I was on the edge, anxious, anticipating the next dose of punishment. There was running water, my hair was being cut off. How did it get so long? *Remember*, I tell myself. His face, the Monster's face interchanges with the face of the man in the photo. The photo of that cop and me. Mom and dad? Mom and dad will be mad. Mom and dad? I never called Them that before. They were always Mother and Father. A word forms on my lips again and I whisper, "dad". I reach out for him but he's not there. Only the Monster.

All the Evil Scatters

And yet, he is here and I know that Man and that Woman were not my parents. They had taken me. Far away from my home. And now, dad was hunting *me* instead of saving me from the Monster.

81

RJ skirted around the house, looking through windows for any signs of their suspect. He ended up at the one with the light on. He parted the branches, pushing his way through the gnarly, needle-like system, and peeked through the window. He saw him, Gabriel Santis, his back toward him, small-statured and seemingly non-threatening, very much like Donald Spielman.

As he was about to go back and find the door, he heard it, a faint, muffled cry coming from somewhere inside, from down below the house. There was a door leading to where the noise was coming from. *The basement,* he thought and put his ear against it. There it was again, a faint scratching. He looked around for something with which to pry the door open. There was nothing. He shoved his body against it, but it wouldn't give.

Where is everybody? I've gotta go in. If he has more victims inside and I do nothing, I'll never forgive myself.

He scurried back to the kitchen window and saw Gabriel lift a syringe and apply pressure to the flange, releasing a clear liquid. RJ dropped his head back down.

*

The whispering wind carries itself noisily through the trees, shaking the leaves as if to waken them from their nightly slumber. In the distance, I hear a dog bark. Branches scrape against the window and I see His reflection in the mirror before He ducks. It happened fast, but I know it's Him, familiar and unfamiliar at the same time; the lead cop on my case and the man in the photo, my dad. Twigs break under a footfall. *Snap.*

I am pleased He found me, it's only fitting. Now I know why I was drawn to Him. I wanted him to know me. To come to me. To come and save me.

I grab the knife.

All the Evil Scatters

I hear the kitchen door clicking open and tighten my grip on the knife. I know it's Him without even looking. "You found me," I say and remain with my back to him.

"Gabriel Santis! Put down your knife and turn around," dad said.

"Are you sure you want to see the monster that I've become?" I turn slowly, savouring the moment when I will see him face-to-face.

RJ looked at him puzzled and said, "I said, drop the knife. You're under arrest."

"Before you arrest me, tell me why?"

"Why what?" RJ said.

"You never came for me."

"Came for you?"

"I waited. I endured. Until I became this…this monster that you've been hunting."

"I'm here now, Gabriel. I won't ask again. Put it down!" RJ said and with the gun pointed at his killer moved toward him.

82

Melissa turned off the lights to her unmarked cruiser and eased it onto the gravel shoulder to the right of the long driveway of their suspect's house. She'd heard on the car radio that the rest of the team were fifteen minutes away; she'd missed the accident that had blocked the northbound lanes of the highway.

She spotted RJ's car. *He's already here,* she thought and ran her fingers through the end of her ponytail. *I have to tell him.* She got out, moved toward his car, and was dismayed that RJ was not inside. *Surely he hasn't gone to the house? Not without backup! Oh RJ. I wish you'd returned my calls so that I can tell you the truth about the man inside the house.* She released the clasp on her revolver case.

The hundred-year-old clapboard house appeared to be well-maintained: the lawns neatly manicured; the window frames painted a dark colour, possibly blue, but it was hard to tell at this time of night. Only the junipers, wildly out of control, marred the home's neat appearance as they hugged the lower half of the windows, blocking her view. A faint light filtered through one of the windows.

All the Evil Scatters

She stepped around the bushes bordering the driveway and saw the Oldsmobile. The plates were the same as the ones they'd identified. Millions of stars shimmered in the clear night sky, keeping vigil with the moon, and guiding her toward the house.

Melissa went to the window from which she'd seen the light and peeked into a kitchen. She saw RJ, his face a combination of sweat and dirt; his clothes looked as if he'd been rolling around in a grassy or wooded area. A collection of twigs and leaves had embedded themselves on his wool jacket and pants. He was talking to a man, likely their suspect. He had a knife pointed at RJ; RJ had a gun pointed at him.

"RJ," she whispered under her breath and moved toward the entrance.

83

Gabriel made a barely discernible turn of his head as Melissa entered. RJ blinked and said, "Mel! Don't come in. Mr. Santis and I are having a chat."

Gabriel released an eerie, menacing laugh and moved toward her.

RJ slightly moved his finger on the trigger.

"RJ! Stop!" Melissa said, focused on Gabriel. "Ryan. Stop!"

Both RJ and Gabriel took a step back and looked at her in surprise.

"You've never called me Ryan before, Mel," RJ said surprised, and eased his finger from the trigger.

"Not you," she said and cocked her head in Gabriel's direction. "I'm talking about him. I tried calling you. To warn you. To tell you —."

"To tell me what? That he's a monster who destroyed the lives of so many families?" RJ said, his words full of venom.

Gabriel tensed upon hearing the word *monster*.

She watched the two men lock eyes; two men with the same eyes. A smile played on Gabriel's lips. *He knows RJ is his father.* Confusion mottled RJ's face. Melissa heard faint, muffled cries, barely audible from the whirring of the refrigerator, coming from below the floorboards. "Who's down there, Ryan?"

"My finale," he said.

*

All the Evil Scatters

RJ stared at Gabriel Santis. Melissa had called him Ryan. *Had we gotten the name of our killer wrong? Of course, a stolen identity!* He wondered, shook his head from side to side, taking in the face: the dark brown eyes; the cleft chin; the curly jet-black hair that fell in a matted mass on his shoulders. He saw the scar along his brow, the one that Chen had described. "Stop this now! Set whoever you have down there free."

*

I smile and remain still. The man before me, dad, familiar, yet strange, older than in the photo and then that name, Ryan, insinuating itself into the room. He doesn't know who I am. He forgot me long ago. "Jesus Christ is victorious, and all the evil scatters by Him. Jesus Christ is victorious, and all the evil scatters by Him. Jesus Christ is victorious, and all the evil scatters by Him."

*

"RJ. There's something you should know," Melissa said.

"Go ahead. Tell him," Ryan said. "Or should I?"

"Tell me what? Is this some kind of a riddle?"

"This man who calls himself Gabriel is Ryan. Your son. He's been alive all these years. I matched the blood we found near Donald Spielman's place to those of an old case. That case was Ryan's. The blood analysis came from the shirt that was found in a pool of blood."

RJ looked from one to the other, processing what she was saying, "Ryan is dead."

"I'm sorry RJ. He's alive and right here.

"That's impossible. I saw all that blood. There was no way he could have survived that."

"That's why he drained my blood! To make it look like I was dead so that you'd stop looking for me," Ryan said.

"What are you both talking about? You've got to be confused, Mel. This is our killer and he's got other people here. Ready to kill and you think he's my son?"

"You're a stupid man," Ryan said, sneering at RJ. "You never see the truth. Do you?"

"And what truth is that?"

"That I am your son, Ryan!" He laughed, an eerie, haunting laugh.

All the Evil Scatters

"My son is dead. How dare you," RJ said as he looked from Melissa to Gabriel and then back to Melissa who nodded her head.

"Look at that photo on the table," Ryan said, angling his head toward it.

RJ grabbed the photo, looked at it and said, "Where did you get this?"

"You gave it to me, don't you remember? We were camping in Algonquin Park."

"I gave it to my son. Why do you have it?"

"Because I am your son, Ryan."

RJ recoiled as if he'd been slapped.

"You have to believe it RJ. He's your son, Ryan," Melissa said. "He's been alive all these years."

"That's impossible. This monster is not Ryan! My son is dead. This… this monster…" RJ said, his body tensing as the reality of what was being said pounded on his head like a hammer. "No! No! No! You're lying! What could you possibly gain by saying this? Mel?"

She nodded confirming the reality he couldn't accept.

"Of course, you wouldn't want a monster for a son, would you?"

RJ's disbelief was replaced with an overwhelming sense of loss. The memories of his young son flooded back unbidden like the tears streaking down his cheeks.

"No! Put down the knife and come with us!"

*

Melissa moved toward RJ, but stopped in mid-stride when Ryan said, "Don't move or I'll kill you in front of him."

She poised her gun at Ryan, assessing the situation. He was no more than 5'8" which was consistent with their eyewitnesses. His scraggly hair was a matted mess as if he hadn't washed it for a while. The light of the moon reflected off his dark eyes, eyes so familiar, eyes that were the same as those of her colleague. Her colleague who'd just discovered that his supposedly dead son was none other than the killer they'd been hunting for weeks.

Ryan moved toward her; RJ aimed his gun at him. "You are not my son!" He wrapped his index finger around the trigger but did not discharge his gun. "Gabriel Santis! Do not move. Stay where you are. If you move I won't hesitate to shoot you."

All the Evil Scatters

"Ryan. Please don't do this! I don't want to shoot you." She needed to tread carefully. She did not want to be the one responsible for killing RJ's son.

"I'm not afraid of you."

"We can help you. Put down the knife," Melissa said.

"Hahahaha," he laughed.

"Your father will get you help. He loves you."

"Love? What does he know about love?" Ryan said. "If he loved me, he would have come to my rescue. I waited for him. So many nights. So much darkness."

"He never stopped looking for you."

"He should have tried harder."

"He, we, can save you now. Get you help," Melissa said.

"Hahahahaha! You can't save me. Not now. Not ever."

Ryan wielded the knife at her. RJ stared as if frozen by Medusa's glare, understanding finally entering his eyes.

"You don't want to do this," Mel said.

"How do you know what I want? I was a little boy. They did horrible things to me. Torture, mutilation, deprivation. I sat in my shit for days on end. I want to repay Him for that," Ryan said and pointed the knife at RJ.

"I can't imagine what you went through, but it doesn't have to end like this. We'll get you help," Melissa said.

"The time for help is long gone." Ryan smiled at her, shrugged his shoulders and said, "You know exactly who I am. I am a monster. Shoot me!"

"Mel?"

"Your father and I will get you help. I promise."

RJ and Melissa locked eyes, a common understanding now between them, stemming from years of working together. No verbal cues were necessary. They needed to bring their killer in alive. They would get him help.

"Ryan? Son?" RJ said, noting a flicker of surprise on Ryan's face. "I don't want to shoot you. Melissa is right, let us get you help."

"Help? You're a little late for that, aren't you?" Ryan said.

"I promise. I'll do everything that I can to make this as easy as possible for you."

"How could you have left me with that Monster? Why didn't you look for me?"

"You have no idea how we and the entire police force looked for you. For months. Years. I kept your memory alive, looking for clues, scouring the ravines, examining what little evidence I had."

"And then you forgot all about me. Went on with your life as if nothing had happened."

"You have no idea what I, we, went through."

"What YOU went through? What about what I went through?"

"I want you to tell me everything, but first we need to go to the station. Sort everything out. Get you help."

"Don't you want to know why I killed them?"

"Okay. Why?" RJ said.

"I had to snuff their evil. They were monsters, like Him. Like me."

"Those people did nothing to you. They were innocent."

"I was innocent."

"You're not anymore. You killed six people"

"*You* never *came* for me. You never searched for me. Instead, you left me to rot in that monster house with those people who made me believe that they were my parents. They did horrible things to me."

"I can't imagine what they did to you. I want to know everything. I want to get you help." RJ said and looked at the door. There were noises outside. "Stand down everyone. It's under control," RJ yelled out.

Ryan moved toward RJ, knife pointing directly at him.

"Ryan! Don't," Melissa said and aimed her gun.

"Put that down!" RJ said. "I don't want to shoot you. You've already been hurt enough."

"Hahahaha!" RJ heard the evil in his cackle and watched in horror as Ryan lunged at him.

RJ fired his gun.

Shock registered on Ryan's face as he stared down at the blood seeping through his clothes; understanding and fear clouded his face as he crumbled to the ground.

"No! No! No!" RJ said and moved to where Ryan lay on the floor holding his stomach.

All the Evil Scatters

Ryan looked at his blood-stained hand and garbled, "thank you," as the blood trickled from the side of his mouth.

"What did I do?" RJ said, pulled Ryan to his chest and cradled his head.

"I can't be helped. Not...not anymore. I am e...e...evil. I am bad."

"No. No. We can help you," RJ cried. "Stay with me."

"Bad...evil...monster," Ryan coughed, gagging on his blood.

84

Melissa watched as if in a dream, father and son, reunited through a horrific and inexplicable chain of events. She heard pounding on the door and rose to let the team inside.

Paul, Greg, and Heather entered en masse, taking in the scene: RJ weeping, his bloodied fingers combing through Ryan's hair. Scores of police officers and then Tara entered the premises.

"I'll stay with him. I think you need to go downstairs. There might be more victims," Melissa said and returned to comfort her colleague and friend. Blood seeped through Ryan's t-shirt, forming what looked like a Rorschach inkblot. RJ's hands were covered in his son's blood.

She put her arms around RJ and heard him whisper, "Remember all those times when the two of us looked through that microscope and saw the cells splitting on the pinprick of blood?"

Ryan could barely move his head, but said, "I... re...re...remember... you told... me to lo...lo...look at life in sm...smallest particles? *All in the de...de...details* you s...s...said."

"That's right, son," RJ said.

"Not... your... son. His son. Son... of... Monster."

"You will always be my son." RJ held his son's head against his chest, rocking back and forth, tears streaming down his cheeks.

"Jes... Jes," Ryan started, his words were barely audible.

RJ leaned in and said. "Don't talk. Save your strength."

"*Jesus Ch...Ch...Christ victorious...all evil. Ch...ch...chased...away by H...H... Him.*"

As if in a dream, Melissa watched the flurry of activity around her: Paul and Greg carrying two kids, alive; Tara removed scores of videotapes

All the Evil Scatters

from a shelf; Heather gathered news articles and photos that were strewn on the kitchen table and put them into a plastic evidence bag.
    Melissa looked back down at father and son and put her arms around RJ. Together they heard Ryan's last exhalation.

All the Evil Scatters

Epilogue

Melissa looked over at her nephews, enjoying their Sunday morning pancakes; she picked up Ari's news article on the serial killer, known as *The Suturer*.

Toronto. In a case that plagued the Toronto City Police Force for over a month, the city can now sleep comfortably knowing that the serial killer named, *The Suturer*, has died from a gunshot wound to the abdomen. The serial killer has been identified as Gabriel Santis, but his real name is Ryan Otombo. Ryan is the son of Staff Sergeant RJ Otombo, one of the lead investigators on the case. As the police put the pieces of the killer's life together, it is believed that Ryan Otombo was abducted by Gabriel and Eugenia Santis eighteen years ago. His family believed he was dead. For reasons we may never know, during his captivity Ryan assumed the identity of the Santis's dead son, Gabriel. Perhaps the Santis's used Ryan as a replacement for their son, whose skeletal remains were recently found in a shallow grave in Orangeville.

Videotapes and news articles documenting the serial killer's horrific crimes were removed by the police from the Gabriel Santis/Ryan Otombo home. These, along with other evidence taken from the farmhouse, suggest that *The Suturer* suffered extreme trauma at the hands of his abductors. Through this spate of serial killings, experts believe that he was reenacting the events that had caused him so much pain and suffering.

An autopsy performed on the killer revealed that he'd been castrated. Severe lacerations on his back and other parts of his body suggest that he'd been beaten; a belt believed to be the weapon used for these injuries was recovered at the farmhouse. There were also self-inflicted wounds along the killer's arms, legs, and abdomen. Experts believe that self-harm is a coping mechanism that people use to shift focus from the emotional pain, anxiety, depression, or other psychological disorder that they are experiencing. The pain that he caused to both the victims and their families is unimaginable, but one

might sympathize with the pain the killer endured at the hands of his abductors, Aidan and Eugenia Santis.

As police continue to investigate, doubt has been cast on another case, the death of Aidan Santis, who was believed to have died at the hands of an arsonist, Frederic Gauvin who is now serving time for manslaughter.

In a case where the pile-up of bodies never seems to end, the decomposing body of a female victim was discovered buried behind the wall of a makeshift washroom in the basement of Gabriel Santis's residence. The victim's eyes had been sutured shut. An autopsy is underway to determine the cause of death. Police wonder if she was *The Suturer's* first victim before he developed his MO and began targeting couples like the Olsens, Smikowskys and Lawsons. There was no male body found on the premises, but police won't discount that there may be other victims.

Before becoming a paramedic, Gabriel Santis/Ryan Otombo worked at an eatery on the Danforth. The owner Stavros Patris died of an apparent heart attack. An article about his death was found among The Suturer's belongings. Although not consistent with Santis's modus operandi, police will exhume the body to determine if there was evidence of foul play and if Patris fell prey to the depravity of Gabriel Santis.

On a positive note, the two children who were found at the farmhouse are safe and sound. It is believed that they would have been Ryan Otombo's next victims.

Neither Staff Sergeant Otombo nor his wife, Carla were available for comment, but we can only guess at the horror of discovering that their son was not only alive but had also been responsible for the deaths of six to nine people.

In Canada, over 40,000 children disappear each year, some are abducted, others run away, and some never return home.

Melissa folded the paper, looked up and watched Ari playing with his kids. She rose and went to help her sister-in-law with the breakfast dishes.

*

All the Evil Scatters

RJ read Ari's article with horror, loss and sadness. He couldn't believe that his son, Ryan, who he'd thought to be dead, was the serial killer that they'd been hunting. He couldn't equate the serial killer's heinous acts to those of his innocent young son who had disappeared long ago. That was the boy he wanted to remember, not the boy who had grown up to be a monster.

Was there something more or different that he could have done to find his son and save him from the hands of his tormentors? These tortured thoughts would plague RJ until the day he died.

All the Evil Scatters

Citations

The Pit and the Pendulum, Edgar Allan Poe, 1842

To His Coy Mistress, Andrew Marvell, 1939

Hyperostosis frontalis interna (HFI) and castration: the case of the famous singer Farinelli (1705–1782) Belcastro, Fornaciari, and Mariotti, 2011

Bible, King James Version, Revelation 6:8

https://www.rcmp-grc.gc.ca/en/gazette/just-the-facts-missing-and-abducted-children

All the Evil Scatters

Acknowledgements

Many say that writing is a lonely proposition, but I neither felt alone nor lonely while I wrote this novel during one of the darkest times in recent history. Writing this book would never have happened if not for the supportive book lovers and writers in my life who I call *my village*. They encouraged and pushed me when I was stuck or lacked motivation, listened to my readings and gave me the necessary feedback to move the story forward. I worked endlessly with my writing group that I met at the Humber School for Writers in 2013 along with our mentor, the late, Wayson Choy. We've been meeting monthly since then, forging strong relationships as we developed our craft as writers and as constructive critics of each other's work. Thank you Douglas Schmidt, Phyllis Koppel and Nadja Lubiw-Hazard for helping me uncover what worked and what didn't. When the manuscript was ready, I sent it out for review to my brilliant beta readers: Diane Bickers, Jeffrey Osborne, Peter Papoulidis, Susan Ritchie, Peter Maher, Shirley Silva and Margaret Williams. Their insights and thoughtful feedback helped me to refine the story. My acknowledgments would not be complete without thanking the virus, COVID-19, that plagued our world and gave me the impetus to finish this book. I also want to thank my high school English teacher, Russell Adams. He recently died, but I think he would have been proud that I pursued my dream of writing. I want to thank my parents. Dad gave me the gift of story-telling when on Saturday nights the family gathered around the living room to hear about his tales from the old country. Mom introduced me to the horror and mystery/crime genres — Friday nights at the Roxy Theatre hold a special place in my heart. Lastly, my yiayia (grandmother) who would often utter the Greek version of the words *Jesus Christ is victorious, and all the evil scatters by Him* and mock-spit three times whenever I didn't feel well because someone had cast upon me their evil eye.

Made in the USA
Middletown, DE
28 October 2022

13626884R00142